Teresa is a writer and gamer at heart. The genres she is interested in are love, romance, and adventure. She is a people watcher and loves to sit and watch people to see all walks of life. She is very observant at times and loves the outdoors, especially the trails in the parks. Her favorite animals are horses, dogs, and cats.

To Aaron Rave, my soulmate, who has recently left this world.

Teresa

CALL OF THE DRAGON

AUSTIN MACAULEY PUBLISHERS™

LONDON * CAMBRIDGE * NEW YORK * SHARJAH

Ordering Information
Quantity sales: Special discounts are available on quantity purchases by corporations, associations, and others. For details, contact the publisher at the address below.

Publisher's Cataloging-in-Publication data
Teresa
Call of the Dragon

ISBN 9781643788609 (Paperback)
ISBN 9781643788593 (Hardback)
ISBN 9781645365419 (ePub e-book)

Library of Congress Control Number: 2021909857

www.austinmacauley.com/us

First Published (2021)
Austin Macauley Publishers LLC
40 Wall Street, 33rd Floor, Suite 3302
New York, NY 10005
USA

mail-usa@austinmacauley.com
+1 (646) 5125767

Chapter I

On a pleasant summer day in July, where Victoria Lancaster stood in front of the mystical formation of stones called Stonehenge. Staring at this amazing creation, she could barely contain her enthusiasm. She was born on a warm summer day in June 25 years ago and, most of her life, she had been interest in this amazing structure. It was a dream come true when she was told a couple of weeks ago that she got the job she had been working so hard for. The excitement she felt staring at this enigma that confounded people for centuries was unmeasurable. England's past intrigued her ever since she was a child and it all started when she saw a documentary of this magical place.

Raised by her grandfather, living in the Dakota's, he felt the best college for her to go to was Boston University, but that meant she had to go to Boston, M.A. A feat he had a hard time to deal with. She spent seven years there and received her master's degree in archeology and anthropology. Her grandfather was amazed at how she could finish both in such a timely manner, but he knew that she was a very fast reader and absorbed everything. When she was young, he would always catch her watching documentaries about England and saw that she became very interested in Stonehenge. There was something about this place that seemed like it was calling to her.

Mahlon Featherhawke, a handsome Indian with long black hair was from the Lakota tribe, was called Hawke by his friends and family. He was left to raise his granddaughter when she lost her mother at the age of three, but her father still lived in England. When she was ten, she took a trip to London for the first time since the accident. He had told her, "This is the place where I married your grandmother." Victoria never met her grandmother; she died when her mother was only three years old. She had seen a picture of her and thought she was beautiful. The picture was in black and white and was the only picture he had of her. Her grandfather would describe Victoria's grandmother to her. He told her that she had long, golden, blonde hair and eyes like the color of the blue sky that hovered over Stonehenge that day.

Hawke told Victoria that this place had magical powers, this was the great spirits hunting grounds and she needed to be very careful not to stay too long. Standing there thinking about what her grandfather said made her giggle. She loved him very much and took in everything he said. He had kind of an accent because he was Native American; she loved the way he talked. Her grandmother was from Amesbury and had gone on a holiday to the States. She met Hawke in the Dakotas when she got lost on his reservation. The stories he would tell her were so romantic to her, she could listen to him for hours.

Victoria's mother, Hope, was the product of Hawke and Isadora's undying love. Hope was a beautiful child; she had brown hair with streaks of a golden blonde, woven into her long locks. Her eyes were the color of her mother's and she inherited her father's olive colored skin. Hope was Hawke's pride and joy he loved her very much. But something terrible happened, he had lost Isadora when Hope was three years old, then twenty-two years later, he lost Hope the same way. At that time, Victoria was only three and her father, Carver Lancaster, was so heartbroken that he would keep himself away with his work. Victoria looked a little like her mother, except her hair was a little darker with golden blonde highlights. She also had this strange thumbprint like birthmark on the inside of her wrist. Victoria believed that since she looked somewhat like her mother, it caused her father great pain to the point that he could not come home to spend time with her.

Victoria was told that when her mother was three, Isadora longed to go back to England, so Hawke saved up the money and brought her there. They stayed in England for a lot longer than expected. It was her love for England, especially Stonehenge that kept them there longer. Hawke would take her there many times, but one time, something horrifying happened and Hawke would lose the love of his life there. Hawke would not go back to the states because of the incident, so he raised Hope in England. It was as if he was waiting for something. As Hope grew and became interested in men, she fell in love with the handsome Carver Lancaster. This man was the catch of the county with his dark hair and sapphire blue eyes. They had gotten married when Hope had turned twenty-one and she became pregnant shortly after. Carver and Hope visited Stonehenge quite often and started taking Victoria with them when she turned three. One warm summer day, they went to Stonehenge, but Hawke took Victoria to see the opening of the Channel tunnel. Later that day, he would get a call from Carver telling him to come to Stonehenge immediately. Hawke arrived just in time to see what happened but could not do anything about it. Ever since Carver lost Hope, he found it difficult to take care of Victoria, so he asked Hawke to watch over her, but they had to leave England and never come back. Hope was met with the same fate as her mother and has been gone for nearly twenty-two years. Ever since that time Hawke raised Victoria on his land in the states. For those twenty-two years, he kept her away from all the pain and fears that would follow them in England.

Hawke wanted Victoria's life to be full of happiness, so he would never talk about the incident to Victoria and Carver remained quiet about it too. Living on his hundred acres, Hawke would teach Victoria the ways of his people, his ways were interesting to her and she willingly learned it. He showed her how to make many different weapons from scratch and he also taught her some of his healing secrets. Victoria was a fast learner and became so interested in his culture that she decided to go to college for archeology and anthropology. When she graduated from Boston University, she was given a job through National Geographic to do some research for them on the secrets of Stonehenge. Not wanting to leave her grandfather alone, she asked him to come with her. He did not want her to go and tried to talk her out of it. He was afraid that she would be met with the same fate as her mother and grandmother. There was no other choice for him but to go with her.

Victoria looked at her iPhone to see what time it was. She could hear footsteps coming up behind her and she smiled. She turned and gave this elderly man a hug and kissed him on the cheek, "You are always here at the exact same time every day this week, grandfather." Hawke put his hands-on Victoria's face smiled and gave her a kiss on the forehead, "Oh, yes. Same time always. Your grandmother and I spent our last moments here. At this precise time." A sad look came across his face as he looked pass Victoria and stared at the formations of rock known as Stonehenge, "You know if I didn't know any better, I would say you were waiting for her to come here." Hawke looked down and replied, "No, it has been so long, she is not coming back." A surprised look came across her face at his words and Victoria asked, "Wait, what?"

"It is nothing, just the ramblings of an old man," he enveloped his hand around hers then patted them.

"Grandfather, please tell me some more stories about how you met grandmother?"

Hawke grabbed the two folding chairs that he brought with him and unfolded them. He then proceeded to sit down, "Not today, maybe tomorrow I will tell you."

"Why not today?" Victoria pleaded. He patted the chair next to him and said, "Here, sit with me. I brought your favorite sandwich." He took the bag he had strapped over his right shoulder and opened it. In the bag were two sandwiches made with fry bread, mustard, mayo, lettuce, ham, and cheese. It was her favorite sandwich because he made them with fry bread, which she loved and try to make them herself, but he did a better job. He grabbed a Pepsi and a napkin and handed them to Victoria. She sat down and proceeded to carefully unwrapped her sandwich. The two of them sat there quietly eating their lunch.

There was a nice warm breeze that lightly danced around them. At times, it would pick up strands of Victoria's hair and made it flow gracefully around her head. There were many clouds in the sky and the sun would peek through them and shine down on the golden highlights of her hair, which made it shimmer. Her thick hair was up in a high ponytail and was still long enough to come down to the middle of her back. She always seemed too busy to get her hair styled in the new fad looks, besides, it was easier for her to just brush it than pull it back into a ponytail. Since she had her hair pulled away from her face, the sun had been beating down on it and turned her skin a soft olive brown. She was even getting a sunburn across her nose and forehead.

It was such a nice day, so Victoria had worn her pink lacey tank top layered on top of a purple tank top. It was nice out but a little chilly for shorts, so she wore her A.G. skinny Jeans. The weather in England was a lot cooler than in the Dakota's, so she had to wear her Eileen Fisher cardigan sweater. She wasn't sure about the weather in England, and she brought her deep brown Hera Gladiator sandals but founding out soon enough that her feet would get cold, she decided to wear her white Nike Air Force 1 shoes instead. Hawke didn't make enough money to afford Victoria's schooling and clothes, but her father did. He would rarely come to visit but he always sent her letters and pictures. Carver was very well off and even though he still couldn't bring himself to see Victoria he still provided for her.

Victoria finally broke the silence with a question, "Grandfather, why do you keep telling me that this place is a magical place?" Taking the last bite of his sandwich, Hawke wiped his mouth with his napkin. He crossed his legs, then crossed his arms on top. Looking down he shook his head then looked back up at Victoria and sadness was in his eyes, "Not today, Tori, I want to remember this day with just you."

Victoria knew there was something he was holding back, he also seemed to be a little nervous when talking about this place. But, out of respect for her grandfather, she did not push the subject. In time, she thought he would tell her. His past must have been awful for him not to want to talk about it. Yet, it seemed kind of strange that he would come out here every day at the same time. It was almost like he was waiting for something or somebody.

Looking around, Tori could see that there were a lot of people at Stonehenge that day. She decided that it was too busy for her to get any work done. She started packing up her equipment and gathered up her research papers. Hawke tried to help her, but she told him to just sit there and enjoy the day. As she was walking back to her car, her birthmark started to bother her, then there was this strange noise that began to echo throughout the area, it kind of sounded like trumpets. Looking back toward Stonehenge, she saw a strange flash of light. She shrugged it off and figured that with all those people there, it must have been flashes from cameras, but the noise she had no idea what that was. She started back up to go help her grandfather with his folding chairs when she saw him walking as fast as he could toward her. Hawke had this look of terror on his face, and he said to Victoria, "Get in the car, let us go." He grabbed her arm and guided her to the driver side and practically threw her in the car.

"But, grandfather, what about your folding chairs?" Victoria replied, pointing up where the chairs were.

"Just forget them, let us go."

She got out of the car and started to walk toward Stonehenge where the chairs were. Hawke followed her and grabbed her arm, "Victoria, no, let us go quickly."

"Grandfather, you are starting to scare me. What's wrong?" Hawke grabbed both of Victoria's arms and looked at her with pleading eyes.

"We must go, trust me."

He grabbed her hand and led her back to the driver side of the car.

"Please, Victoria, let us go."

Victoria got in the car and started it up. As they were leaving, she could see another flash in her rearview mirror, "Did you see that? I thought it was camera flash but there is something different about it and what was that strange noise?" Looking at her grandfather, she could see that he had turned pale. He began sweating and put his hand on his chest. Thinking that he could be having a heart attack, Victoria placed her hand on his chest and drove her grandfather to the hospital. She completely forgot about the noise and the flashing lights.

Standing in front of the Pepsi vending machine at the hospital, Victoria looked at the European money she had in her hand. She wished she had studied more about the British currency; it was all too confusing for her. All money was confusing to her; it didn't serve a genuine purpose. For somebody who had two master's degree, you would think she could at least figure out British money. Out of the corner of her eye, she could see that somebody was standing nearby so she stepped aside to let them use the machine. When he didn't go up to the machine, she looked up and saw that he was watching her. He was a handsome man with golden blonde hair and sultry green eyes. He was wearing a pair of navy straight fit belted Chinos with a Ralph Lauren Oxford shirt and a pair of signature wing cap Brogue shoes. From the looks of his five o'clock shadow, she could tell he had been at the hospital all night. He smiled at her and asked with a sexy English accent, "Diet or regular?"

"Sorry, what?" Victoria queried. When he smiled, she could see how perfectly white his teeth were. She stepped aside as he stepped toward the machine and proceeded to put money in it, "Your Pepsi, how do you take it? Diet or regular?" She was so enamored by how handsome he was, she began to stumble over her words.

"Oh, you are talking about the pop. Yes, I mean, regular. No. Diet. Regular."

"Which is it?"

"Regular, I like regular Pepsi."

The man pushed the regular Pepsi button, and you could hear the pop cans shifting around than one dropped down into the slot. The man bent over to pick it up then handed it to Victoria. "Thank you, here, let me pay you for that," he smiled at her and closed her hand that had her money in it, "You looked like you were having trouble figuring that out. New here I take it. Trust me, it does get easier. You just visiting or are you staying for a while?"

"Oh, no, my grandfather is here. He was feeling a little ill, so I brought him here."

"Sorry to hear that, I hope he is doing okay, but I meant are you just visiting England or are you staying awhile?"

"Oh, right. No, I will be here a while."

Feeling a little childish, she rolled her eyes and stated, "I'm doing research for National Geographic on Stonehenge."

"Stonehenge, I've been told it has mystical powers."

"Really? I have been told that, too."

She was interrupted by a nurse that came out of a doorway which had the words labor and delivery above it. "Mr. Emsworth, your wife and baby are ready to see you," he turned to Victoria smiling, "I'm sorry, but I must go. It was nice meeting you. I hope you have a pleasant stay."

With that, he touched her arm then turned toward the nurse and disappeared behind the doors. She stared at the door for a minute, then with great disappointment, turned around and walked down the opposite hallway toward her grandfather's room.

The doctor was standing over Hawke's bed, telling him he needed to take it easy. The doctors diagnosed him with Myocardial Infarction due to excessive release of norepinephrine at myocardial nerve endings. He wanted Hawke to stay at the hospital for a couple more days to make sure they got his condition under control. Victoria didn't want to leave her grandfather alone and thought she should call her boss and arrange to spend some time at the hospital for a while.

Victoria sat by her grandfather's bedside and was watching him rest. An hour went by and she thought about the work she needed to do and how she hadn't called her boss yet. Her mind kept drifting back to the pop machine and Mr. Emsworth. She thought it was too bad he was married. *Strange*, she thought, the feeling she got when she stared into his eyes, it was as if their souls knew each other. Thinking about this made her heart leap and it made her smile. Sitting there, she glanced up and saw a man standing outside the room on his phone watching her. To her surprise, it was Mr. Emsworth. She got up the nerve to go out and talk to him. As she walked out of the room, she didn't notice a man mopping up some water that had spilt on the floor. Victoria was just inches away from Mr. Emsworth when she stepped onto a wet patch. She slipped and almost fell when Emsworth dropped his phone and reached out for her. He caught her and held her in his arms making sure she was okay. Victoria stared into those enchanting green eyes and smiled. He made sure she was steady on her feet before he let her go.

"Oh, I am so sorry, I didn't see that."

"That's quite all right. It's not every day a beautiful lady falls into your arms."

Victoria gave a nervous smile and replied, "Thank you, Mr. Emsworth, was it?"

In his British accent, he replied, "Very good, I'm surprised you remembered that, but please, call me Richard. And you are?"

Suddenly, she felt like a stalker and wanted to turn around and leave, but her feet wouldn't move, "I'm a stalker. I mean." Victoria was really embarrassed now, her face turned red, and she rolled her eyes trying to cover up what she said, "I am so sorry, pleased to meet you, too." Stumbling over her words and feeling a little awkward, she realized he was waiting to hear her name, "Oh, right, my name. It's Victoria, Victoria Lancaster."

"Really, well, at least I know why you can't meet me today. Sorry, N.G. assigned me to you as your assistant. When I first met you, I had no idea you were Victoria."

He put his hand out and shook hers.

"N.G? Oh N.G, National Geographic. You're to be my assistant? Oh, I don't understand, why?" she replied still holding on to his hand.

"Yes, might I have that back?"

"Yes, what's that?" she then realized she was still holding his hand and she let go as a slight blush of red came over her face. He smiled and said, "Do you have time to go somewhere private?"

"What, why?"

"To discuss our new assignment."

"Oh, right," Victoria rolled her eyes, not knowing why this man flustered her so. He took her by the arm and walked her toward a waiting room.

"I gather your grandfather is doing okay. He is going to be okay, is he? This isn't an inconvenient time; I am sorry to bother you like this."

"No, he is going to be ok. They want him to stay and rest for a couple of days," Victoria started to relax as Richard guided her to a chair, "So, you will be helping me with Stonehenge?"

14

"Yes, they gave me your number to call you. But all I got was an answering machine," Victoria fumbled for her phone in her pocket and saw that the battery had died, "That's strange, I just charged this phone overnight, it should be fully charged."

"That's all right. Is it okay for us to talk?"

"Sure, we can talk, but don't you need to be with your wife and baby?"

"No, they are fine and resting. Here, you need to see this," Richard took an iPad out of his bag and handed it to Victoria. As he bent over her, she silently inhaled deeply and could smell his sweet musky fragrance. He smelt so good that she found it hard to pay attention to what he was saying. She snapped out of it when she saw the video of a dig site not too far from Stonehenge.

"They want us to go to this site. Some of the team used a G.P.R. and they believe they found something. They wanted the experts, us, to check it out."

"Can we go there now?"

The thought of finding something that nobody has touch sent sparks of excitement through her body. She nearly jumped out of her chair from the adrenaline surging through her, "I should let the nurse know what I am doing. Wait, my phone is dead, how are they going to contact me if something happens?"

"We can give them my number."

As he looked at the crack in his phone, he checked to make sure it was still working. The two proceeded to leave their information at the nurse station and then headed out to Victoria's car. She fumbled around her pockets searching for her keys. Not finding them, she closed her eyes and bent down to look in the car. When she opened her eyes, there were the keys, still in the ignition. Victoria lightly hit the window; she was really embarrassed about the keys being locked in the car. She sheepishly looked at Richard and he smiled at her showing his beautiful white teeth, which caused Victoria to get lost in his appearance again. How handsome he was, and those eyes were so hypnotic. Richard pulled his keys out of his pocket, jingled them, and gestured her to follow him, "Come on, we can take my car. It's just over here." She started to walk toward his car and remembered, "But my tools. They are in the car." Richard gently grabbed her arm and said, "Don't worry, I will share mine." They got into the car and drove to the site.

Upon approaching the site, there were several people from the team there. They were all excited to see what was down there. While the teams were setting up, the ground had collapsed and revealed a tunnel. Nobody was hurt but their G.P.R. had fallen through. They had been rigging up a pulley system to lower somebody down to retrieve it. Richard and Victoria raced up to them and told them that they would be the first to go down. As they were getting hooked up, Victoria couldn't stop smiling, she was so excited. The two were lowered down the large opening in the ground armed with flashlights and Richard's tool roll.

It was so dark down there even with their flashlights, they were almost afraid to move their feet for fear of stepping on something crucial. The small flashlights they had barely cast enough light to see around the dark tunnel. Not wanting to go any further in the dark, they had the crew lower down some lights. Richard asked a few workers to come down and help with the light. The air in the tunnel was rather stagnant, but the longer the site was exposed to the fresh air above, the sooner the smell dissipated. Victoria had her little flashlight and slowly worked her way further down the tunnel. She came across a marking on the wall that was just barely visible, and she asked Richard to come look at the marking. Richard shined his light on it, and they were able to make out a red cross. Victoria gasped, and then cover her mouth with her free hand, "Richard is that what I think it is." With disbelief in their find, Richard smiled and started hugging Victoria, they were so excited from what they found they could barely contain their selves, "Knights Templar, Victoria we found a Knights Templar's ruin."

"Richard, I can't believe we found this. It's like all these years it was waiting for us to find it," Victoria traced her finger on the Templar's Red Cross, finding something like this was a dream come true for her, "It's a marker, there must be something nearby. I read they marked spots with a red cross for other Templars." Taking her light and shining it on the wall, she looked carefully for something out of place. Proceeding down the tunnel, she noticed something different about a section of the wall. She instinctively stepped back to get a better look, "There is something strange about this part of the wall." Richard stepped back with her and looked, and then he stepped closer to the wall and started to feel it. He felt a stone out of place and pushed on it. He could hear a faint sound of gears moving and he backed away. Then there was this hissing sound like air being released and he quickly shielded Victoria with his body pushing her down to the ground. Suddenly, the wall sunk in and started sliding to the right.

With Victoria on her back and Richard on top of her, they watched as the wall opened. Richard looked down at Victoria smiled and said, "I keep finding myself in the strangest positions with you." He got up and helped Victoria to her feet; they turned toward the wall and walked in. It was a small chamber with markings on the wall. At the far end of the room were two torch sconces about four feet apart from each other. There were two others on the right and left side of the room. Observing closer, they noticed that there were words deeply engrave into the wall between the torches. Richard studied the words on the far wall "*In nomine patri,*" the right wall, "*et fili,*" and the left wall "*spiritu sancta.*" Victoria translated, "In the name of the father, the son, holy spirit." Richard grabbed both sconces and turn them away from the words, hearing cranking sounds, he went to the one on the right and did the same. He heard more gears then went to the left wall and did the same as the others. Again, they heard a hissing sound and watched the far wall open.

"How did you know that would happen?"

Richard shrugged his shoulders and said, "I don't know, I just have a knack for puzzles, it felt right."

As they walked into the second chamber, there, in the middle of the room, was a chest. It was made of oak and well preserved. There were carvings of what appeared to be Knight Templar's carrying their shields with the Templar cross on them. In between the Templars was a carving of a woman with wings. The two grabbed a package that had white cotton gloves in it. Putting the gloves on, Victoria traced her finger on the wings of the woman and said, "The symbol of the Virgin Mary." Richard looked at the woman on the chest and said, "The Virgin Mary looks an awful lot like you." Victoria looked at him and grimaced, "Don't be silly, I don't have wings." Richard responded by saying, "Well, last I heard, neither did the Virgin Mary." With that, they open the chest and inside was a small book that was bounded in leather. It was roughly five by eight and it had approximately 200 pages in it. Richard carefully picked up the book and opened it. There was a list of names. It showed their full name shorten to just one name. From Victoria's research, this was one of the requirements; men had to give up their full name to become a Templar. As they looked through the names, Victoria saw a name with a line through it, "Why would they put a line through this name?"

Richard tried to make out the name, but it was illegible because of the line, "I don't know, maybe he died or something." He shrugged his shoulders and continued looking. "But wouldn't there be others like this if they died," exclaimed Victoria.

"Maybe there is a ledger in here that will explain why they did that. It's hard to read in this light," Richard stated as he carefully closed the book. He grabbed a plastic bag and gently placed the book in it. The two were so focused on the book they didn't notice what it was laying on inside the chest. The Red Cross caught Victoria's eye, gasping, she reached for the tunic and carefully unfolded it. Underneath the tunic was chain mail armor, a sword, and a shield, which were made of iron and had been placed in the chest too. Richard saw something in the corner of the chest. He picked it up and saw that it appeared to be Templar's ring.

He looked around to see if anything else was in the room, "This room must have been tightly sealed for these things to be so well preserved." Searching the room, he spotted something behind the chest. It was a rolled-up piece of vellum. He grabbed another bag and gently placed the vellum in it. Happy with their find, they wrapped the chest up and carefully hauled it out of the tunnel.

"This is a big find Richard, do we tell N.G. or the press? I am not sure what to do, it's my first find. I dreamt about this for years while studying and now that it has happened, my mind has gone completely blank."

"Well, there have been many people who out of sheer excitement claimed they found something amazing. Like, what's that chap's name, that Geraldo fellow?"

"Geraldo Rivera, you mean the time he thought he was going to find something in Al Capone's secret vault," Victoria rolled her eyes when she thought of how humiliated Geraldo was.

"Yes, exactly. I don't want that to happen to us. You know, in case this is not authentic. Let's get it tested first and then go from there," Richard looked down at the chest, and then gave her a smile.

"Smart move. You are right Richard; I would hate to have that happen to us."

They both were brought up out of the tunnel and started to walk to Richard's car. Victoria walked to the back of the Range Rover, turned to Richard, and said, "Hey, thanks for letting me use these." She then placed the tool roll in the back of the car, "Richard, I just wanted to thank you for the best day of my life."

"You are most welcome, but the day is not quiet over yet."

"Oh, it's not?" Victoria was surprised and confused by his statement.

"Well, yes," holding up the baggy with the rolled-up vellum he replied.

"We need to see what is on this parchment. What do you think it is; a love letter?" he said teasingly, he raised his eyebrows and opened his mouth in surprise.

Victoria giggle at his gesture, "Yes, what if it was a love letter." Richard adored her little laugh; there was something very special about Victoria, "Hey, I need to stop in and see my wife and baby. How about we meet up somewhere."

"Good idea, because I would like to check up on my grandfather, maybe we could meet in the waiting room."

Richard smiled and said, "It's a date."

Richard drove them to the hospital, and they talked about their find all the way there. The two walked down the hallway of the hospital, then went their separate ways. Victoria went to her grandfather's room to find him resting peacefully. She didn't want to wake him, so she talked to the nurse to find out how he was doing. The nurse said he was doing well, and he could be going home soon. Victoria decided she would go to the nursery, she wanted to see Richard's baby. She walked down the hall toward the room that had the pop machines. Across from the machine was the doorway that read "Labor and Delivery," she figured the nursery should be through those doors. She walked through the doors and just as she was rounding the corner, she could hear a man and woman talking. She slowly peeked around the corner and saw Richard standing next to a woman with short dark hair. Not wanting them to see her, she ducked back around the corner.

Richard was looking at his son with his arm around his wife. She didn't seem very excited about the whole baby thing. She stood there with her arms crossed and a frown on her face. Richard was smiling, then looked at his wife, and the smile faded.

"What's wrong, Sophia?" Sophia was a French woman with short dark hair and brown eyes. She was pretty and spoke with an accent.

"Richard, I don't want to do this."

"Don't say that, you're just tired. Give it awhile."

"No, I really don't want to do this. I will be the one stuck with the baby while you go out on your little adventures."

"That's not fair, you know what my job entitles me to do."

19

"Yes, but I thought I could get you to change that, by having this baby," Richard turned to her and put his hands on her shoulders. Sophie went to pull away from him, but he held on, "Sophia, I will be there, I just need to finish this one job and I will ask for a short leave, so I can spend time with you and the baby."

Sophia jerked away, and this strange sort of evil look came over her face, "I said no, I don't want to do this. Just go, leave me alone." Richard did not want to push it, so he let her go. He turned and looked at his son, putting his hand on the glass, he smiled a little, and then a sad look came over his face.

Victoria didn't want him to know she overheard what they were saying so she quickly turned around to leave. But being a clumsy person that she was, she didn't see the wet floor sign and tripped over it. She squealed a little and caught herself before she could fall to the floor. It was a kind of dance she did to stop herself from falling and when she turned around, she saw Richard smiling at her, "I guess I am not very graceful." Richard laughed and made sure she was study on her feet. "Well, you don't seem to have much luck with wet floors," he was smiling at Victoria but then his mind went back to his conversation with Sophia. "I…I'm," Victoria felt bad for him and put her hand on his shoulder, "I'm sorry, I didn't mean to hear that. I just wanted to see your baby; I didn't think you two would be out here."

"That's all right, she was standing here when I came around the corner," Richard looked sad, Victoria hated to see him like that. She didn't know what to do to help ease his pain. He then looked at her and smiled, "Do you want to see him, my son?"

"Yes, I would love to see him," Richard put his hand on her shoulder and guided her to the nursery window. He pointed out a beautiful baby with dark hair, "That's him, my son, William."

"Oh, Richard, he is beautiful."

"Thank you, I just wish Sophia, my wife, was half as excited about him as you are."

"Oh, I am sure she has told you that he is a beautiful baby," Richard shook his head no and said, "She has said nothing but looks at him with distaste." The two turned toward each other and Victoria put her hand on his shoulder, "You know, I heard that some women who have babies get something called postpartum. I am sure she will come around." Richard smiled at her for trying to help him feel better, but he knew it was something more, "Come on, let's go check out this parchment."

"Are you sure you want to do that, maybe you should go talk to Sophia."

"No, it will be okay."

"I insist that you give it a try, Richard. It couldn't hurt, your family is important, right," Richard looked at his son, then down the hallway where his wife's room was.

"Really, Richard it's okay, I want you to work this out. I wouldn't be able to work well knowing that you have some issues with your family. Family is very important, Richard, please, don't give up."

Richard gave in but insisted that he give her a ride home since her keys were still in her car. She accepted the ride and the two walked back to his car. Victoria showed him where she was staying and the ride there was very quiet. She felt bad for Richard but there was just a little bit of contentment in her heart. She really cared a great deal for him, even though they just met. It felt like they were together in another life. Like they truly belonged to each other. But she knew nothing could happen between them because he was married and had a baby. It's just the kind of person she was. Victoria was a kind soul and would never come between families like that, even though they were having problems. When she got out of the car, she waved goodbye. Watching him drive off, a sad look came over her face. She knew she had to get off this assignment and leave England. Her grandfather was right, England had sad memories for them.

Chapter II

Standing in the fog, Victoria could just barely make out Stonehenge. Nobody was there, she was all alone. She started hearing these strange sounds coming from every direction. It sounded a little bit like trumpets. Flashes of light were shooting all around Stonehenge. Victoria could hear somebody yelling her name. She turned around and saw her grandfather running up the hill wearing a hospital gown, Richard had the look of confusion as he was running up behind him. They were yelling at her to come away from there. The fog started to bellow, encircling her and she could feel this force pulling her. She reached out for Richard but as she was getting pulled in, he was getting pushed back. The light kept flashing then became steady. It was so bright that she had to put her hand up to shield her eyes. Between her fingers, she could see the silhouette of a man on a horse.

She opened her eyes and was back in her room, the sun was peeking through the curtain and she put her hand up to shield her eyes. Looking at the time, she saw that it was 10:00, with haste, she jumped out of bed and ran to the bathroom. She turned the shower on and threw off her T-shirt and as it landed on the floor, she jumped into the shower. The warm water felt good on her face, she turned to saturate her body with the warmth of the shower. Lather herself up, she had to be quick, she was supposed to call N.G. early this morning to let them know that she had decided to go back to the states. But since she slept in, she was going to have to go through the day with Richard.

Grabbing a piece of peanut butter toast and a cup of coffee, her phone rang. Looking at the phone, she saw that it was Richard, "Shit, maybe I should just ignore it." She rolled her eyes up to the ceiling and in frustration answered the phone, "Hello, Richard, I am so sorry I overslept."

"I figured that much since I didn't hear from you."

Victoria looked confused, why would he thank he would hear from her, "I don't think this would be a good idea, Richard." On the other end, Richard smiled and knocked on a door, "Hang on Richard, I have somebody at my door." As she walked to the door and was about to open it, Richard said, "I know." She opened the door and there standing in her doorway was Richard. "It's me," she looked at her phone then at him. He smiled at her and put his phone in his pocket.

"You look a little confused."

"Yes, why are you here?"

"Well, I figured since your car was at the hospital, you would call and ask for a ride. But since you didn't call, I thought I would stop by to see if everything was okay." Feeling a little foolish and still holding her phone up to her ear, she said, "I forgot that my car was still there." Then he slowly took her phone away from her ear and walked to a small table in the entryway to place her phone there. "You mind if I come in," she smiled and said, "Yes, I mean no."

Richard did a half smile and said, "Well, which is it, yes or no?" Victoria couldn't understand how this man made her so nervous. She felt like a high school girl with a crush, "No, I don't mind if you come in." As he headed toward her living room, she followed behind him. She tripped over her shoes and caught his shoulders for support, "Oh, I am so sorry, I don't know why I am so clumsy." Looking the place over, he turned around and smiled at her, "Are you always this way, or do I make you nervous?" She looked down and took a deep breath, "Yes, I mean no, yes, no."

"Well, which is it, yes or no? Am I going to be asking you this question often?"

Victoria's eyes got big; she didn't want him to know that he made her nervous. It was very unprofessional of her and he was married. Just then her phone rang again, and it was the hospital, "Mrs. Lancaster, this is Nurse Williams from Salisbury District Hospital."

"It's Miss."

"Sorry, what?"

"It's Miss, I am not married."

"Oh, well, your grandfather is much better, but the doctor wants him to stay another night, just as a precaution."

Victoria gave a sigh of relieve and said, "That's great." She looked at Richard and decided she better cut this short, she's kept him waiting long enough, "Could you tell my grandfather that I will be at Stonehenge with Mr. Emsworth."

"Mr. Emsworth, Richard Emsworth?"

"Yes."

"Is he with you now?"

"Yes, he is."

"Mind if I had a chat with him?"

"Oh sure, of course."

She handed the phone to Richard. He took the phone, put his hand in his pocket, and slowly walked away. Not knowing what to do, Victoria started putting things in her bag. She watched Richard pace back and forth across her apartment. He looked distressed and suddenly sad. He looked at her and cracked a forced smile. Then he walked toward her and handed her the phone.

"You seemed troubled, is there anything wrong?"

He looked at her and she put her hand up and said, "I am so sorry, it is none of my business."

Richard shook his head and said, "It's okay, I just… Do you mind stopping at the hospital first?"

Victoria looked down then looked back up and smiled, "That would be find. I could visit my grandfather."

"I just really need to stop by there first."

"That is okay, do what you need to do. I am really sorry you are having problems."

Victoria looked down and a piece of her wet hair fell onto her face, as she looked up, Richard walked up to her and slowly placed the hair behind her ear and said, "Thank you, I just have to check something out and then we can go somewhere and assess the parchment."

The drive to the hospital was a quiet one. Richard seemed very melancholy, which Victoria believed had something to do with his wife. As they walked through the hospital door, the chief of staff needed a word with Richard. Richard told Victoria he would meet her upstairs in the waiting room where they first met. Not sure how long that would take, she stopped in to visit her grandfather. Walking into the room, she saw that he was asleep. Victoria thought this was strange for him and went to the nurse's station. There was a different nurse there, she looked about fifty years old, and she was looking at the computer. When the nurse finally looked up at Victoria, she asked, "Can I help you?"

"Yes, hi, I am Victoria Lancaster and Mahlon Featherhawke is my grandfather. Is he all right?"

The nurse seemed kind of flaky and asked, "Are you related?"

Victoria looked at this nurse with disbelieve and said, "Yes, he is my grandfather."

"Well, you can visit him, but I cannot give you any information."

Getting just a little upset Victoria replied, "But he is my grandfather, and it is not normal for him to be sleeping now."

"I'm sorry but I am not allowed to give out any information. Doctor, patient confidentiality."

"But I have been conversing with the doctor since he got here the other day."

For some reason, this nurse did not seem to like Victoria and was making things difficult for her, "I am sorry but unless there is a release or next of kin, I can't give out that information."

Now Victoria was really pissed and raised her voice just a little out of retaliation. "I am his next of kin, you dumb bitch." The nurse looked at Victoria and got on the phone to call security.

"Look, I am sorry, I am just a little worried about my grandfather, this is not normal for him."

Victoria was getting upset with this nurse and decided to leave before she really lost her temper. As she turned around, she ran right into Richard. Seeing that she was really upset, he asked her, "Is everything alright? Is your grandfather okay?" Victoria put her face in her hand and replied, "No, I went in to see my grandfather and he was sleeping, this is not normal for him. So, I came out here to find out what is going on and this woman won't tell me anything."

The nurse was still looking down at the phone and responded, "I cannot give out any information, doctor-patient confidentiality."

This nurse hit a nerve with Richard, and he responded by saying, "Oh don't give me that rubbish, Nurse Kally. Miss Lancaster has been conversing with the doctors about her grandfather since they got here, which means she has every right to know what is going on." The nurse was about to retaliate when she looked up and saw that it was Richard. Richard just happens to be the son to the chief of staff. He normally wouldn't use that as leverage, but he has been told by his father that this woman has been causing trouble at the hospital. He also didn't like to see Victoria upset; he held a special place in his heart for her. He just couldn't understand why. Richard is a very loyal man and to put another woman, besides his wife, in his heart just was not him. Nurse Kally frowned and replied, "Sir Duke Emsworth, I am sorry, I didn't see you there. Of course, let me get that information." She didn't really need to get any information; she was just stalling because she did not like the duke. She thought he was a pompous ass because he wouldn't date her daughter back before he got married.

"Yes, oh right, he got belligerent, so we had to sedate him."

"What, who's we?"

"The doctor and I."

"The doctor, you're lying, he would not have given that order without contacting me first."

"Well, we tried to contact you but didn't get an answer." Victoria looked at her phone and it was fully charged. The last call on there was from the hospital but she had answered it. Showing her phone to Richard and the nurse, Victoria said, "There has been no call, what's going on, why was he sedated? I want to speak to the doctor."

"I had to sedate him because he was trying to leave, he said somebody was in trouble. I couldn't get him to calm down."

"What was going on? What upset him?"

"I don't know why he was upset. All I know is when I came into the room, he was getting out of bed. He had pulled his I.V. out and tried to leave, so I gave him a shot."

Shocked by her grandfather's actions, Victoria calmed down, "I understand why you did this. I'll let it go this time, but under no circumstances are you to ever do that again."

"Yes, ma'am."

"Something is wrong; I should try to talk to him."

"It could be a couple of hours before he wakes," the nurse responded, then went back to her work on the computer.

"Richard, I can't leave him like this."

"It is okay, we can go to the conference room down the hall and work on that paper there."

"Are you sure that is okay with you?"

Richard looked at the nurse who was watching them and took Victoria by the arm. He walked her down the hall and into a room that had an oval table and some comfortable chairs. There was a coffee machine, water, and some snacks on a table against the wall. Across from the door were windows with a very nice view of London. Richard shut the door behind them, then pulled out a chair for Victoria to sit in, "You just sit here, and I will get a couple of laptops, the book, and parchment. Help yourself to some coffee or water. There are some snacks too if you would like some." Richard left the room to retrieve their work. Victoria got up and walked over to the window. Looking out the window, she could see the beautiful countryside of London. Turning away from the window, she saw that there was a T.V. in the room. She picked up the remote and turned the T.V. on.

There was a rerun of Charmed on and she stood there watching it. She used to watch this when it first came on in 1998. She was only seven years old, but she loved watching Charmed because of the magic powers. Piper was her favorite because she could freeze people and blow-up demons. She stood there for nearly the whole episode when Richard finally came in with a cart. He had it loaded with laptops, the book, the parchment, some gloves, and a few other things they might need. As he walked in, he saw Victoria watching Charmed, he said, "I didn't know you were a Charmed fan." Victoria turned and smiled, "I loved watching this. I always thought it would be so cool to have their powers. As a little girl, I used to pretend that I could freeze people, so I would put my hands up, like Piper did. The only thing I didn't understand was why they would scream when they saw a demon. Why would you scream when you had all that power? I remember when I was younger, my school mates didn't like the way I played. The girls would freak out because I would try to freeze them, hoping it would work. Even some of the boys were afraid of me, they believed I could freeze them. But some of the boys liked playing with me, they said I had some great ideas."

"Sounds like you were a blast when you were younger."

"Most girls that I knew didn't like me very much. I always thought they were very boring," Richard chuckled at that and so did Victoria, "Well, I got sent to the principal a lot. I was bored at school, they believed it was because I caught on to things really fast, they even had me skip a grade."

"So, you were very smart?"

27

"I don't know, I guess so, things just came really easy to me. My grandfather said I had a photographic memory, but I was told that there is no such thing as a photographic memory."

"There isn't?"

"Well, they say there is no actual proof," Victoria replied, shrugging her shoulders.

"Seriously, you just seem to remember everything, and they have no proof of that?"

"Well, it's not just instant memory. It is only if I am interested in it. Otherwise, I must go into a sort of trance to pull out what I read or have seen. They ran these tests on me and I got so bored that I just started making things up. I just wanted to get out of there and I was missing my favorite show."

"Your favorite show?" he pointed at the T.V. and said, "Charmed? From the way you talk, I take it Piper was your favorite." Victoria smiled and shook her head yes.

Victoria loved the way the English talked. If her father would have raised her, she probably would have not noticed the accent and would have had that very same accent. She thought maybe she wouldn't even have been allowed to act the way she did if her father raised her. The only time she sees him is on her birthday, Father's Day, and Christmas. She would love to spend more time with him, but they were both very busy. When she was younger, one time, he spent the summer with her in the states. She just couldn't understand why he didn't want her here, in England. Both, her father and grandfather, hated the idea of her working in England. Victoria believes that it was because of what happened to her mother and she feels that both her father and grandfather were hiding something from her. She felt something was wrong, because all her life she had the feeling of something missing.

Richard was setting things up on the table and Victoria grabbed some gloves to look at the book. It looked very old but as she was looking at it, she got this feeling that she has seen something like it, but she just couldn't place where. The leather-bound journal looked like something Hemingway would use. This could not be because the dates made it impossible for a Hemingway journal to be in a Templar chest. She was about to ask Richard about it when she noticed a look of distress on his face. Then she remembered the phone call he got earlier, she wanted to help him but didn't want to pry. She got up the courage to ask him, "Richard, I don't mean to pry, but is everything alright? Ever since that phone call, there are times that you seemed a little melancholy."

"No, it's all right. I must admit I don't normally get others involved. But I need a woman's perspective," Richard replied.

"Oh, are things okay with Sophia and William?" Richard winced a little because he really didn't like talking about his problems. But it was really bothering him, and he found it hard to work, "I really don't want to bother you with this."

"Well, I couldn't help but notice that you have been staring at the same page on your laptop for the last ten minutes. I know that feeling and I can tell that something is bothering you enough to cause you to stray from your work."

This time it was Richard's turn to stumble, "Yes, no, I mean yes, yes, something is bothering me."

"Well, I find that if I talk about it and get it off my chest, it doesn't haunt me as much. Now, I am not an expert on marriages or babies but maybe somehow, I can help, if anything, by listening."

Richard smiled at Victoria and got up from his chair, he put his hands in his black chinos pockets and began to pace around the room. He put one hand on his chin and looked at Victoria, and then he places both hands on the back of the chair next to her. "Okay, you mentioned something about women having post-partum syndrome after having a baby. Well, unfortunately, Sophia has been this way ever since she found out she was with child." He pulled the chair out and sat on it then put his face in his hands, "She left, she just walks out of the hospital without a word to where she was going."

"Oh my God, Richard, did she take the baby too? Do you need to go find her?"

"No, my father is chief of staff here and well, she left a note. Victoria, she left me and William, she said she did not want this kind of life and stated not to look for her. She said that I wouldn't be able to find her. She took 90,000 Euros and disappeared. My father was trying to find her through train, plains and buses, even rental cars. There is not a trace of her."

"Oh, Richard, I am so sorry. 90 thousand euros, is that a lot because it sounds like it?" Richard chuckled a little remembering Victoria's problem at the vending machine, "It's really not that much, okay, well, it is a lot, it's around $100,000 in American money." He responded as Victoria was taking a drink of her water. Victoria's eyes got big and began choking on her water. Richard surprised reached over and rubbed her back saying, "Are you okay?"

To her, 100 thousand dollars was a lot of money. She wasn't poor, but she didn't have a lot of money. Her father provided for her but just enough to get by. Her grandfather worked for a long time but had to retired just before she went to high school. They had been living on his retirement and money from her father. Both her father and grandfather paid for her college. They wanted to make sure she had a good education. They felt with her special abilities she should be able to go to the best college and get her masters. When Victoria was able to talk, she said, "A hundred thousand dollars it's almost like she put a price on the baby." After saying that, she realized what she said and with great sorrow, she too, retracted, "Oh, Richard, I am so sorry, that sounded so terrible, please forgive me." Richard put his hand up and said, "No need for apologies, I thought the same thing." There was an awkward silence, then Richard said, "Come on, let's get this started."

For hours, they sat there trying to figure out this book and parchment. The parchment looked like a letter of some sort, but large parts of it was smeared. Some of the parts, they could make out didn't make any sense. Victoria started to wonder about its authenticity and thought that the handwriting was a bit familiar. She also noticed that the writing was the same for the book and the parchment, "Whoever wrote in this book, wrote on this parchment, but it doesn't make any sense. It almost looks like somebody wrote it, then threw it in that room. We need to get the dating on this."

Richard was looking at the book and the parchment and seemed to be in deep thought. Then something came to him. "Wait, I had it dated. A colleague of mine said he could get it for me right away," he grabbed his phone and called his friend. As he listened, a look of bewilderment and shocked came across his face. He said a couple of uh hums and I see, then hung up the phone. He looked at Victoria and put his hands on her arms, "This book and parchment is approximately 2600 years old." Victoria couldn't believe what she heard; it was impossible. The writing and the words seemed a lot recent. They didn't talk that way 2600 years ago; they didn't even write like that.

"I don't understand; this can't be right. Is he sure the test he did was accurate?"

"He said he was just as shocked by the date, so he did it again, he took three testing, and they all came out conclusive."

"Something just isn't right; I need to go back to the site."

"It's kind of late. You won't be able to see much."

"It is," looking out the window, she saw that it was dark out. She didn't realize that they had been working on this all day. Time seemed to just get away from her and she felt like she needed some air. She needed to get away for a few minutes to clear her mind, "Look, can we call it a day and start on this tomorrow, I need to clear my head."

"Sure, you go get some rest and we can meet up tomorrow with clear heads and clear minds," Victoria got up, looked at Richard and smiled, "I will see you tomorrow. How about we meet here?"

"Don't you need a ride?"

"No, I had called earlier when we took a short break to have somebody get my keys out of the car. I asked them to leave the keys at the nurse's station if they couldn't find me."

"Ok then, I will see you tomorrow."

Victoria left and went to the nurse's station. She talked to the nurse and thanked God it wasn't the one she argued with earlier that day. She got her keys and took a sneak peek at her grandfather. She had visited him earlier when he was awake, she stayed with him for a while, but he told her to get back to work, that he was fine, and she didn't need to babysit him. When she saw that he was asleep, she left his room and walked out to her car. As she was walking through the parking lot, an elderly lady came up to her and handed her a piece of paper. The woman held her hand and smiled saying if you see them please call. Victoria glanced at the paper and saw some faces with names and at the top of the paper it said "Missing." She said she would call and folded up the paper and put it into her pocket.

When she got home, she took her phone and the piece of paper out of her pocket and placed it on the hall table. She kept thinking about the parchment and the book. Some of the words kept ringing in her head.

'So, you see, you must come back. Go to Stonehenge, all the answers are there.'

This alone did not make any sense; did they call it Stonehenge back then? And come back to where? Lying in her bed, she tossed and turned. She rolled over and reached for her light. Turning it on, she had two picture frames, one of her mothers and one of her grandfather and grandmother. She grabbed the picture with her grandmother and grandfather.

Her grandfather was such a handsome man. He had long, dark hair and there was a feather on the right side. The picture was black and white, but she could tell he was much darker than her grandmother. Her grandmother had blonde hair and you could see in the picture that her eyes were very blue. As she looked at her mother, she had the same blue eyes. It was strange that her mother nor her had the same color eyes as her grandfather. Those blue eyes were very prominent and continued down the line. Putting the picture back on her nightstand, she wondered what it would be like if her mother and grandmother was still alive. If only she could remember her mother and that day of the accident.

She found it very difficult to fall asleep; so much was going through her head. The parchment, book, grandmother, and her mother. She had a flash of a little boy with the same fair skin as her grandmother and those blue eyes. She was not sure why she had this memory and couldn't understand why she couldn't pull it out. She has a very good memory but this one has been giving her problems. She never told anybody about it, she kept it to herself. All she sees is wind blowing, her grandmother smiling and her mother with the look of terror on her face. She wasn't sure if it was a memory or something she concocted in her head.

She laid there thinking about these things and then slowly drifted into sleep. Her dreams were the same, over and over with her mother, grandmother, and this pale, little boy with dark hair. Something wasn't right, something felt wrong. She heard her mother screaming and then she heard a voice say mommy. She wasn't sure who said it. Suddenly, there was this bright light and she had to shield her eyes with her hand. It was so bright and there was this strange noise, like trumpets.

As she opened her eyes, the sun was once again shining through the curtains. She laid there thinking she needed to move the bed to a different spot in her room. That was the second time the sun woke her up this week. Looking at the time, she decided to get up and get ready for the long day she knew she was going to have. She needed to figure out this parchment and that book, so she needed to get going and meet Richard at the hospital. But first she wanted to stop at Stonehenge to see if she could find some clues there.

As Victoria was headed to the door, she went to grab her keys on the table in the hall. Next to her keys was a folded piece of paper. She unfolded the paper, then remembered it was the missing person paper. Missing since May 29, 2008; Elizabeth Jones age 16, brown hair, green eyes. Last seen at Stonehenge.

"Last seen at Stonehenge. That was about eight years ago," Victoria stood there thinking where she has seen that name before. Victoria started moving her fingers on her left hand as if she were sifting through files. This was a process she would go through to remember what she has seen. Her mind was like a picture film showing information, pictures, places, and designs. As she was sifting through it all, she stopped at the name. It was in a book with other names; alongside her name was a hyphen then one single name, Eppiny. In her mind, she closed the book, and it was the one they found at the dig site. "What the hell, this isn't possible," Victoria was so confused; she couldn't make any sense of this.

Instead of stopping at Stonehenge first, she was going to make a stop at the police station. It was a long shot, but she had this strange feeling about Stonehenge and missing people. She would give Richard a call when she was done at the police station to fill him in on her theory. Victoria knew he was not going to believe it mainly because she scarcely believed it herself. Grabbing her keys and the paper, she headed out the door.

Chapter III

At the police station, Victoria asked for a list of missing persons last seen near Stonehenge. It had to be dated back thirty years. She wasn't sitting there very long when a woman came to her with a large envelope. She handed it to Victoria, "That didn't take very long?"

A little confused Victoria reached for the envelope, "Oh, well, earlier this week, an elderly man asked for the very same thing."

"Do you know who he was?"

"No, but he was a Native American. He never came back for it, so I figure you could have it since it was already here."

"Thank you, I do appreciate it," Victoria placed the envelope in her book bag. It was a large leather rectangular bag that she used for her papers, books, and other things to put in. It had a long strap, so she could hang it over her left shoulder while the bag hung down her right side. She didn't really carry a purse, so she would put her billfold and keys in there too.

Victoria went to her car and sat in it with the look of confusion. Why would her grandfather want a list of missing people? Something was not right, she could feel it, something bad was going to happen and she began to panic a little. Her mind was flooding with all kinds of memories and her head started to hurt. She grabbed her head and closed her eyes. As she opened her eyes, she noticed that a man was staring at her. A little embarrassed, she smiled and looked down at her bag. She grabbed the bag and took the envelope out. She sifted through a couple of pages, then her hand went up, and the process for finding her information started up.

In her mind, she could see the names in the book with a single name next to it. This made no sense to her at all; she needed to find the underlying cause of this, so she headed for Stonehenge. On her way, she decided to call Richard and let him know what she has discovered. Richard was at the hospital and just happened to be standing next to Victoria's grandfather. He had been trying to help calm him down. Hawke was out of his bed and had put his pants on. He still had the hospital gown on and some slippers. When Richard had told him that Victoria was on her way to Stonehenge, Hawke ushered Richard out of the room and had them running to Richard's car.

Following behind them were the nurse, doctor, and security guard yelling at them to stop. Richard was still on the phone with Victoria trying to make out what she was saying. She kept breaking up and he could only hear every other word. As he was reaching for his keys, Hawke grabbed the phone from Richard and kept yelling at Victoria to stay away from Stonehenge. He kept trying to explain something to her but on her end, they kept breaking up too. Hawke asked Richard to drive fast and kept trying to explain to both what happened the year Victoria's mother disappeared. Victoria was confused and started asking, "What do you mean disappeared? Mother died, I thought."

Hawke was trying to explain but Victoria wasn't getting it all, the closer she got to Stonehenge, the worse the reception got. As Victoria pulled up to the parking lot, her phone died. She put it on the seat of her car and grabbed her bag. Leaving her keys in the car, she walked toward Stonehenge. Off to the right, there was a woman selling journals and other trinkets. Victoria had never noticed this before and stopped because something caught her eye. As she looked at the merchandise on the table, she couldn't believe what she was seeing. There, in front of her, was a book that looked exactly like the one she found at the dig site. She grabbed the book and looked through it, it was just a blank journal. She didn't have time to ask about it, so she reached into her bag and got her billfold out. She paid for the journal and set her billfold down to put the journal into her bag.

Suddenly, there was this loud trumpet like sound followed by flashes of light. Forgetting her wallet, Victoria started to run toward Stonehenge. The vending lady yelled, "Ma'am, you forgot your billfold." Victoria looked back, but the flashes of light were flashing longer, and she was curious, so she ran toward it. As she was running up to Stonehenge and the light, she could hear her grandfather, "Victoria, stay away, do not go near it." Victoria stopped to see her grandfather running toward her still wearing the hospital gown, his pants, and slippers. His hair was down and flying behind him. He still had long dark hair with streaks of gray in it. She saw his face and there was a look of terror on it.

Richard had no idea what was going on, but he didn't like what he saw. He ran past Hawke and tried to catch up with Victoria. The only thing that ran through his head was what Hawke had told him. Victoria's mother did not die, she disappeared.

Earlier, Hawke told Richard that he had just got back with Victoria just in time to see these same flashing lights and trumpet sounds. He remembers that Carver, Victoria's father was knocked down by a blast of wind. Then the sight, he would never forget, Hope was pulled into this light along with Victor, Victoria's twin brother.

"Victoria has a twin brother; does she even know this?"

Hawke shook his head *no*, "She does not even remember him. So, I would never bring him up, I did not want her to remember that day."

"Well, don't you think that could be harmful eventually," Richard exclaimed.

"I saw nothing wrong with not telling her. She went into shock that day. She was catatonic for a month and when she finally came out of it, she did not remember what happened. I told her that her mother died in a car accident and she did not ask about her brother. I thought it best she did not know of him."

"You should have told her. She felt something missing in her life but couldn't figure out what it was," Hawke looked at Richard and said, "Did she tell you this?"

"She mentioned it one time but shrugged it off."

"Oh, my God, Victoria, I am so sorry," Richard started thinking about Victoria's special talents and asked Hawke, "Is that about the time she started showing her special talents." Hawke looked surprised and asked, "Did she tell you what she could do?"

"Well, yes, she said she had a photographic memory."

"I see; she did not tell you all of it. She has more than that."

"More than that? Like what?" Richard pried for more answers.

"She could freeze people."

"What? She told me she pretended that she could freeze people," astonished in the answers he was provided.

"Yes, that has happened many times, but I told her they were pretending to be frozen."

"Oh, my God, don't you think others would have noticed?"

"No, I convinced them that they were just playing," Hawke responded, shrugging his shoulders.

"I am not one hundred percent sure, but I think she could predict things," Hawke responded with doubt.

"I think you are right about that, but I don't think she realized that herself. My God, she couldn't blow people up, could she?"

"No, she could not do that, but she could heal things and move things with her mind."

"Wait, if she could heal things, why didn't she heal you?"

"I asked her not to, I told her she could not keep me alive forever, it was not right."

"And she listens to you," Hawke thought about it and realized that maybe he was supposed to die. He remembers her touching his chest but doesn't remember much after that.

They drove up to the parking lot and saw Victoria's car. As they were about to get out of the car, Hawke said, "There is one more thing, Carver Lancaster is not really her father. He found out years later that he could not have children. Even knowing this, he still paid for Victoria's schooling and care. Hope told me one night when Carver was on a business trip, a handsome man with hair so blonde, it looked white came to her. When he came to her bedside, she could see that he had one blue eye and one green eye. For many nights, he would hold her in his arms and comfort her. Then one night, he told her what was about to happen to her. With her consent, he laid with her and when he left, he held her tight, kissed her and told her to be brave. Then shortly after she said her mother and a pale man with dark hair came to her. He forced himself on her then they left her crying, curled up in a ball. Soon after, she became pregnant with the twins. I did not believe my Hope. I thought she was going crazy."

"So, you sound like you believe her now, what changed your mind?"

"When Victoria was about ten, Carver had a test done, it proved that he was not the father but there was something else unusual in her blood. Something the doctors could not figure out. I would not let them test her anymore."

Richard was intrigued and asked, "So, what did they find?"

Hawke looked at Richard and said, "Something in her blood was not of this world they said."

Just then, Hawke saw Victoria and shouted for her. Both Hawke and Richard ran for her, Hawke had to stop her, he could not bear the thought of losing what was left of his family. As they were running to her, they heard this trumpet sound and saw the flashing lights. The lights and sounds had frightened the people visiting and they started running away from Stonehenge. A man ran past Hawke and knocked him down. Richard reached down to help him up. Hawke shrugged it off and yelled at Richard to hurry and stop Victoria.

Richard tried to run but he felt like he was running down an endless hallway. He could see Victoria in front of him, but she felt miles away. Suddenly, the wind started picking up and he had to dodge the people that were running away from Stonehenge. He shielded his eyes from the dust and debris that was flying around. Somebody tried to grab him and pull him away from Stonehenge, but he freed himself from their grip. He had to get to Victoria. There was something about her, he couldn't stand the thought of losing her. Why did she seem so important to him? As he got closer, he reached his hand out to her.

Victoria got closer to Stonehenge and as she was looking at the stones, a memory flashed in her head. She could see her mother yelling for her. One hand was reaching out to her and another hand was holding onto that little boy. Suddenly, she remembered him, she now knew who that little boy was. That was her twin brother, Victor. How could she forget her twin brother? Why would her grandfather and father let her forget him? She began to cry and looked back at her grandfather. "Why, why would you let me forget him?" she wanted to know what was going on. She looked at Richard and reached for his hand. The lights were flashing faster, and the trumpets were getting louder.

Victoria put her hands over her ears and closed her eyes. She began to scream and opened her eyes. Richard could almost touch her, all she had to do was to reach out for him. Tears were flooding her eyes and rolling down her face. Her head started swimming and she felt like she was in a dream. She began to reach out for Richard. Their hands were just about to touch when a blast of wind knocked him back ten feet. It felt like something grabbed her and pulled her in. The last thing she saw was her grandfather on his knees and slamming his fist into the ground.

Hawke started singing in Lakota, still on his knees, he starting to raise his hands up to the skies, then back down to the ground. Richard sat up in disbelief, looking toward the spot where Victoria disappeared. He got up and walked over to Hawke who was still singing. Looking back at the spot, Richard could not believe what he just witnessed. Then he remembered what Hawke told him in the car, "You should have told her, maybe she would have used better precautions if she knew the consequences of getting too close when the lights were flashing." Hawke put his hands over his head and buried his face in the ground. Maybe Richard was right, he should have told her. Maybe if she knew she would not have accepted this job. Richard reached down to Hawke and said, "Come on, I need to try and decipher that parchment and the book. My answers could be in there."

As they were walking back to the car, a woman came up to Richard and handed him a piece of paper. He looked at it and smiled at her then put it in his pocket. It was a quiet drive back to the hospital and when they got there, the nurses took Hawke and Richard went back to the conference room. He sat there for hours trying to make since of the paper and book. He stood up and walked to the window looking at the England landscape. He put his hands in his pockets and felt something. He pulled out that piece of paper and looked at it. It was a picture of a young girl and above her picture were the words "Missing Person." Richard continued reading, *Missing since May 29, 2008 Elizabeth Jones age 16, brown hair green eyes. Last seen at Stonehenge.*

Where had he seen that name, he sat back down at the table, placed the paper down, and started thumbing through the book. Just then he saw it, the same thing that Victoria saw. *Elizabeth Jones—Eppiny.* He grabbed his phone and called the police station. As he asked for the list of missing people's names only missing near Stonehenge thirty years back, the voice at the other end replied, "Another one? You are the third person who has asked for that."

"The third person, do you know who the other two were?"

"Well, one was a Native American man, looked to be in his 50s and the other was a…"

"Never mind, I think my question has just been answered, thank you."

With that, Richard hung up the phone and continued looking through the book. Close to the end of the book, two pages were stuck together. Richard carefully separated them as not to damage any of the writing. He read what was on the page, then closed the book in disbelief.

He picked up the parchment and tried to read what was said. Some of the writing was hard to make out so he grabbed his magnifying glass to make it out better. The writing wasn't small but some of it was illegible. He could make out some words but not enough to make any sense of it. As he was looking at all the stuff on the table, he spotted a notebook that Victoria was writing in. He brought it closer to the parchment and noticed that the handwriting was the same, "Impossible! This is Victoria's handwriting." As he scanned the parchment, some words made sense to him. He looked at it again, then read it aloud, "Rich, Richard, don't look for me." Richard stood up and looked out the window. England just didn't look the same to him anymore.

Victoria opened her eyes and her head started swimming. She lost her balance and fell to her hands and knees. She closed her eyes, then opened them slowly. Her heart began to race in a panic when she saw that everybody was gone. What the hell happened, where did everybody go? Stonehenge looked different, there were more stones and none of them were tipped over on the ground. It looked new somehow, but where were the sidewalks and where did all those trees come from? As she slowly got up, she saw that there were no signs of buildings, no sounds of cars or people. Then behind her, she heard this weird thumping sound. She turned to see what it was and could not believe her eyes. There was a man on a horse, normally that wouldn't seem too strange except for the fact that he was wearing the strangest outfit. It looked like he was wearing armor and so was his horse.

As the man got closer, Victoria could see that he had golden, blonde hair and sultry, green eyes. Such an enigmatic facial expression came over her face, which caused the rider to pull hard on his reins and made his horse rear up. As the rider steadied his horse, he put his hand up and said, "Caidil." A strange feeling came over Victoria and she closed her eyes and gracefully fell to the ground. The man got off his horse and walked over to Victoria. Her long hair had fallen over her face and the man knelt next to her and gently brushed it away. He had never seen a woman as beautiful as her. Victoria slowly opened her eyes and said, "Richard?" The man gently caressed her face and repeated the word "Caidil," which caused Victoria to fall into a deep sleep.

The man did a side smile then scoop Victoria up in his arms. He walked over to his horse and climbed on. He had a half days' ride ahead of him, so he kicked the sides of his horse, which made the horse jump into a gallop. He left behind him a structure that looked like Stonehenge, only there were other pillars and stones. It seemed unstable with flashes and the sounds of distance thunder. The stones were in a circle and a whirring sound would cause the whole thing to turn in a clockwise rotation. The man looked back at the structure and a worried look came over his face. He hoped that the woman he had in his arms was the one that the head mage was looking for.

As the sun was racing ahead of him, Cullen came to the clearing where you could see the outline of Mage Mountain. Looking down at Victoria, he could smell a fresh clean aroma coming from her. The sun was glistening off the golden highlights of her hair and he noticed that the clothes she was wearing were a little strange. Then he remembered what Ipion, the head mage told him, that the woman they were looking for will be wearing strange clothes. The clothes were only strange, because he had never seen a mage wear clothes like these. Normally mages wore mage robes, at least the female ones did. Mage robes were long but fastened snug around the waist. On the back, there was a hood to cover their heads. They came in several assorted colors, black, green, maroon, blue, and gold. The robes were made of cotton, leather, or silk. He had no idea what the women wore under them, but the men wore leather pants and a cotton shirt, and they all wore leather boots.

Victoria's shoes looked normal to him, maybe just a little fancy. She was wearing the boots she likes to call her Xena boots. They were black leather and laced all the way up to her knees. She had on a pair of black skinny jeans and a white sweatshirt. Cullen pulled one of his gauntlets off to feel the material of her pants and shirt. He never felt material like this before as he ran his hand down the side of her leg. Then he pulled his hand away when he realized he was touching her leg. A flush of heat rises to his face and he suddenly felt ashamed. He only meant to feel the material; he wasn't touching her for pleasure. Cullen whispered, "Maker's breath, forgive me." Then he put his gauntlet back on his hand.

For several hours, the ride was through a beautiful forest, the trees were so tall they seemed to touch the sky. Every couple of miles, there would be a small stream. Some streams had little waterfalls, which was an indication that they were slowly ascending. They were nearing the foothills and getting closer to another clearing. Many magical beings lived in this forest of foliage and every now and then, you could see a hut. Little firefly like bugs were floating around the rows of wildflowers that had grown in the areas where the sun could peek through the trees. The flowers were colorful with reds, purples, blues, and pinks and the aroma lofting from them was very pleasant. The trees were green and had a soft look to them. Beautifully bright colored birds flew from branch to branch as they curiously watch Cullen riding by. This forest was a magical one as little Flitters that looked like fairies flew by stopping every now and then to check on a hurt animal. They had shimmering wings and long hair. Their clothes were strands of sheer cloth, with many pastel colors. Running around on the ground were these little guys with their pots of honey, they were called Honey Nabbers. They gathered honey from the blossom that were scattered on the forest floor.

As they got closer to the mountain, you could see the tower. The tower holds a little over 1000 people, which consisted of mostly mages and guardians. It was carved into the mountain and stands over 800 feet tall. There are at least 500 rooms that ranged from mage dorms, bathing rooms to dining halls and workers quarters. All the ceilings were 20 feet high with windows halfway up the walls and the only windows there were, were at the front and sides of the tower. At the very top of the tower is a larger circular room where the more advanced mages are taught to control and test their magic for graduating. The stone walls had a blue hue to them and were protected with magic. There are many floors that consisted of ward rooms where at least ten mages share. These rooms have ten beds in them and several dressers to share among the mages. In the back of the room is an area for them to relieve their selves and freshen up. The floors had two sides to them, the east ward, and the west ward. The women are in the west ward while the men were boarded on the east ward. The wards are divided by a large sitting room and a huge staircase. Other floors consist of single rooms for the more important mages. Some of the rooms had large canopy beds with huge dressers and large wardrobes. They also had their own private bathing rooms.

On another floor, there was a huge library with thousands of books in shelves that line the walls and reached the ceilings. There were tables and chairs to sit at and candles that you could light when reading. Hanging from the ceilings are circular rod iron chandeliers with about twenty candles around them. These chandeliers were hung throughout the whole tower. On the main floor, there was a huge dining area that only sat hundred mages and 150 Guardians. The mages had to eat in shifts depending on their teachings. The newest mages had to be up first, they got cleaned up, dressed, had their breakfast then headed off to their instructor. Then there was a second group, a third group, then a fourth. There were at least ten cooks that prepared fresh food for each group. In the back of the kitchen were rooms that boarded the cooks.

Up on the second floor, deep in the mountain were the hot springs. There were 20 different hot springs throughout that area. This is where all would bathe after a grueling day of learning how to use their magic. It was needed as some of them smelled of sulfur from there magic spells that produced fire. They would finish their last lesson then go to the springs, after which they would have a nice hot supper. But as usual, in any place where clothes would be removed, the men were always separated from the women. The only time a man was in the same room with a naked woman was if it was a guardian. They watched over the women with their heads down, if anything happened, a guardian could sense it and can react in time.

All guardians were men; they were given enough magic to stop a rogue mage. This kind of thing would happen at the tower but not often. A mage who couldn't handle their magic would sometimes go crazy. The power they had would be too much for them and the only way they could release the pain from that power would be to hit others with it. If not stopped, they could kill somebody, then the power would begin to blacken their heart. A guardian can put a mage in a deep sleep, long enough to detain them. If a mage cannot be cured of the insanity, he or she is removed of their magic. Once the magic is removed from them, they are released from the tower to live their lives as a normal person. Ipion, the head mage, is the only one who could remove the magic.

Not all mages come to the tower, some try to teach themselves and live out their lives as outcast. People fear mages that have not been trained by the tower. They believe that magic is unstable and only the tower can teach them properly. There are some mages that learn magic on their own and have no problems. But some mages couldn't handle the power and become evil. These mages seek protection with Aldabus, the Darkheart.

Aldabus is a dark evil elf of the ancient mages, he surpasses Ipion by many centuries. He has tried many times to destroy Ipion, but Ipion has a power far greater than Aldabus. Ipion had Aldabus's daughter, Velatha's heart. Velatha was a good elf growing up, but when she married Ipion and had a baby, they thought the evil blood that ran through her veins came out and made her mad, or so he was made to believe.

Velatha was a very beautiful elf with long, dark hair that shimmered like the feathers of a crow in the light. Her skin was dark but not as dark as Aldabus, she had lush full lips and big sky-blue eyes. Her frame was small, and she was very agile, which made it easier for her to dart around like a deer. She was the best bowmen in the land, and nobody could outshoot her. Velatha had fallen in love with Ipion, and they had a child. But having this child, they were made to believe that it caused her to lose control of her power and her mind. Ipion was faced with a decision he never wanted to make.

Since she was from ancient magic, he could not remove the magic from Velatha but had to stand by and watch her go mad. After several days of reading the ancient books, he could only find one way to help her. He had to remove her heart and change her form. The form she took was a dragon. Ipion had no idea that a dragon was the form she was to be changed into. It was never written in the books what she would be turned into. But if he had her heart, she could do no harm to him. The only thing that worried him was the cure.

Most of the books he had, he got from Aldabus, so he knew that evil had the recipe. The cure was the blood of the cursed bloods first child. Ipion had to protect his daughter at any cost, so he sent her into a realm that no evil could enter. Even though Velatha seemed evil, there was still a part of her that remembered her love for Ipion. Because of this, you could sometimes see her circling the tower.

Cullen was only a few miles away from the tower and he just caught site of a dragon leaving, "Velatha." In the distances, he could see the bridge that crossed Vanishing River. It was called Vanishing River because whoever or whatever fell into it would be swept away and vanishes forever. The river started around one side somewhere at the top of the mountain. The massive fall splashed down and wrapped around the front of the tower than flowed down to the other side of the mountain. It had a strong current as it streamed down to the bottom of the mountain which had a drop off disappearing inside the other side of the mountain. At the back of the mountain from the bottom to about 200 feet high was rock that was smoother than ice. The tower had only one way in and one way out that people knew of and that was at the front. At the entrance to the tower were two large iron doors that stood 15 feet high. There was a cranking mechanism that was operated by ten dwarfs, which opened these two large doors. Only the dwarfs from Davenshaw caverns could operate these doors. They had these special crystals used to run the mechanism that would start up the cranking action which helped the dwarfs to open it. The dwarfs were the ones that invented these doors and trusted nobody other than themselves to run it.

Crossing the bridge, Cullen could hear the cranking of the mechanism and shouting from the dwarfs. As he got to the stables that were off to the side, a young elf boy held the horse while Cullen climbed down. He looked down at Victoria to make sure she was still asleep, then entered the doors that were finally open. It took a couple of minutes to get the doors open, but only seconds to shut them. Walking through the front entrance of the tower, Cullen was met by Ipion.

Ipion wore a long, white robe that covered his feet. The sleeves were narrow at the shoulders then flared out at the elbows. He always walked with his hands in each sleeve, almost like he was cold. The robe was a little snug from the shoulders to the waist then flared out enough to adjust to his gait. Around his waist was a gold belt that had small vials of liquid placed in slots. He stood six feet four, which made him the tallest man there. He had long gray and white hair and a long beard and moustache. Some of his hair was pulled back into a braid while the rest just flowed down to the middle of his back. He had kind blue green eyes and a prominent nose. As he spoke to Cullen, his voice was deep but soft, "Let's see what you have there." Ipion looked at Victoria's face and he smiled, he could see the resemblance and he knew that they finally found her. Cullen looked at Ipion and asked, "Is she the one?" Ipion looked at Victoria's wrist and saw the birthmark, he then patted her hand and replied, "Yes, she is the one. You did an excellent job, Cullen. You must take her to the wards and have one of the maidens find her something else to wear. We mustn't let anybody see her in these strange clothes."

"Master Mage, where does she come from? How—"

"Remember, Cullen, no questions. You are better off not knowing, they are all better off, at least for now."

"Yes, sir, I will see to it that she gets taken care of right away."

He adjusted Victoria in his arms and headed up to the wards.

Cullen took her up to one of the wards that had enough beds for ten people. As he laid her on the bed, he instructed one of the maidens to get her something to wear. Maidens were women that cleaned up, washed clothes, made beds, and at times, helped newcomers with proper clothes to wear. While she was getting Victoria some clothes, Cullen sat at the end of the bed and took her boots off. He tilted his head a little when he saw her foot covers. He had never seen any like those before. He pulled them off her feet and put them in a satchel. When the maiden came in with some clothes, he instructed her to put

45

all of Victoria's clothes in the satchel and set them outside the room. He was to dispose of those clothes, so that nobody would see them. The maiden wouldn't say anything because they are magically bound to secrecy if anything odd comes about.

As Cullen waited outside the room, he could still smell her on him. She smelt so good and the memory of her made him do this side smile. He couldn't help but wonder who she was and where she was from. There has never been any special woman in his life, he never thought he would find that one for him, one of the reasons he became a guardian. Guardians are dedicated to their work and sometimes never marry. But this woman was different, he couldn't stop thinking of her. As he stood there, thinking about the way she smelled and how pretty she was, he didn't notice somebody standing next to him.

"Well, that's an interesting look on your face," Cullen looked up and standing in front of him was a Satyr named Clark. They don't usually take Satyrs into the tower, but he begged Ipion for sanctuary as a little boy. Ipion was not only just any ordinary mage, but he also had many talents, one of them being the gift of foresight, he knew that one day Clark would become very important to Victoria. When Ipion sent Cullen up to the wards, he sought out Clark and asked him to help Victoria. He let Clark know that Victoria will seem a bit frighten and very confused. Always glad to make new friends Clark trotted up to the wards, "Clark, what brings you up here?"

"Master Ipion sent me up here, I take it we have a new mage," Cullen looked at the close door and said, "Yes, Master Ipion sent you?"

"You sound surprised," Clark smiled.

"Yes, well, I guess Master Ipion knows what he is doing."

"What she like? Did you see what magic she could do?"

"No, I cast the sleep spell on her before she could do anything. She seemed surprised," responded Cullen as he looked back at the door. A little confused, Clark asked, "Then how do you even know she is a mage?" Cullen sheepishly answered, "I just knew, there was something about her." He blushed a little as the maiden stepped out the door. She was surprised to see them standing there. Cullen looked at her and said, "Where is the bag?"

The elf was acting strange but quickly replied, "Forgive me, my lord." She ducked back into the room and seconds later, she came out with the bag. Looking down, she said, "She is ready, commander." Taking the satchel and hanging it on his shoulder, he told Clark to go in and wait for her to wake.

46

Clark was told to bring her to Ipion the minute she wakes. Just as Cullen was about to walk off Clark touched his shoulder and asked, "What's her name?"

Cullen looked down then back at Clark, "I don't know."

Clark smiled as he stepped into the room with the satchel that Cullen had, Clark was quite the pick pocketer. As he placed the satchel on the floor next to an oversized armchair, he paused when he saw Victoria lying on the bed. The maiden had put a drab looking robe on her that looked like it came out of the soiled bin. He saw her boots sitting on the floor and he picked one up and smelled it. It was different; everything about this boot was different. The smell, the way it was made, and this strange contraption on the back of them. He had never seen a working zipper before, and he carefully slid it up and down the tracks. He remembered his mama showing him an old dress she had with one, but it was broken, and this was the first one he seen that worked. He placed the boot down and pulled up a chair to sit on. He knew that since Cullen placed the sleep spell on her, it could be a while before she woke.

Chapter IV

Victoria was standing in front of Stonehenge; it seemed a little quiet and the surroundings did not look the same. She heard this thumping sound and as she turned, she saw a man on a horse. As the man got closer, she thought it was Richard. The eyes and hair were a little different and the man was wearing armor. His armor reflected the sun, which caused Victoria to shield her eyes with her arm. She tried to look at him, but he was too bright. Closing her eyes to moisten them from the glare, she slowly opened her eyes. When she opened them again, she realized that the sun was shining in on her and she stated, "I have got to move this bed."

Then a voice said, "Yeah, you could do that." Shocked at hearing a man's voice in the room, she jumped out of bed.

Looking around, she noticed that she was not in her room. Where the hell was she? Scanning the room, she saw that there were other beds, a few single ones and several bunk types looking beds. The bed she was laying on had your basic wood, sled head and foot boards. The bunk beds were made of heavy oak post with ladders on the side for accessing the top bunk. Looking at the walls, she could see that they were made of stone and had a strange blue color to them. The windows were very high from the floor and the ceiling was just as high. She concluded that she must be in a castle. When she looked at her bed, there was something or someone next to the bed that she had never seen before. Thinking maybe, she was still dreaming she calmly asked, "Who are you and what are you?"

Clark walked up to her and said, "My name is Clark, and I am a satyr."

Victoria's hand went up and she did that thing with her fingers like she was rifling through pages. In her mind, she was going through pages and it stopped when she saw the word Satyr. When she saw the description, she said, "Satyr, a fictional character. A lustful, drunken woodland god. Greeks saw them as a man with a horse's tail and ears. Roman's seen them as a man with goat ears, tail, legs, and horns."

Victoria looked at Clark and said, "The Roman's way."

"What's a roman and I am not a drunk. Also, what is that thing you do with your hand," he asked pointing to her hand.

"It's a thought process," Victoria answered as she lowered her hand.

"So, you are not afraid of me?" Clark surprisingly asked.

"No, because you are not real, and I have finally lost my mind."

"I am so real," Clark retorted, then reached over, and pinched Victoria on the arm.

"Owe, why did you do that?"

"Ah, you felt that."

"Well, yeah, it hurt."

"Then that proves it, I am real. I win, you lose," Clark turned around and walked toward the door. He turned and said, "Well, come on, follow me."

Victoria picked up her robe that she just noticed she was wearing and walked out the door with Clark.

"By the way, what is your name?" Clark smiled, waiting for an answer.

"My name is Victoria. Clark, where am I."

"Can I call you Tori?" Victoria smiled remembering that her grandfather would call her that. Then she realized the last time she saw him he was at Stonehenge, "Oh, my God, my grandfather!"

"Oh, that is so sweet, you have a grampy, I wish I had a grampy," then he stops and in a pitiful way, he whined, "I never knew my grampy, I never knew my daddy either." As he was talking about his needs for a father and grandfather, Victoria noticed he had kind of had the personality of an actor in a movie she liked to watch. What was his name, right, Hollywood from the movie "Mannequin." Then she heard him say how his father wants to kill him, "Wait, what? Your father wants to kill you, why?"

"Because I like men," Victoria looked at him with a blank look on her face, she batted her eyes and said, "He wants to kill you because you like men? I don't understand, why?"

"Well, I am a satyr," Again, a blank look from Victoria. Clark rolled his eyes and smiled, "You know nothing about this world do you."

"No, I don't. And how is it that you know I am not from this world."

"You have that scent about you like my momma."

"Your mother? Is she here with you?"

"No, my daddy killed her," Clark had the look of sorrow and anger on his face.

"He killed her! What kind of place is this?" she looked at her surroundings and said with great sarcasm, "I guess I am not in Kansas anymore."

"Oh, funny Dorothy Gale, and where is your little dog, Toto," with surprise, Victoria looked at Clark, "How?" Clark smiled and said, "Girlfriend, please, my momma told me the story about the wizard of oz."

Confused, she was about to ask him how he knew these things, but he answered her before she could ask, "My momma was from your world, that is why they sent me to you."

"Your mother was from my world? Were there any others from there? And who is they?"

"Oh, yes, thousands of them, maybe even more. Oh, but none of them had mag…" Clark's eyes got really big, and he put his hand over his mouth, "Oh, I wasn't supposed to talk about that."

"Talk about what, mag, mag, mag…ic? There is no such thing," Clark looked at Victoria, closed his mouth tight, and looked away. Then he tried to change the subject, "So, how do you like the clothes they picked out for you." Victoria stopped and a disgusted look came over her face. The gown she had on wasn't exactly her style and kind of ugly. It was sort of gray and had no style at all. This was usually what they had the first-year mages wear. The robe kind of wrapped around your waist and was tied with a rope. The sleeves were long but didn't quite hit her wrist. As tall as she was, the robe still dragged on the floor mainly because it was too big for her. There was a short cape that draped over her shoulders and went all the way around from front to back. On the cape was a hood attached to it that was hanging in the back.

"What is this thing I am wearing? It's ugly, too big, and it is itchy."

As she grabbed the sides of the robe, she caught a whiff of it. Her eyes got a little big and she wrinkled one side of her nose, "And what is that repulsive smell." Clark lifted his arm and smelled to see if it was him. Upon discovering that it wasn't him, he looked at Victoria, "Oh honey, that's you."

Victoria grabbed a piece of the robe and smelled it. She gagged at the odor it gave off. It kind of smelt like sulfur and sweat. The maiden that put this on her was not one of the maidens that worked there. She was a spy put there from Aldabus and Ipion had his suspicions about her. He sent her to dress Victoria,

50

and he would know for sure she was a spy if Victoria was not wearing the right clothes. The maiden had grabbed the robe from the men's soiled pile. She didn't really work at the tower, so she didn't know where to get the right clothes. She was only sent there by Aldabus because of a vision he got. The vision wasn't clear, but he knew his answer could be found at the tower.

The maiden was an elf with the power of fire and ice. She could throw flames to scorch a person, or she could throw a blast of frigid wind that could freeze. She couldn't use her magic, or she would be discovered. Magic taught at the tower had an unusual color from magic taught on your own. When magic is cast, each level has a distinct color to it. Pure evil would cast a green hue. Magic taught by evil cast a turquoise color. If taught on your own, it was light blue and taught by the tower, it had a light bluish-purple color. Very powerful and good magic had a violet color.

As the elf made her way toward the exit of the tower, she came down the long corridor that led to the entryway of the tower. She paused briefly when she thought she saw Ipion coming toward her. When she blinked, she found herself in front of the doors and the shouting of the dwarfs. She wasn't sure how she got there but she shrugged it off; thinking she was just so nervous about getting caught. As she left the doors and headed toward Vanishing River, she turned and smiled. She couldn't believe she didn't get caught and started on her trek to Aldabus with the information she collected.

Clark and Victoria got to the staircase and proceeded down them. Clark was looking at Victoria's feet when he noticed that she didn't have any shoes on. He gave her a confused look and asked, "Where are your shoes? You're not even wearing foot coverings." Victoria looked down at her feet and responded, "I didn't know where they were. This is how I woke up, in a strange place with strange clothes. Clothes that stink." Clark had her sit down on the steps and told her to wait right there. Thinking this was going to take a while, she crossed her leg and put her chin in her hand. No sooner did she do that, Clark was right by her side with her foot coverings snatched from the satchel and her boots. Victoria was glad to see her socks and boots that she almost forgot how quick he got there. She looked at him and said, "How did you do that and so fast?"

"I'm a satyr," Victoria raised her eyebrows and winced at his answer, "I forgot, you don't know anything about this place. My momma was the same way, but she learned a lot and told me everything. Satyr's are very fast." When she finished putting her boots on, they continued walking down the stairs. Victoria wanted to know more about his mother, "She sounds wonderful, your mother." Clark smiled a kind of sad smile, "She was; she was all I had." Victoria felt a little lightheaded, so she grabbed Clark's arm and sat him down with her, "Tell me about her."

Clark looked up as if he were looking at his mother; a sort of happy peaceful look came across his face, "My mother was a beautiful woman. She is what you would call a hefty woman. Not too heavy but not very thin. She had the prettiest face I ever saw. Her eyes were big and light brown. She said where she came from she was called a black woman."

"A black woman, I am sure she said African American," Clark looked at her with a blank look on his face. Realizing that this was a strange place Victoria had to ask, "What year was she born. Did she ever tell you?"

"Girlfriend, she was my momma, of course she told me the day she was born," he smiled and said with profound respect, "Jan-a-wary 18, 1945." Victoria smiled when he said January wrong but didn't say anything. Clark continued with his story, "She said she was 15 when she came here. She was a smart woman and very social like. She learnt ever thing she could about this place. She kept to herself and never drew any attention."

Clark looked at Victoria and raised his eyes, smiling, he said, "I never believe that part. My momma talked to ever body. When I was a little boy, I could tell the men liked her. They would tell her how pretty she was. But momma was only here for me. She had to keep me hidden. She said from the day I could talk and walk, she knew I was going to be different."

"I would have noticed the day you were born," Victoria sarcastically responded. Clark quizzically answered, "What?" Changing the subject, Victoria asked, "So, did your mother fall in love with your father."

"Oh, hell to the no, honey. My daddy was what she called a pervert. Still not sure what that is."

Victoria turned her head and did a half smile, then looked back at Clark, "Please, continue." Victoria said gesturing with her hand for him to continue, "What, what does it mean?" Victoria shook her head back and forth and said, "I am sure she would have told you if she wanted you to know. Please, continue."

Clark kind of pouted his lips and frowned a little before he continued, "Well, she said he broke her flower, she said he came at her like a frighten train on a track, whatever that means." Victoria was sure he meant a freight train, "And then, she had me. But I believe he got his privates up when he saw her, then backdoored her. I have seen a few satyrs do that to other women before. Mama tried to shield my eyes, but I know what I saw." Clark looked sad when he suddenly remembered his last day with his mother, "The last day I was with her, she handed me her bag that had her books in it and told me to run as fast as I could and never look back."

"Books? She wrote books."

"Girlfriend, my momma wrote ever thing she knew about this place. Everything. She had over ten years of writing in that bag. She told me one day she wanted me to give these books to the mage at the mountain that looks like a tower."

"How old were you when she had you run."

"I was only twelve."

"Twelve! You were only a child; wait was that when your father wanted to kill you. I don't understand."

"Let me give you a lesson on satyr. All satyrs are men; you will never see a female satyr. Satyr only like women, they lust after them and get them into bed, this is how they make other satyrs. Satyrs cannot mate with women from your world because for some reason, they all end up only liking men. I don't see nothing wrong with that. The other thing is that they don't get the goat legs, only the hooves. If a satyr likes a man, the daddy of that satyr must kill him because he is considered an abomination. A satyr stays with his momma until he turns ten and then the daddy comes and takes them. I don't know why, it's just a rule, a stupid one if you ask me. Well, when my momma discovered this rule, she had also heard that if the young satyr likes men, they would be killed. She kept me hidden from my daddy for two years. When he finally caught up with us, the night before she died, she told me we were going to the tower. She was sure they would keep us safe. But when he caught us, he grabbed a hold of me, and my momma swung her bag at him. Don't laugh, that bag was heavy, and the weight of it surprised him enough to knock him right off his hooves. That was when she yelled at me to run and never look back. So, I grabbed the bag and did as she said." Clark had tears in his eyes and was wiping them with his hand, "Later that day, I came back when I knew it was safe and found my momma dead. He horned her to death with his horns, but from the look of her hands, she must have put up a really good fight. Such a waste, she was only 28."

"Wait, 28? How old are you?"

"23."

"23, that doesn't make sense."

Victoria felt so bad for Clark, she grabbed him and slowly held him close to her. She cradled him in her arms and tried to console him. She felt a closeness to him that she couldn't explain. Tearing a piece of cloth from her robe, she handed it to Clark. As she looked at his face, she could see that he was quite handsome. He had almond shaped golden amber eyes and long dark eye lashes. His eyebrows were straight with a kind of sadness to them. There was hair on his chin that connected to a thin moustache. He had light brown skin and straight jet-black hair that was braided down to the middle of his muscular back. Horns grew out of his temple area and his ears were long and pointed, kind of like elves.

For clothes, he had a vest on that stretched across his broad shoulders. The vest was opened so you could see his chest and stomach. Carved into his stomach were muscles from many days of hard working. On his chest, he had some hair and just a little on his arms that bulged, from muscles. There was a line of hair that started from the bottom of his navel and disappearing underneath his belt he had on. He had a piece of cloth on to cover his bulging penis and some of his butt. He was very well endowed from the looks of the bulge and he had a very nice well-rounded butt. Since he came from a woman from Victoria's world, his legs were not goat like. From a distance, he looked like he had black pants on, but it was a soft fur. The fur started just below his navel and went all the way down to his hooves. Just above his hooves were tuffs of hair that flowed down to the pastern part of the hooves. He didn't have the dewclaws like most satyrs have but his legs were very muscular like a man on steroids.

Clark wiped his face with the piece of cloth and tried to hand it back to Victoria. She smiled and urged him to keep it. They both stood up and started down the stairs again. As they were walking down the stairs, Victoria sighed at the size of the steps and wondered how much further they had to go. Clark sensed the urgency in Victoria and figured she wasn't quite acclimated to her unfamiliar environment. He stopped Victoria, fluttered his eyebrows with a smile and said, "Hold on." With ease, he swept her up in his arms and ran down the stairs. Everything went by so fast that Victoria screamed with excitement at the ride. Her screams and their laughter rang through the whole stairwell.

At the bottom of the stairs were Ipion and Cullen. They could hear the screams and the laughter all the way down there. Ipion had a bit of a smile on his face when he heard her sounds. He felt joy in his heart that he hadn't felt in a long time. Cullen, on the other hand, was a bit serious and was shocked at Clark's exuberance. Cullen was always chasing after Clark when he showed his child like personality. The two of them had a love hate relationship, Cullen hated the way Clark acted and Clark loved getting a rise out of Cullen. "Maker's breath, I do wish he would grow up."

"Then who would you have to keep in line," Ipion replied in a soft tone and a bit of a smile. Ipion and Cullen watched as Clark hit the floor with a skidding stop. Both were still laughing when they looked at Ipion and Cullen's face. "Clark, must you show such childish displays to our new guest," retorted Cullen.

Ipion looked at Victoria and smiled. He took her by the hand and said, "Welcome, Victoria." Victoria tilted her head a little and replied, "How do you know my name?"

"Come, hold on to me," he looked at Clark with a smile, "You may join us as well." Holding on to Victoria's hand, he slowly raised his other hand and next thing Victoria knew, she was in a spacious room with a big desk and oversized armed chair. Over to the right was a long table with many chairs pushed against it. The chairs looked heavy with high backs, cushioned seats, and thick arm rest. She turned to hear a door opening and Clark walking through it. Behind Ipion was Cullen who only had to touch Ipion's cloak and was whisked away to the room as well. Ipion walked over to a cabinet and opened it. Inside were some clothes about Victoria's size. Looking over at her, he said, "You might prefer these over the dirty laundry you are wearing." Victoria wrinkled her nose and made a noise of displeasure.

Then she walked over to the cabinet and began rifling through the clothes. She pulled out something small that had straps, it almost looked like a bra, but she wasn't sure. Pulling it out she asked Ipion, "What is this?" Cullen's face turned red and he looked away. Ipion cuffed his hand and brought it up to his mouth, then cleared his throat, "That is a binder."

"A binder? You mean a bra?"

"We call them binders here," Victoria felt to see if she still had her bra on. The imposter maiden did not take Victoria's under clothes off, just her outer clothes, "Oh, I have one, so I won't need that." Ipion walked over to Victoria as she was putting the binder back. Ipion retrieved the binder and handed it to her, "Victoria, you are from a different world. We don't want others to know this. I need you to blend in." Usually she would fight this, but his eyes were pleading, and she thought maybe it would be best that she did dress the part, at least until she could get back. She continued going through the clothes and found something that looked like boxer briefs. Looking at Ipion, she knew she had to wear those too. The more she looked through the clothes, the more she noticed that they were her size. Were they expecting her? Just how long do they think she's going to stay here?

She came across a pair of black leather pants that felt light and when she ran her fingers across it, the material shimmered. Looking at Ipion, he said, "All your clothes are enchanted, they will protect you from fire, ice, lightening, and any other spell that would be cast on you."

"Magic? Are you saying there is magic here?" she rolled her eyes and turned back to the wardrobe, "That would explain getting in this room the way we did." There was a shirt that looked like leather, like the pants but they felt like silk. She had never felt material like this before. Victoria spotted a belt that had slots for vials, it looked heavy but when she grabbed it, it was light. There was a breast plate that was made of the same material as the belt and just as light. In the back of the cabinet, she spotted a long coat. It was black with buckles up and down the arms. There were four buckles from the breast down to the waist, which cause the coat to be snug but not restricting. The coat opened at the waist, then flared out which would flow down to the top of her feet.

Ipion ushered her to a screen where she could change into the clothes she picked out. She was concerned about how long she would be staying here, so she asked, "I see that all those clothes look my size, just how long do you suppose I will be here, because I need to get back to my grandfather." There was no reply, so she peeked around the screen. Ipion quickly said, "We will discuss that later, for now, we just need to get you properly dressed." It took her awhile to put these on but when she was done, she came out from behind the screen. Cullen gasped when he saw her. She looked so beautiful, he had never seen a woman or a mage that look as attractive as she did. Her hair was so beautiful as it fell past her breast to her waist. The pants showed her small but curvy hips and her skinny legs. She had a small waist, and the shirt made her breast pop out more then what she expected. As she put the coat on and fasten it up, you could still see her waist, the shape of her inner thighs and her long skinny legs. The top part of her breast where still showing over the top of the coat and Victoria pushed her hair aside and looked at the men in the room then stated, "Now how is this part protected when it is exposed like this." She was waving her hands around her breast in a desperate anticipation for an answer.

Ipion smiled and said, "That is what is protecting you. People tend to hinder their attack when their target is a woman. Especially one so beautiful and gifted as yourself." Ipion looked over at Cullen and saw how enamored he was by her presences, "Don't you think so, Cullen?" He finally blinks and looked at Ipion. With his face blushing from his reaction, he said, "Maker's breath." He turned around and left the room. Ipion smiled and looked back at Victoria, "Don't worry, he obviously liked it. Cullen is a very respectable man; I am sure one day; he will make somebody a good husband."

Clark walked up to Victoria and looped his arm into hers, "Girl, you look so fine. Let's go show that sexy bod off to some of the guys." With little resistance, Victoria looked back at Ipion, "But, I really have a lot of questions."

"Go, I will find you later and we will talk. Let Clark show you around. Get to know the place. You must be hungry; Clark will show you the kitchen."

Ipion was right, she was hungry and with little resistance, Clark was able to pull Victoria out of the room. He was so excited to show her some of the classrooms, the bedrooms, hot springs, and the dining room. But first, he thought he would show her what are the best dishes in the house were and which ones to stay away from. The cuisine was prepared for each diverse species in the tower. There were elves, dwarves, and humans. There were other species in the land, but they were of old magic and felt confident in their own teachings. Clark tried to help pick out the right kind of food for Victoria, but she insisted that her eyes knew what she liked, and she could smell it too. She grabbed something that looked like meatballs in marinara sauce. It smelt good, so she took it even against Clark's advisement.

Clark guided her to a table where they sat to eat. Victoria took a couple of bites and thought it was good. She couldn't understand why Clark didn't think it was a promising idea. It was gross to Clark because he was a vegetarian. She took another bite and proceeded to ask Clark, "So what is this, it taste really good." Clark made a disgusted look, leaned in, and said, "They're Harpy balls."

"Oh, like ground up meat and rolled into balls."

"No, I mean Harpy balls, as in testicles."

Victoria started to do her hand process when Clark grabs her hand and said, "Trust me, you don't want to look that up." She made a face but could still taste the tender meat lathered in sauce. She shrugged her shoulders and said, "Well, that is gross, but they taste really good, and I am starving." Clark grabbed a hold of his balls and said, "Girl, I am keeping my jewels away from you." Victoria laughed and continues chewing her food. As she looked down the table, she could see Cullen. When he looked up her way, he felt a little ashamed for staring at her. He was so handsome, and his personality made him more exciting to her. Clark saw her watching him and stated. "Honey, he is one fine man," he leaned in and whispered to her, "And I have seen him naked." Victoria choked a little and laughed, "You did not."

"Oh, honey, yes, I have. I peeked one time when we were in the hot springs."

Victoria hit him with the back of her hand and said, "Clark."

"Ow, don't hit me, I bruise easy," he looked at her winked and smiled, "You should get some of that, hm, hm, hm, so good."

"How, I can hardly get him to look at me," Clark looked down the table and pursed his lips, "Oh, that is because he likes you."

"How can you tell?" she turned and looked at Clark. Clark chuckled and grabbed a napkin. He reached over and tried to wipe some sauce off her mouth and said, "Honey, I wouldn't look at you either if you going to slop your food all over your face."

Victoria's face turned red, and she grabbed the napkin and started rubbing her mouth.

"Here, give me that, you going to rub those lushes' lips right off and then how he gonna kiss you," he took the napkin and wet it with his tongue and wiped the sauce off her face. She looked at him with disgust from the spit on the napkin.

"What, it's just a little spit. My momma said nothing cleans better than a little spit. There, that is much better. Why don't you ask him to come down and sit with us?"

"Oh no, I couldn't," in a high pitch voice, Clark hollered for Cullen. Cullen hated it when Clark did that, so he got up and walked down to them.

"Hi sweet cheeks, Victoria said you should come sit with us."

"Maker's breath, Clark, must you always draw attention," Clark looked at Cullen and batted his eyes, "Well, yes, how else am I to get noticed." Cullen looked at Victoria and said pointing to the seat across the table from her. "May I?" Victoria started to smile but checked her teeth with her tongue first then continued, "Please, sit."

"I can only sit for a while; I have my duties."

"Cullen, is it, I am Victoria."

She stretched her hand out to shake his. He gently grabbed her hand and smiled. He was so handsome; his hair was a wavy golden blond that was pulled back and tucked back in his armor, so she couldn't tell how long it was. The color of his eyes was a hypnotic green, and he had a scar that ran from the bottom of his cheek and through the right side of his top lip. He had this strange looking armor on which look very light and when he moved it was as if he were wearing nothing. On the chest was something she recognized, it almost looked like the Templar tunic and armor that she and Richard had found. On his hand was a ring, just like the one in the chest. The only thing different about it all was the material, it was different, it wasn't made of iron.

"I would love nothing more than to spend more time with you, but I really must get going."

"Oh, you have to leave so soon."

"Yes, Master Ipion is expecting me," he got up and gave Victoria that side smile and said, "Enjoy your meatballs."

"You mean my Harpy balls," Clark choked on his food and chuckled a little. Cullen looked at Clark and said, "Always up to no good." With that, he walked away. Victoria realized that Clark was just messing with her, then suddenly her face turned red, and she covered it with her hands. Clark just chuckled and said, "What a sexy man." Smiling, he looked at Victoria as she pulled her hands away from her face, then slugged him in the shoulder. "Ow, that hurt," Clark said rubbing the spot where Victoria hit him, "You totally deserved that. How embarrassing, I said balls to him. How uncouth was that." By now, Clark was laughing so hard that he stumbled out of his chair. Putting his hand out to Victoria, he said, "Come on, let me show you around, before I have to get you back to Master Ipion. At least you got his attention, as if you didn't have it the first time, he brought you in here." Victoria wanted to be mad at him, but she just couldn't be. Clark's personality made him too likable, and she got up and followed him.

Clark took her around the tower and showed her the magical rooms. They went to the hot springs and Clark had to back her out when he saw that there were guardians in there. Victoria caught a glimpse of one and saw that he had very long hair. Were they hiding all that hair in their armor? As Clark walked her out, she asked, "Why do they hide their hair behind their armor?"

"So, you won't know how long they have been here," Victoria questionably furrowed her brow and before she could ask, Clark said, "When a guardian first comes here, his hair is cut short, and that will be the last time he gets a haircut. It's a kind of cleansing they go through. As you saw, some have very long hair, which means they have been here for a very long time. I think it kind of sucks because they are sworn to celibacy as long as they are guardians."

"How long has Cullen been here?"

"Let's see, I was 12 when I got here, and he was 16, so about ten, maybe 11 years."

"16? He was just a kid. Didn't he have a family?" Clark looked at Victoria and said, "I think I will let him tell you those things, that way you two have something to talk about."

He continued to show her around the tower before he took her back to Ipion.

Chapter V

In the back of the staircase were lifts that were operated by more dwarfs. You couldn't hear them until you came around to the back of the stairs. These lifts were used for faster access to the higher floors. Clark showed them to her last because he liked showing off his strength and speed. He let her know that she could use these, instead of him hauling her around. Clark was a bit of a jokester, but it was all in genuine fun. She really couldn't tell when he was or if he was ever serious. But he did tell her that the story about his mother was true. Clark instructed the dwarfs to send the lift to the sanctuary; they were headed for the top floor. Ipion believed that even though Victoria was a beginner, it would be best to teach her up there. He didn't want others to see what she could do. People might think she was their secret weapon but Ipion was protecting her.

This floor was only used when mages graduated and since nobody would be graduating for six months, Ipion would spend that time teaching Victoria. It was a round and open space, which had windows all around it so that natural light could pour into the room. Above was a stain glass dome with a picture of dragons flying around. There were several dragons; one was a close likeliness to Velatha. The center dragon was larger than the others and was white. The dragons had special meaning to Ipion and felt this would be the proper place to teach Victoria. Ipion never taught anybody, Victoria was special so he and his assistant, Saphon, would be teaching her.

Saphon was a handsome man that looked to be in his 40s. He had hair so blonde it looked white. He had one blue eye and one green eye. He stood about 6'2" and was carved in muscles. He was wearing black leather pants and a white cotton looking shirt that was snug to his form. He had a long coat on that had straps, buckles, and other secret compartments to it. On his feet were black leather boots that had straps all the way up to his knees. He was always seen with a staff that he used for close combat. Saphon was the best staff fighter in the land, when he moved, he flowed like the river. The staff he had was made of a very hard wood. This wood was not easy to burn and was just as hard to break. An old ancient elf gave him this staff because Saphon saved his life. Days before Victoria arrived, Saphon had visit that elf to ask him to make another staff, just like it but molded for a woman.

As Clark and Victoria arrived at the top, they were met with Ipion and Saphon, "Aw, Victoria. Come. I would like you to meet Saphon." As Victoria came closer, her body began to tremble. There was a strange pull coming from Saphon that stopped her in her tracks. Saphon whispered something to Ipion, and he replied, "No, it will be all right. She will get use to the pull."

Victoria furrowed her brows, how did he know there was a pull, what was going on?

"Come Victoria don't be frightened," Ipion put his hand out to her, and Victoria reluctantly took his hand, "I know you have many questions, but the only way I can get you to understand is by showing you."

Ipion circled his hands as if he were rolling a ball in them. A violet glow started to form in his hands and then a ball of fire appeared. He threw the ball at Saphon whose hands glowed almost the same color then doused the fireball with a gush of water. Victoria could not believe her eyes, this was impossible, there was no such thing as magic, not like this.

"What is this? Am I no longer in my world? How did I get here? Will I ever get to go back?"

"The answer to some of your questions is magic. The other answers will come in time. When I feel that you are ready," Victoria was frightened and confused, none of this could be real. She wished she would wake from this dream.

"You are not dreaming, Victoria."

Ipion brought his hand up to his face and began stroking his beard. He looked toward the shadow of the room and said, "Maybe another way. Cullen." Out of the shadows came Cullen. For some reason, Cullen gave her some calmness and inner peace. He seemed to be a close connection to her world and Ipion knew this, "Cullen, would you please take Victoria out of the tower and show her around. Take her to a few of the towns nearby."

"Yes, headmaster," Cullen took Victoria by the hand and led her to the lifts.

As the lift descended quickly, Cullen mustard up the courage to talk to Victoria, "Please try not to be afraid." Cullen put his hand on the back of his head and rubbed it a little. What was he thinking, tell her not to be afraid, of course she will be afraid? Ipion told him everything about Victoria and swore him to secrecy or until Cullen felt the right time to tell her. Ipion told him he will know that time. Now that he knew everything about her, he had to be careful what he tells her. He did not want to cause her any reason to distrust him. She needs time; she had to adjust to her new surroundings. "What can be achieved by showing me around?" Cullen did his side smile and said, "Trust me, seeing is believing. Your own eyes will not lie to you."

The lift stopped, and Cullen stepped out, he bowed a little and said, "My lady." He stretched his hand out toward Victoria. She could not resist his charming and debonair personality and took his hand.

The dwarfs saw Cullen coming and they began shouting and the process of the doors opening began. A kitchen aid came up to Cullen and handed him a large satchel with meat pies and jerky. There were a couple of apples and some grapes in there as well. She had two flasks in her hand, and she handed him the flask of wine first. He opened it and smelled it, then told her that he will take the water instead. She handed him the other flask that had the cool water from the cold springs that came higher up in the tower. This water was a lot colder than the hot springs water and it had a sweet taste to it. They made their way out of the huge doors and walked toward the stables. An elf boy was standing there with Cullen's horse and another one for Victoria. His horse was a big, beautiful, black Friesian. The mane was long and flowed down to the top of the horses' front legs. The tail was just as long and nearly dragged on the ground. There were also tuffs of hair that covered the hooves of the horse. Victoria gasped at the site of the horse standing there patiently, "What a beautiful horse. What's her name?" Cullen smiled and said, "His name is Thunder."

"Such a majestic name for an extraordinary creature," Victoria replied as the horse shook his head up and down than stomped the ground several times, "It suits him well. And the other horse?"

"For you, my lady."

"Oh, that might be a problem, I have never ridden a horse before."

Even with all the land that her grandfather had, they never had the time or money to have horses. She always wanted one, but her grandfather didn't think it would be a good idea. He was very protective of her.

As they drew closer to Cullen's horse, he leaned over and said, "Change of plans, forgive me, my lady."

Grabbing her by the waist and hoisted her up on his horse and gestured to the stable boy to take the other horse back. He then hopped up on his horse behind her and they began to trot away. Crossing the bridge, Cullen explained to Victoria about Vanishing River. Suddenly, the air filled with the sounds of the dragon that always circled the tower. As they looked up, Victoria could not believe her eyes, flying above them was this magnificent dragon. Cullen slowly walked his horse into the trees that was just slightly ahead of them. He knew not to run because that would have drawn her attention. He was not to let Velatha see Victoria yet.

Riding through the trees, Victoria witnessed things she couldn't explain. There were plants that seem to come alive as they rode by. Cullen pointed out some little guys that were smaller than the dwarfs. They were carrying small pots of what looked like gold but was honey. These guys loved honey; you could find them running around in the forest collecting the sweet nectar. The honey gave them the ability to make bridges out of rainbows. This helped them to cross great distances a lot faster. The Honey Nabbers were the perfect bee charmers and always kept the bees safe. If they felt bees were in danger, they would bring them to a safe place.

Further down the road, Cullen spotted the flitters, he told Victoria in her world she would call them fairies. The Flitters helped the plants to grow and populate, they also healed the ground and took care of the small animals. They would go to other places and bring rare and strange plants into the forest. He explained that they along with the Honey Nabbers have been under strict supervision because they like to escape to her world and cause havoc. There were many places in this world that led to her world, but he told her that would be explained to her later. Seeing these creatures explain a lot about some of the stories she would have heard. She thought those people were crazy and now she feels like she has lost it too. This world was going to take time for her to get used to. But if those little creatures can go between her world and this, there must be a way back for her.

After several hours of riding, Victoria was starting to get anxious, and her butt was beginning to go numb. Cullen was enjoying the ride; he could smell Victoria's sweet fragrances. He noticed that she was adjusting more now and knew it was time to get her off the horse. Not too far away, he could see the town of Hamesbring. In the town, there were many different people, but Victoria saw nothing abnormal about this place. Cullen brought Thunder up to a building that had a sign made of wood. There was a picture of a mug carved into it. He got off the horse and reached up for Victoria. She gladly slid into his arms and only looked away for a second. To her amazement, she caught site of something she had never seen before. At first, she thought she saw a man on a horse, but it was a man with a horse body, a centaur. Half afraid and partly shocked, Victoria held onto Cullen. When she looked up at Cullen, their face was very close to each other. Cullen smiled and said, "Maker's breath." Then he came to his senses and said, "Forgive me of my boldness, my lady." He then released her and led her into the tavern.

Still looking back at the centaur, she turns to look inside the tavern. There was a bar inside that was U shaped. Half was inside while the other half went outside, this was for centaurs or any other large creatures too big to come inside. There were tables place throughout inside of the building, at one of the tables were a couple of elves and a human. At another table was a human, elf, and a dwarf. Most of the people in the bar were men but there were a few women too. They all wore leather or some type of armor, some had a mixture of both. A handful of them were carrying swords others bows and arrows. Some even had double blade axes or a staff. These axes looked to be very heavy, and the bigger and stronger looking creatures were carrying them. The strangest creature she saw was the man and woman at the far end table. She had never seen anything like them. The man was very large with a shoulder span of two feet. He had a thick muscular neck. On his head looked like horns from a dragon. His skin looked strange, kind of thick, like it would be hard to pierce. His hands were large, but his nails looked like claws. On his back, he was carrying a double-edged axe. In the middle of the blade was a carving of a dragon's head. The staff and handle of the axe was the body and tail of the dragon. Victoria noticed some strange looking slits in the man's back too.

"That is what we call a dragataur. We believe that they were bred from the blood of a dragon."

The woman had the same features as the man, but she was slightly smaller and looked like she had flakes of gold in her skin. Victoria took another look just in time to see a drunk man harassing them. The male dragataur stood up and roared a mighty roar. It was like the sound of a dragon but throatier. This sent the man sailing ten feet across the room. The Dragataur sat back down to finish his ale as if nothing happened. Victoria had so many questions, "Where am I? Surely this is not in the past, is this a different realm or world?"

"Those answers will come in time. For now, just know and learn what you could be up against. These people are with us. There are others that are against us and if they knew of you, you could be in danger."

"Then why am I out here?"

"You need to see that this is real and what Ipion and Saphon are about to teach you are real and for your protection."

"I don't understand, why me, why would I be in danger?" she responded, glancing back at the dragataur.

"In time, Ipion will tell you everything."

"Do you know everything?"

"I do now, but it is not my place to tell you. At least not yet."

All this was getting to be too much for her, she placed her face in her hands and tears started to fill her eyes. To see her like this nearly broke his heart. He gently grabbed her hand and walked her out of the tavern. As they were leaving, an elf sitting in the shadows of the tavern placed their hood over their head and slowly walked to the door. The things they were saying caught the elf's attention. The elf wanted to follow them to see who this woman was.

Cullen took his horses reins in one hand and still holding Victoria's hand he walked down the road. There were several roughly made buildings along the road, they were made of something like shiplap and thatch roofs. A few of the buildings were two stories high, like the tavern. The tavern was the largest building because it had rooms for rent upstairs. There was a wooden sign on another building that had a needle and spool of thread on it which indicated that this was the tailor. Across from that was a sign that had a sword on it. Cullen told her that is where you can buy all sorts of weapons. Outside of the building, there was a sort of opened shed connected to it. Inside the shed was a blacksmith, he was a large man with big thick arms from pounding and molding what she thought was iron. He was sweating and had soot all over him. Above, hanging from the rafters, were all kinds of swords and axes.

On the opposite side of the shed was a thin elf that was surrounded by many size and shaped staffs. He was carving a dragon head onto a piece of wood. Victoria stopped to watch him carving this staff with great speed that he made the wood seem soft as a bar of soap. The wood was a very hard a solid wood made from a tree that only elves can fell. The elf looked up at Victoria and smiled, then he looked back down at his work. Victoria looked away for only a few seconds and looked back where the elf had been sitting. He was gone. This place was starting to become very amazing to her, she felt so calm and not as afraid. Cullen was still holding onto her hand and he gave it a squeeze. As Victoria looked up at him, he smiled. The way he looked and smiled at her made her melt, she thought she would follow him anywhere.

As they continued to walk down the road, they saw a few more signs, one for potion making, which was the home of an alchemist. Another building with a sign indicating armor, it too, had a blacksmith pounding away outside. Then there was a small building that smelled good. It was a restaurant with several large tables and a few small ones. There were women waiting on the tables and some in the back cooking. All the places had people working in them, some dwarf, elves, and humans. Victoria wondered if these people were slaves to the owners and asked Cullen. "The people that work here and the tower, are they slaves?"

"No, they are indentured servants. Poor people who need to work for a living. You will find no slaves here. But…"

"But what?" Cullen had led her to the edge of the town. There was a waterfall with the sweet smell of flowers and a grassy knoll close to the fall. Seeing such a beautiful site made her forget what she was asking. Letting go of her hand, Cullen reached for the bag of food and flask of water. He gestured for Victoria to come sit down to eat. They sat there, eating the food provided for them. Cullen told her all about the land, he felt very comfortable with her and she with him.

He told her the land spread everywhere with many bodies of water. Some bodies of water were so large it took weeks to cross them. The land was beautiful with lots of foliage. There were other parts of the land that seem dark and were forbidden to go to. Some of the trees were leaf barren and some were overtaken by this black ivy. These lands were home to Aldabus, the Darkheart. He did not have indentured servants, he had slaves. Ogres and orcs roamed this land. There were dark elves, like Aldabus, but not as powerful. He had a castle carved into a place that is called Death Mountain. The river flowing around this mountain was not water but lava. The castle had a dungeon that kept his prisoners and some of his unworthy slaves.

Cullen told Victoria about the evil man that worked for Aldabus, his name was Zeddicus Payne. He had long, dark hair that he would pull back with a piece of cloth. His skin was pale with a gray tinge to it. His eyes were amber colored but turned red when cornered. Next to Aldabus, he was thought to be the evilest man in the land. It is said he held a woman captive in a tower, this woman had given birth to his son. The captive woman's mother was also there but of her own free will. The son of Zeddicus was to be the next powerful mage in the land but something unforeseen happened. He was a young man in his twenties. His magic seemed frail and not as powerful as predicted. His long dark hair was comb back and came down to the middle of his waist. He had sky blue eyes and his skin was just as pale as Zeddicus, but it did not have that gray tinge to it.

There was so much to this land and it fascinated Victoria immensely. She wanted to see and hear more about it, "Cullen, what is this land called, can you tell me that?" Cullen did his side smile and said, "*Asimeritian* (Aash mer i tin)." Victoria smiled and said, "That is a beautiful name. I would really like to see more of this Asimeritian."

"You will, in time."

"Can I ask some question about you?" Cullen put his hand on the back of his neck and said, "Sure, but why would you want to talk about me?"

"I feel comfortable with you and I would like to get to know you more," he did his side smile and said, "What would you like to know?"

"How long have you been a guardian?" Clark had already told her this answer, but she wanted to hear it from him.

"I have been a guardian for 11 years."

"Is it true that you get your hair cut for the last time when you first become a guardian?"

"Yes."

"Your hair must be very long for eleven years," she reached over to pull his hair out and said, "May I?"

He was hesitant at first then said, "Yes." Victoria came closer and gently pulled his long hair out of his armor. It was so beautiful and came all the way down to his waist. "It's almost as long as mine," she looked into his eyes and smiled saying, "It's beautiful." He smiled and tucked his hair back inside his armor. He was a little afraid that she would not like his long hair. Victoria had one more question, "Why do you tuck it inside your armor?"

"So that our enemy cannot get ahold of it."

"Oh, yeah, that makes since," Cullen looked up at the sun and saw that it was getting late, he needed to get her back before it got dark. They gather up their little picnic and got on the horse. Victoria looked back at that spot and smiled, "I will always remember this spot."

"Yes, I will, too."

They looked at each other and felt a close bond. A connection that could not be severed was created in that spot, that day. They started to draw closer when Thunder neighed and started stomping the ground, "Yes, my friend, you are right, we need to be going."

Cullen was so enamored and distracted with Victoria that he failed to watch out for suspicious characters. They had been riding awhile when Cullen snapped out of his trance by the sound of a rock falling. Without turning his head, he cast his eyes over to the left and on a small cliff was a hooded stranger. Going behind some bushes Cullen got off the horse and gesture for Victoria to be quiet and stay put. Quietly, he snuck up behind the hooded stranger. Pulling his sword out, he placed it in the strangers back. The stranger did a somersault, spun around, and rolled down the hill. Cullen ran after the stranger as an arrow came flying at him. With his blade, he blocked the arrow and it pinged as he pounced on the stranger. The stranger dropped the bow and laid flat on their back. Cullen stood over the stranger with his sword at its chest. He bent over and pulled the hood down to expose a female elf.

"Who are you and why are you following us?"

"Don't get your nickers in a twist."

Cullen was insistent on a direct answer that he pressed the sword into her chest just enough to pierce her skin a little. Victoria jumped off the horse and ran to Cullen. She put her hand lightly on his arm and slowly pulled the sword away. Looking at him, she said, "Please, Cullen, don't hurt her."

"But she could be a spy for Aldabus." Offended at his accusation, the elf got up and rebutted, "What! I would never work for old butt. Everybody knows you can't trust him. Even his own daugh—"

"Who are you and why are you following us?" queried Cullen.

"You're from the tower, aren't you?"

"I asked you, who are you?" Cullen responded sternly.

"Well, who are you?"

"You're hiding something." Cullen replied ostentatiously.

She looked at her hands and said, "Why would you think I was hiding something?"

"Because you keep answering a question with a question."

"So, you are hiding something too. You're doing the same thing." The stranger replied pompously.

Cullen was getting impatient with her and drew his sword on her again. The elf put her hands up and said, "All right, all right. The name's Claire."

Putting her hand out, Victoria lowered Cullen's sword and shook Claire's hand, "I am Victoria, please to meet you." A puzzled look came over Claire's face as she was shaking Victoria's hand, "Victoria? Like in Vic—?"

Cullen interrupted and said, "You still haven't told us why you are following us."

"I overheard you talking about Ipion and Saphon. I've been looking for them."

"Why have you been looking for them?"

"Boy, aren't you the nosey one."

Cullen was about to bring his sword up, "Okay, you're such a pus bucket. Hagmer sent me."

"Hagmer, how do you know him?"

"Well, maybe it's because I am an elf, dragon breath," Cullen cut his eyes at her and she reluctantly answer, "And he's my grandfather."

"Give me the message, I will give it to him."

"Yeah right, not."

Cullen got Victoria back on his horse then hopped up behind her, "Well, you can come with us, if you can keep up." Cullen kicked the sides of Thunder who reared up and jumped into a gallop. Unimpressed by his glibness, she brought her fingers up to her mouth. With a sharp and loud whistle blowing through her tongue and fingers a huge white 20-point stag broke through the bushes. Claire hopped on him and gracefully caught up with Cullen.

The stag was no ordinary stag; he was almost as big as Thunder. He had a royalty presence about him. The inside spread of the antlers itself was well over forty inches. His neck was massive and there was a thick tuff of hair flowing down his chest. Claire was a forest elf from a tribe of elves that have been around for a very long time. Forest elves were different from the elves raised in the small towns. Elves normally stay in the forest, but some become curious about the city way of living and decided to leave. Those elves were poor and had to work hard for a living. Living in the forest didn't seem as glamorous for them anymore but if they would have stayed, everything would have been provided for them. Out of the forest, some of the elves had to sell their selves out as hunters or mercenaries. Others enrolled their selves as indentured servants for the rich people and would have to live among the other servants in the hovel at the end of bigger towns. The hovel had sheds or tents used for their homes, it was dirty and sometimes, could be dangerous, especially at night.

Some of the richer people that had elves as servants were cruel to them. They snub their noses at them and considered them filth. Some were kind to them and gave them rooms in higher parts of their homes. These parts of the house were cold and drafty in the cold seasons and sultry hot in the warm seasons. They were kind to them but still considered the elves below them. Then there were the people that treated the elves like one of their own.

Claire wanted nothing to do with that kind of living, she thought that the rich people in the land were a bunch of stuck-up pus buckets. She had some family members who lived out of the forest and she saw how they were treated; she wanted no part of that. She even had a cousin who was a mage but turned evil. Claire believes that old butt, as she called him, turned her cousin evil. Anybody who goes to him thinks he will protect them, but they are fooled and end up his slave. Some submit after days of torture and some would be found dead in the cell, they were thrown in. Others were just as evil as Aldabus's counterpart, they all tried to climb up the corrupted ladder. You either did as Aldabus wanted or you die.

As they were crossing the bridge Claire heard the dragon, she looked up and freaked out. "What the hell is that?" She jumped off her stag and sent him into the forest while she ran to the doors of the tower. She began banging on the doors yelling, "Come on you pus buckets, let me in." Cullen jumped off Thunder and grabbed Victoria, "Stop, you will attract her attention." It was too late; Velatha was already swooping down to see who this fair maiden was. The doors were open enough for them to squeeze through. Victoria was shuttled through the doors, but she turned in time to be face to face with the dragon.

The dragon tried to get closer, but the dwarfs used the failsafe to slam the doors shut.

"Shite, that was close. What the hell was that, I mean, I know what that was but why do you have a dragon?"

"We don't!" Cullen responded angrily, "That was Velatha."

"Velatha, but" she looked at Victoria and continued, "Then she must be…"

"Silence, that will be enough, can't you see she…" Cullen looked at Victoria who was just standing there looking at the door, "Maker's breath. Are you all right?" Victoria stood there still staring at the door responded. "I saw into her eyes. It was like she knew me. There was a sort of sadness." Victoria turned toward Cullen and he held on to her.

"Forgive me, my lady, I am so sorry you had to endure that."

Victoria looked up at him and said, "I'm okay, I don't think she would have hurt me." Running up to them was Ipion and Saphon.

"What happened here?" Ipion's voice thundered for the first time.

Cullen returned with, "It's okay, she is all right. But it was Velatha. She saw her."

Calming down his voice to that soft whisper, Ipion replied, "Well, they have seen each other."

"Do you think Velatha will inform Aldabus?" Saphon inquired with his deep but sultry voice. Ipion closed his eyes and sighed deeply, "No, she was just curious, but she knows who she is now. She won't let Aldabus know."

"Could somebody tell me what the hell that fire pit was doing here?" Claire retorted.

"Aw, Hagmer's granddaughter. Claire, is it?"

"Yeah, and I didn't come here to become a roast chicken," Claire had a raw glibness to her but sometimes, she would miss her mark on the punchline, "Well not that I am a chicken, because I'm not, right. Shite, what has my grandfather gotten me into this time?"

Claire was pacing back and forth throwing her hands in the air while she was talking, "I'm supposed to give you a message, but I don't know what it is. He said you would know when I got here. Shite, pus buckets, ass biscuits, how does he get me into these things?"

"What's she going on about?" Cullen enigmatically asked. Ipion gestured for a kitchen servant to take Claire to the dining room and get her something to eat. Claire followed still spouting colorful metaphors.

The rest of the group went up to Ipion's office where Clark was waiting for them. He was so glad to see Victoria back at the tower safe. He freaked out a little when he heard that Velatha came down to take a closer look. Victoria was very amused by Clark, even when he was upset, he managed to make her laugh. But now was not the time to lose control, now they really needed to let Victoria in on some things. It was time for her to see what she can do. She was still having a challenging time believing that she had any magic in her. She had gone all these years leading a normal life and she really believed that they had the wrong person. There was nothing special about her. Her mother was normal, and so was her father. Little did she know that she was not who she was raised up believing she was.

Ipion told her that she needed to get a good night's rest. There were things she had to know but they could wait until morning. He wanted her to have this one last night of normalcy, for it would be her last. Her life was about to change, and she needs to be ready for it. He did tell her that she will not know everything because she is going to need time to accept who she is now. She left Ipion's office with Clark and they headed off to her room. Ipion had a single room prepared for her. He thought it would be easier for her to adjust if she had her own room.

Clark helped with the room and hoped she liked it. It was a palatial room with a beautiful king size canopy bed. The posts were a dark, walnut color that was twelve inches around. You could stand on the bed with your hands up but still not touch the top. The top was cover in a violet velvet, the curtains around the bed were of the same color and material. There was a large dresser filled with clothes. In the wardrobe were other outfits for her to wear. In the back was a beautiful dress. It was a spaghetti strapped, rose, pink, mermaid sequins dress, that would be snug to her body then would flare out just above the knees. There was a two-foot train that would flow beautifully behind her. When she saw this dress, she thought when she would ever wear this.

"There is a party in Cantlos."

"Cantlos? What's that?" she asked as she sat on the bed.

"It's the time of song," Clark said with a smile, "Oh, let's see if I can remember what my mama told me. She was so smart, she had it all figured out." Thinking about it, he gestured for her to wait a minute. Clark left the room and came back with a book almost the size of a large dictionary. Inside this book was all kinds of information. It translated everything from this world to Victoria's.

"Here, take it. Study it. My mama wrote everything down. And look she drew pictures too."

Victoria took the book and started to leaf through it. She chuckled a little and said, "It looks like a book of shadows."

"A book of what?" Clark almost looked offended, but Victoria reassured him that it was a good thing, "I will leave you alone, so you can read it. Oh, by the way, I found your satchel with all your strange things in it. It's over there in that chest."

"Thank you, Clark."

Clark smiled and said, "You're welcome, my friend."

With that, he left the room closing the door behind him.

Victoria jumped off the bed and ran to the chest. Opening it, she found her bag and the clothes she came in. She smiled and thought how naughty Clark was, but was very happy to see something normal to her. She took the bag and put it on the bed as she sat down. Pulling herself up to the head of the bed, she sat crossed legged and proceed to dump her bag. In the bag was the list of missing people, some pens, a candy bar which she opened and ate it. There were also two warm cans of Pepsi. She opened one and began to drink it. She didn't even care that it was warm, it still tasted very good. As the semi warm Pepsi, glided down her throat, it caused her to release a very resounding belch. She smiled and said good stuff. Then she thought, there must be a way to make this here. How could she go without her Pepsi? The water was good, but she needed something different occasionally and she wasn't a beer drinker.

Spending most of the night going through her bag and reading Lucy's book, Victoria started to get tired. She wondered what time it was, there were no clocks, and she didn't have her cell phone which she used occasionally as a time piece. How was she going to live in this world? She was so accustomed to things just being there for her she wasn't sure she could adjust. She couldn't think that way, she needed to keep an open mind, "I mean really; how bad could it be." As she was reading the words started to get blurry, the more she tried to read, the sleepier she got. It wasn't long before she laid back and fell asleep to the sound of singing.

Chapter VI

Victoria awoke with the sounds of a door opening and closing. As she opened her eyes, she was thankful that the sun wasn't blinding her. Sitting up on her elbows, she saw a small elf girl standing over the table in her room. She noticed that she was undressed and only in her underclothes. Looking on her bed, she began to panic, her bag and the book was not there. She glanced over at the elf girl who looked even more panic stricken had cast her eyes down and said, "Forgive me, milady, I did not mean to wake you." Victoria jumped out of her bed, which frightened the girl even more. She put her hands out in front of her and said, "I am so sorry, I didn't mean to frighten you."

"No, milady, it is I who is sorry."

Victoria felt she was getting nowhere and said, "Okay, a lot of sorrys, moving on."

"I beg your pardon, milady; I don't understand..."

"It's okay, I just need to know what happened to my clothes and the things that were on my bed."

"Oh, I came in last night and put you to bed, milady, and the things on your bed are over here on the table." Relieved that her things were still in her room, she walked over to the table. As she was walking to the table, she noticed the elf was trying hard not to look at her.

"Is something wrong?"

The girl cast her eyes to the floor and with fear in her voice said, "Forgive me, milady. I did not mean to stare."

"No, you're fine. Please tell me; what is it that intrigues you so about me?"

The girl did not understand Victoria's words and with great discomfort, murmured, "I do not understand the question."

"You seem puzzled about me; what do you not understand about me."

"We are not allowed to ask," the elf responded with fear.

"Well, I give you permission to ask whatever you want to know."

"They say you are very powerful and not from here."

"Hmm, not from here is true; but powerful, I don't see how."

The elf looked at her with big eyes that made Victoria ask, "Do you know how?"

"We are not allowed to talk about it," the elf got uncomfortable and started looking at the door.

"Well, I said you can," Victoria answered with a stern voice but regretted it because it scared the girl even more.

"Please, milady, I must not. May I leave?" the girl was on the edge of tears and began to shake. Feeling bad about how she made the elf feel, Victoria sighed and said, "Yes, I am sorry I did not mean to frighten you, you may leave." With that, the girl ran to the door, opened it, and ran into Clark. She fell to the floor and got up on her knees and crawled away fast. Clark looked at Victoria and squinted his eyes. Victoria tried to cover herself and shouted, "Clark, please, I am not dressed." Clark rolled his eyes and shooed his hand at her saying, "Oh please, as if." Victoria looked at him bewildered and Clark responded, "Hello, honey, I don't see a penis between those skinny legs of yours. So not interested."

"Oh, right," Victoria exclaimed relaxing. Looking back at the door, Clark inquired, "Geez, Victoria, what did you do to her."

"Oh, my God, nothing. Why are some of these people afraid of me?"

"Because you so fine that's why." Clark said as he snaps his fingers. Victoria chuckled and looked over at the table. She could see her other can of Pepsi sitting there and said, "I sure wish there was a way to duplicate Pepsi. You wouldn't happen to have Pepsi here, would you?"

Clark smiled and walked over to his mother's book. He rifled through the pages, then stopped at a page that had a picture drawn of an old glass bottle of Pepsi, "Are you kidding me. My momma loved her pop, she called it. She found an alchemist who mimicked the taste and wrote it down for her." Clark held the book up showing Victoria the picture and ingredients, "Is that hard to make?"

"You would be better off letting one of the alchemists here make it for you. Come on, I will take you to him."

Victoria started to walk out the door with him when Clark looked at her and said, "You settin' a new style?"

"What?" Victoria looked down at her attired and realized that she was still in her underclothes.

"Oh shit." Clark walked over to the door and shut it then turned to Victoria's closet.

"I guess I better put some clothes on."

Most of her clothes consisted of the same thing but there were some in white some in black then there was that dress which she didn't think she would ever wear. As she was getting dressed, she began to hear this strange noise, it almost sounded like trumpets. Victoria furrowed her brows and asked, "What is that? I've heard that noise before, it sounds like trumpets."

"What noise?" Clark looked up and said, "Oh that's just Velatha. Don't know about trumpets, but you have heard her before when you and Cullen were on your outing."

"No, I heard it before I came into this world."

"No, you couldn't have," Victoria finished buckling the boots she found in the closet, she grabbed Clark who still had his mother's book in his arms, and ran to the door, "Come on, I need to talk to Ipion."

"What you gotta do that for?"

"I am tired of being in the dark, I want to know what is going on."

They went to the back of the stairs and rode the lift to Ipion's office. As she stormed into his office, Clark coward behind her, "You need to tell me everything that is going on. If you want me to help you with this war between good and evil, I need to know everything." Ipion glanced at Clark with his eyes over the top of his glasses.

Clark put his hands up and said, "Don't look at me, I didn't say anything."

Just then, Cullen walked into the room, "Makers' breath, forgive me, I did not know they were in here."

"Please, Cullen, come in," Ipion gesturing Cullen to come in. Ipion decided to tell her some things but not everything. For her safety, he would not tell her all. Clark adjusted the book in his hand, which caught Ipion's attention. Ipion put his hand out and the book was pulled out of Clark's arms and placed into his hands. He began to look through it and asked, "What is this?" Victoria winced and looked at Clark with a sorrowed look on her face, "It's mine."

Ipion looked at Victoria and gave a smile, "I think not. Clark? Was this your mothers?"

"Yes, Master Ipion."

"Come forward," Clark sheepishly walked over to Ipion, "Don't be afraid. This is a very handy book. I wish you would have told me about it. It looks like it could help Victoria tremendously." He handed the book to Victoria and said, "Finish this book, all your answers you need to know are in here. From the looks of it, Clark, your mother did an excellent job of putting it together. I know she was not from here. She came from Victoria's place. Are there anymore?"

"Yes, she spent her whole life here writing everything she knew about this place. She did it for me, I believe she knew, one day, my father would catch up to her."

"When Victoria is done with this, show her the others and if it would be okay with you, I would like these books to be place in the special addition section in the library."

"Oh yes, she would have been honored by that, master. Thank you so much."

Clark puffed up his chest with delight of his mother's work being place in a very important section of the library.

"Yes, oh, you might want to go see Uwrick, he can make that drink for you and have it available in the kitchens. I believe there could be recipes in that book that you would like Victoria, the kitchen will know how to make them."

"Wait, Ipion, that noise, I have heard that noise that the dragon makes. At least the muffled sounds from inside the tower," she paused and looked at him then responded, "I heard those sounds when I was in England." Ipion had a very worried look on his face and then he nodded. He looked over at Cullen and said, "You must tell her the next step, it is time."

"Yes, Master Ipion."

Cullen gestured for Victoria to lead the way and they all walked out of Ipion's office. Ipion raised his arms and a swirl of purple lights in circled him. When the lights faded, he was outside on top of the tower. This area wasn't as big around as the rest of the tower, it was more of a landing pad that nobody but Ipion knew about. Above him was Velatha circling, when she saw Ipion, she carefully landed in front of him. She was huge with wings that nearly stretched across the landing pad. As she folded her wings in, she brought her face down to Ipion. She was nearly twice the size of a T-Rex and almost had the same built except her front arms were longer, the tail was a little thinner and she had wings. She had a serpent like neck that came out of her body,

78

curved up then down to her head. She had a long thin snout that had razor sharp teeth in her mouth. At times smoke, would smolder from her nostrils. Her eyes were almond shape and had a soft violet color. Around the outside of her head were spike like horns that are used to protect herself from predators. On the top of her head were two long horns that can be used to disembowel her enemies. As Ipion stared into her eyes, he could see how sad she was. He put his hand between her nostrils and petted her, "I am so sorry, my love; I did not mean for you to suffer like this." A tear fell from her eye, which she left for Ipion, then she spread her wings and flew away. Ipion picked up the tear that was hard like crystal and placed it into a vial that had several other tears in it.

Victoria, Cullen, and Clark walked into Uwrick's lab and showed him the book with the recipe for Pepsi. Uwrick gathered all his ingredients and began making the potion. It didn't take very long and with a few puffs of smoke it was done. He said he would send a batch down to the kitchen. They decided to call it Victoria's drink, so that the kitchen staff would understand the importance of this drink. The three of them headed down to the kitchen and were met up with Claire, "You three look like pus buckets waiting for a vacuation." Victoria looked at her and chuckled because she understood the allegory of her sentence, but she had a word wrong, "You mean vaccination."

"Yeah, wrong way 'round, means the same thing."

Clark puzzled by what Claire said looked at Victoria and asked, "What is she trying to say."

"Don't worry about it."

Victoria got her drink and something that looked like potato chips. To her surprise, the recipes in the book were already sent to the kitchen and some things were prepared. They all grabbed something to eat and drink then took a place at a table. Cullen was really intrigued by the drink of Victoria's that he asked if he could try it. As he was about to put the cup up to his lips, Clark knocked the drink out of his hand. The drink spilled down the front of him and splashed Claire in the face. "Don't drink it!" Victoria was really shocked by Clark's reaction and responded, "What the heck did you do that for."

"My momma said it was bad for you. She said it was addictive and I shouldn't drink it." Victoria began to laugh. It was the typical axiom that a mother would tell her child, "Clark, it won't kill you. Your mother was just probably concern about your teeth and the sugar rush it would give you. You know, because you are so hyper and really fast."

"Are you saying my momma lied to me, my momma would not lie to me."

"It wasn't a lie per-say, it was more of a white lie," Clark looked at her with big eyes and disbelief.

"The sugar would have made you extremely hyper and I am sure you were a handful already. It wasn't meant to be dishonest, just a little deception to keep you from drinking it. She was just being a mother, that is what mothers do," Clark looked over at Cullen who looked a little mad. He tried to help Cullen wipe the drink off him, but Cullen shooed him away. Claire licked her mouth where some splashed on her, "Hey, that's not bad, I'll have a go at it."

Victoria thought Cullen was going to leave, she didn't want him to go. As Cullen got up, he walked over to the kitchen helpers and asked her to bring a round of Victoria's drink. Then he sat back down this time across from Victoria and gave her his side smile. The smile that just melted Victoria's heart. Nothing in the world existed except for him when he smiled like that. The kitchen helper came with a round of drinks and they all took a drink of it. Victoria thought it was missing something. She thought if only it was just a little colder. Her hands were cupped around the glass as she was thinking this. Suddenly, the cup got colder and so did the drink. She put the cup down and said, "Did you see that."

"Blah, blah, blah, so you can make things cold big deal," Claire handed her cup to Victoria and said, "Here, make mind cold too." Victoria grabbed the cup and in the same way, she made the drink colder, "Aw right, that shite tasted better." Clark shoved his cup in Victoria's hand, and she made his cold too. He loved the taste so much that he gulped it down. Tears came to his eyes and then a very loud belch came from his mouth. Claire laughed and said, "Awe mother frigging ass bag, that was rot suck."

She replied as a louder belch came from her mouth, "Holy ass biscuits, did that come from me." Both Claire and Clark started laughing. Victoria just smiled and rolled her eyes. They were just like kids trying pop for the first time. She looked at Cullen and asked, "Would you like me to make yours colder?"

He looked at the other two then back at Victoria. "Don't worry, it's not how cold the drink gets that causes that, it's how fast you drink it." Cullen smile at Victoria and slid his glass over to her and she made it cold for him.

They all tried the tubular shape meat she called hotdogs and the sticks of potatoes called French fries. The meat sticks did not appeal to Clark, but the oddly shaped potatoes looked good.

"Oh, you are vegetarian." Victoria responded. Clark looked at her and said pointing to himself, "Ah, goat boy." The strangest thing they discovered was dipping the fries in a strange sauce she called ketchup and putting the ketchup, and something called mustard on the links of meat. As they sat there enjoying their meal, Victoria became very comfortable with this group of people. She felt she was ready to learn more and was no longer afraid of it. The only condition Victoria wanted was that her friends would be up there in the training room with her. It was like they were her muses; she felt more confidant with them around. While they finished their meal, Cullen decided to let Victoria know of a quest they must go on. When the dining hall cleared out and only the four were left, Cullen leaned over to tell Victoria what was about to happen.

"I must tell you what Aldabus has planned," Victoria saw the serious look on Cullen's face and lean in to absorb all that he was about to tell her. Claire heard Aldabus's name and retorted, "Old Butt, we have to tangle with that ass nut."

"Yes, he plans to break through to Victoria's world and enslave all the inhabitants."

"Oh please, my world is far from helpless."

"Can your world fight real magic. He knows they know nothing of it. Their weapons may be great but magical beings can shield their selves from the primitive weapons that they have."

"I hardly think they are primitive."

"Can your weapons freeze or cast spells to make them stop working," Cullen felt bad talking to her like this, but she needed to know, "Are they protected against magic that could control their minds? Your world may know how to fight, but they can't against this."

"But don't they have to be able to get there first," Victoria enquired.

"Ipion believes that Aldabus might be able to send a man in."

"Well, that is good then. One man can't control my world."

"No, but that one man can get ahold of *Le Bijou du Roi*."

"That sounds familiar, where have I heard that before," Victoria tip back on her chair a little then put her hand up to start her thinking process. As she was rifling through her mind, she could still hear Cullen talking.

"We can't let him get it so Ipion will be sending us on a mission to get it before Aldabus's man does."

She went to take a drink from her glass when her mind stopped on *Le Bijou du Roi*, the king's jewel also known as the Hope diamond. With that, she choked on her drink and started to fall back on her chair. Clark reached out and caught her before she fell to the floor. He lifted her out of her seat and started pounding on her back like his mother did when he choked on his food. When Victoria stop choking, Cullen had made it by her side and ask her if she was okay.

"No, I mean, yes, but I am not okay about the diamond. You want us to steal the Hope diamond. Are you crazy, that thing is heavily guarded? Besides what purpose does it have."

"It generates the porthole stones."

"The porthole stones, what porthole stones?" Cullen did his side smile and said, "The place where I found you."

Victoria smile then it faded, and she replied, "Stonehenge?"

"Yes, if that is what your world calls it. The porthole stones haven't been used in a very long time. Nobody has been able to get it to work without the *Le Bijou du Roi*, your Hope diamond."

"Well, then how is it working now?"

"A long time ago, Ipion used it to hide somebody very important to him. But somehow, somebody opened it from your world, and it has been very unstable."

The more he talked about the two worlds colliding, the more Victoria's head began to hurt. All this information started to pile up in her head and she couldn't make it stop. She started seeing all kinds of information, faces, dates, times. She saw her mother and her twin. She had forgotten about that; she has a twin. What does all this have to do with her? How is it that she knows these things? Who is her real father? Her head started to spin then the room began to spin. She held onto her head and cried out, "Make it stop." Suddenly, everything went dark.

Cullen caught Victoria before she could hit the floor. Scooping her into his arms, he carried her to the lifts. He took her to her room and laid her down on her bed. Clark and Claire followed him up and walked into the room behind him. "Go get Ipion!" Clark spun on his hooves and ran to get the master mage. Within seconds, Ipion and Saphon were in Victoria's room. Ipion looked at Cullen and asked, "What happened?"

"I was telling her about the mission. Then I told her about the porthole stones and *Le Bijou du Roi*."

"Ah yes, it must have triggered all the information she had in her brain. Don't worry, she will be okay. It was more than she was ready for, I thought as much. She will be able to control it now, she is a very strong-minded lady," Ipion grabbed her hand and patted it, he then turned to Saphon and said to him, "She is ready now to know the truth about you."

"Are you sure?"

"She will be fine; you know who her father is."

"Yes, and I fear she will hate him when she finds out."

"She might be angry for a while, but I think she will come to terms with it."

"I think it would be best if you were left alone with her," Saphon was a little afraid, but he agreed with Ipion.

As the others left the room Saphon sat on the bed and held Victoria's hand. He always wondered what it would feel like to hold his daughter's hand again. His heart pounded with fear that she would not accept him. He knew nothing about her. He had been kept from her for 23 years. He only remembers one time that he got to spend with her. She was just newly born and Ipion had brought him through, so they may imprint on each other. As Saphon held his daughter in his arms, he placed his finger in her small hand. She opened her beautiful eyes and gazed into his. They both smiled then he touched her wrist with his thumb which left a mark. All her life she thought it was just a birthmark and, in a way, it was, she was marked by her true father.

When Victoria opened her eyes, Saphon took a deep breath and proceeded to tell her who her real father was. He told her how Ipion brought him through to meet her mother. Carver was always away on a business trip, so Saphon had time to get to know Hope. Carver left Hope alone frequently, which caused her to become very lonely for companionship. He told Victoria that he fell in love with Hope in that short time and she had fallen in love with him.

Saphon told Hope that there was an evil man named Zeddicus Payne trying to seek her out. He told her of a prophecy that a great power was to be born to her. He said that if Zeddicus found her, he would force himself on her and she will become pregnant with his child. If that happens, his child will be born, and evil will be able to enter their world. But all was not lost, he told Hope that if they lay together, she will become pregnant with his child and their child will be able to stop this evil man. Saphon told Hope that she was not to let anybody know of either man. She would be put into an institution and evil will come through and steal the child. If this happened, evil would destroy her world. Carver was to believe that the child belonged to him. So, she agreed to lay with Saphon in hopes that she would see him again.

Saphon and Hope had their special night together and he left her bed side with a heavy heart. He knew that they could not meet again because it would put the child in danger. Little did he know that Zeddicus sought her out that same night and force himself on Hope. It was Hope's mother, Isadora, that brought him through. Hope did become pregnant but with twins. One belonged to Saphon and one belonged to the evil man. The prophecy was told that Zeddicus would have a child born to him that would rule the world with the darkest of evil. But the one thing he did not know was that his child would have to be born first. When Hope had the twins, Victoria was born first, then several hours later with great pain and complications Victor was born. Zeddicus had no idea that Victoria even existed; as far as he knew, his son was the only one born that day. Even to the day, they came and took Hope and Victor; Zeddicus knew nothing about Victoria. Hope never told anybody in this world that there was a twin, not even her mother.

Saphon sat there with Victoria for several hours telling her about himself and what he could do. He told her since she was born first, the powers went to the side of good. Evil still had not figured out why Victor was week and not very powerful. He told her that Victor was with Zeddicus and Isadora in Aldabus's kingdom and that her mother was locked away in a tower. Victoria was glad to hear that her mother was still alive. She hoped that she could somehow help her and her brother. There was more that Victoria needed to know but it could wait another day. Saphon needed to train her, she needed to have control of her powers. He let her know that she was very powerful and that he and Ipion would show her how to work her magic.

Riding in the lift to the training floor Victoria rubbed her birthmark. She took her father's hand and pressed his thumb up to the mark. They were a perfect match. She took a deep breath and slowly blew it out. She was about to embark on a new life, a life that would have seem impossible in her world. She wanted Saphon to know that she understood why this was hidden from her. She held onto his hand and walked out of the lift with him to begin her lessons. She was a little afraid because she didn't know what kind of powers she had. Her photographic mind must have been one of the powers because she only had to see something once and she could remember it or knew how to do it. She also believes that healing must have been another power, because she had saved her grandfather's life so many times. Then there was earlier today when she made her drink cold.

She suddenly realized that she had the power of foresight. When Saphon hurled a fireball at her, she screamed and brought her hands up. To her amazement, the fireball froze in front of her. Then a memory of when she was younger came to her mind, a memory when she froze a friend and her grandfather told her that she was just pretending. Her grandfather must have known these things about her; she just couldn't understand why he didn't tell her. She began to wonder if he knew about her real father. She hoped that one day she would be able to go back and ask her grandfather these questions.

For weeks, she continued her teachings, Saphon did well at teaching her how to control the magic inside her. He also showed her how to use the elemental powers for defense and since he was the greatest staff fighter, he taught her how to fight with a staff. Cullen handed her a sword and taught her how to use it. Clark and Claire showed her how to move with swiftness and grace. Claire also showed her how to use a bow and arrow. She was freezing things and throwing things across the room. There were times when the magic didn't work quite well, and things would go wrong, she didn't have complete control of this magic, but she was just learning. It would come with time and plenty of practice.

Ipion had her reading some books in the library, which didn't leave her much chance to read Lucy's books. The more books she read from the library the faster she got. She was going through so many books with great speed that her head started to spin. Reading all about the magic helped but she needed the experience, Ipion saw her frustration and said, "That will be enough, you have learned much this past month. Go with your friends and explore outside the tower for a month or two. We should have plenty of time before we need to get *Le Bijou du Roi*. I believe that Zeddicus has not figured out how to open the porthole yet. I am hoping it is because we have the key."

Victoria was the key to opening the portholes but unbeknownst to any of them, because Victoria is here, Victor now has the power to open the portholes. When Victoria came through the porthole, Victor's power began to grow. He would now be able to bring as many people as he needed to get *Le Bijou du*

Roi. The Bijou du Roi has trace amounts of boron within it. Cosmic ray spallation and supernovae produce this boron. The diamond also exhibits a red phosphorescence when exposed to ultraviolet light. When good magic is cast, there is an ultraviolet light that shines from it but could only be done from the most powerful mages.

Even if Aldabus gets the diamond he won't be able to get it to work without good magic which he does not have. The diamond must be placed in the center of the heel stone. When the sun shines through, it activates the altar stone, which will help stop the rotation. But when the diamond is hit with good magic, it not only stops the rotation it reveals a panel on the altar stone, which will open one of the five doorways inside the circle. Each doorway leads to a different time, place, or realm. Inside these places are more gems that open even more time, places, and realms. If Aldabus was to get access to these places, he could change things and enslave many people. Therefore, the only way in is started by the Hope diamond, which is protected from evil magic.

Because the diamond can only be activated by good magic, Ipion was not worried about Aldabus being able to enter other worlds and taking control of them. But Ipion didn't trust Aldabus; he would feel a lot better if the diamond was safe with him. Victoria was still concerned about taking the diamond, it's not like her world would just stop looking for them. Ipion had a plan, his alchemist had designed another diamond that was a duplicate of the Hope diamond but could not be activated. The main reason is because they synthesize the boron in the diamond, it wasn't true boron and the scientist in Victoria's world would never know the difference. Knowing this, she felt a little relieved but still worried how they would get in and out undetected. Ipion said, "With magic."

Victoria decided to take Ipion's advice and explore this strange world that she was told she would be living in. Bringing Cullen, Clark, and Claire with her, they all grabbed supplies and started their journey outside of the tower. Victoria had not finished Lucy's (Clark's mother) book yet, so she packed it in her bag along with her notebook she had bought at Stonehenge. She also had the packet of missing people she got from the police station, she wanted to see if any of these people were here. She would look at their pictures, so she could remember them. This had to be the most exciting thing that Victoria has ever done. She kept thinking maybe this was a dream and if it was, she hoped she never woke up, because it was the best dream she has ever had.

As the four headed out the door, you could hear the dwarfs yelling to each other. The sound of the big doors opening with clangs and chimes made Victoria smile. How different this world was to hers and how exciting? She heard one of the dwarfs say to another one, "Oh, come on, you bunch of jugger heads put your back into it."

She then heard a response from another dwarf, "Oh, shut ye pie hole, ya fucken wanker." Victoria eyes got big and tried to stifle her smile. The others didn't think anything of it except for Cullen, he just shook his head saying, "Maker's breath, they can get loud."

As they got to the stable, Claire whistled for her deer that she called Thicket. The two of them had been inseparable since Claire found him when they were both young. He was trapped in some overgrown thickets. When she freed him, he began to follow her around, they have been the best of friends ever since. Victoria could have ridden her own horse but remind Cullen that she was not very comfortable riding her own horse, besides, she liked sitting with him on Thunder. Clark would just trot alongside of the others. He was a lot faster than a horse or deer, so he had no need to ride. With the tower at their back, the four set off on their journey.

Victoria looked back and she could see the dragon, they called Velatha. She watched as she saw the dragon circle around then it landed on top of the tower. Victoria thought that was odd, she never knew the dragon landed on the tower. Straining her neck to see if the dragon was still on there, she nearly fell off. Cullen felt her falling and he grabbed onto her and asked her if she was all right. For fear of her falling off, Cullen held onto her arm as they kept riding. Victoria made one more attempt to see if the dragon left but it was still up there. Fifteen minutes later, while riding through the trees, Victoria spotted Velatha above them. They were camouflage by the trees, so she didn't see them. Cullen saw her and stated that she was headed toward Aldabus. Claire heard the name Aldabus, and she chuckled saying, "Old Butt."

Chapter VII

Velatha flew a great distance to get to Aldabus's kingdom. It was dark and dreary with very little colorful plant life. The odd thing about some of these plants is that they glowed in this evil darkness. All the plants in this section of the land were very magical, Aldabus only surrounded himself with magic, but only dark magic. Some of these plants were poisonous to the touch and only a protection spell could keep you safe from its deadly sting. This was a land where ogre, goblins, and orcs roamed, and they were immune to the poisonous stings. With these creatures roaming the dark side of the land, it would be wise not to travel alone. It is best especially for females to always travel with companions, preferably with more than ten.

Ogres are tall, big, muscular humanoids that have ears like elves, but their skin had a green hue to it. It is said that ogres were inbreeds of elves and orcs. The ogres are a little smarter than orcs and fight with tenacity. Some ogres have the bottom tusk growing out of their mouth and some don't. Because they are believed to be cross breeds of elves and orcs these creatures are evil and cannot be trusted. But it has been known of some trustworthy ogres that were raised by elf women who were supposedly raped by orcs.

Orcs are a little shorter than the ogres but a lot burlier. Their intelligence is very low, and they are pure evil. They will eat any kind of meat; they don't care its meat. Their teeth are razor sharp and have tusk growing out of their mouth. Their face and bodies are like that of a gorilla, and they have green skin. Their strength is ten times that of a gorilla and have the taste for blood. Orcs have ears like an elf but theirs droop more. There are stories that say some crazed out elves had mated with orcs creating the ogres. Both ogres and orcs are very unstable and cannot be trusted. There is a time when orcs come into heat or musk and when the male do, they will rape anything they can get ahold of. There have been stories going around that say an unsuspecting female elf did brave the dark kingdom alone and might have been molested by an orc. It is said that all Orcs and ogres were under the command of Aldabus, the Darkheart.

Velatha arrived at Aldabus's castle and was greeted by a woman with youthful skin but gray hair, "Mother, I see you have been to Ipion's tower again." The woman reacted with hatred in her voice as she voiced Ipion's name. The dragon looked toward the west where she came from with sadness in her eyes, "When will you learn that he cares nothing for you." All the dragon could do was roar, if only she could speak she thought, "It's no use Mother I don't know what you are saying." The dragon looked down and a tear began to fall from her eye. The woman had a vial in her pocket and quickly grabbed it to capture the dragon tear. Dragon tears are very rare but are very powerful magic. When the dragon realized what the woman was about to do, she quickly put her head up and the tear fell back into her eye, "Mother! Damn! You know I need that tear why would you stop me from collecting it." The dragon just looked toward the west and ignored the woman. "Forget about him, Ipion doesn't love you anymore. How could he love a dragon?" Velatha turned and snarled at the woman, then spread her wings and flew off.

The woman reluctantly went inside stuffing the vial back into her cloak. Her long, gray hair flowed gracefully behind her. Even though she appeared to be older, her skin was still youthful looking. She was a thin woman, but she had an eerie kind of beauty to her. Her eyes were big and icy blue but had a darkly stare to them. She wore a crown like head piece that had three sharp points on the top and two pieces that came down to frame her face. There was a center piece that came down over her nose to the tip. The crown was made of a black metal and decorated with black diamonds. The cloak she wore was a low-neck, black shirt that fastened just below her breast which pushed them up. The buttons continued down to her waist just above her navel, then the cloak flowed down to the ground and trailed behind her. Under the cloak, she wore black leather like shirt and pants that tucked into her six-inch heeled boots, which lace up and came to a point above her knees. There were six buckles spaced out from the ankle to the top of the boot. As she was walking through the castle, a man's voice peered out of the darkness, "Isadora, did you get the tears?"

A bit startled, she veered around to see Zeddicus standing there.

"No, Zeddicus, I didn't get them."

"Well did you try to make her cry?"

Isadora cut her eyes at Zeddicus and said, "Of course I did."

"Then why haven't you gotten the tear?"

"I think she knows what I am trying to do, and she pulls back."

"She is just a dumb beast, she can't..." Isadora grabbed a knife hidden under her cloak, pushed Zeddicus against the wall, putting the knife to Zeddicus's neck. With great hatred toward the man, she sputtered, "That dumb beast, as you call her, is my mother." Zeddicus put his hands up and spinally said, "Forgive me, your highness, my mouth speaks unkindly toward you, it will not happen again." Isadora cut his neck just enough to make it bleed and sharply says, "Make sure it doesn't." She places the blade back in its holster, flips her cloak, and walks away. Zeddicus puts his hand up to his neck and gathers the blood onto his fingers. As he puts his fingers in his mouth, he loathingly watches Isadora walk away. Even though he is the father of her grandson, they still hated each other. The plan for Zeddicus to be the father was Aldabus's idea, not hers.

Isadora wanted her uncle, her mother's half-brother, to be the father but Aldabus said that it was too close to the same genes and would spoil the magic. He told her to find somebody else. She didn't think the closely related genes would spoil the magic but make it better. She decided to go behind Aldabus's back and continue with her plan, ignoring what Aldabus said. Zeddicus knew of her deception to follow through with her uncle and he voiced this plan to Aldabus. This infuriated Aldabus and expressed to Zeddicus to do what he had to do to stop Isadora's plans. So, before Isadora could follow up with her strategy, Zeddicus killed her uncle. When Isadora informed Aldabus of Zeddicus's treachery, instead of punishing him, he rewarded Zeddicus and had him take the place to be the father. Not only did Aldabus think Isadora's plan would spoil the magic, but he feared that the child born by Isadora's plan would be more powerful than him. There was no way he was going to let anybody be more powerful than he was. Not even his own great grandchild.

As Isadora walked through the corridors of Death Mountain, she stops at a large wood door, upon opening it, she sashayed into the room. Scanning the room, her glance stopped at the balcony. Standing outside was her grandson, Victor. He was a very handsome and strong looking young man but very pale and gothic. His hair was black as night and fell to his waist, "You should not stand so close to the edge, least you fall." The young man replied in a voice that was masculine but taunting, "Would you like that, grandmother?"

She walked up to him and forcefully made him face her, "Of course not, you are my grandson, I care for you."

"Careful, grandmother, they will think you have grown a heart in that black soul of yours."

She slapped the boy in the face and said, "I will not have you talk in that manor to me." Victor squinted his eyes and rubbed his face where she slapped him.

"Have you seen your mother today?" With distain, he replied, "Yes, but I do hate visiting her. What is the point; she cares no more for me than you do?"

"Well, that is too bad, you need to, she is hiding something from us, and I need you to get it out of her."

"What can she possibly be hiding from you? Just face it, the magic was weak in her from being over there. She has shown no signs of magic. For twenty years, I have been going to see her and in all that time, she has never displayed any kind of magic."

"I don't believe that, she is my child, she has to have some magic in her." Victor gave her a smug smile and said, "Maybe she is more like her mortal father than you think."

"More reason for her to show some magic."

"What? A mere mortal with magic?" Isadora got closer to him and cut her eyes at him saying, "You know nothing of our linage. I think it is time you learned. Go to the Hall of Knowledge and learn about our ancestors, you will sing a different tune when you see where we came from." Victor pulled his long dark hair out of his eyes that were as blue as sapphires. Leaning on the railing, he scans the horizon. Something had awakened in him that he had not told anybody, even his grandmother. A beautiful bird took perch on the railing to rest its wings. Victor gently picked up the bird and closed his eyes. As a tear rolled down his cheek, he looked down at the lifeless bird in his hand. Isadora saw him and said, "Really Victor, you need to learn not to cry when you kill something." With that, she slapped the dead bird out of his hand, and he watched it fall until it disappeared.

Victor left his room and climbed the stairs to the top of the tower. He opened the door to see his mother sitting in the window. She looked tired and sad. All she did was to sit in that window and watch the world go by. She was very thin and fragile from not eating much. Her life meant nothing to her, and she wished they would end it. Thoughts of her daughter would dance in her head but when her mother or son came in the room, she buried those thoughts deep in her mind. She had to keep her safe, they must never know about her. They pried into her mind, but Victoria's safety was more important, so she used all the magic she had to keep those thoughts from them. Victor stayed in the room for an hour and when he couldn't pull anything out of her, he left. As soon as Hope knew that he was gone, she took a vial out of her cloak. Opening the vial, she brought it up to her lips and let a dragon's tear hit her tongue, as she held it on her tongue, it soon dissolved and slid down her throat.

Velatha knew what they were doing to her and the only way she could help her was to give her some dragon tears. She made Hope promise not to tell anybody about the dragon tears. It was very important that Isadora didn't get any. Hope promised that she would not tell them. She knew those tears were powerful magic and evil should not get their hands on them.

Velatha did not spend much time at her father's castle, she hated the man. She finally believes Ipion story that Aldabus tricked him into turning her into a dragon. Aldabus couldn't do it because to turn somebody into a dragon you had to love them unconditionally. Aldabus was so evil that his heart could not love anybody without deceit, save one, but that was a very long time ago and she is gone. Ipion and Velatha had that kind of love, so he cast a spell on Velatha to make Ipion believe he had no other choice but to cast the spell that Aldabus gave him. Aldabus told Ipion that this spell would change her into something else which would save her. He didn't tell Ipion that she would be turned into a dragon. Aldabus needed a dragon that could find the other dragons. There were many dragons in the kingdom, but they stayed hidden away. Aldabus had plans to capture them and to harness their powers then use them in his great battle plan.

When Isadora was brought back to this world, she found out that her mother had been turned into a dragon by her father. This caused great hatred in her heart that she vowed to get even with her father. She heard there was a way to transform Velatha back into human form but Aldabus didn't want her to be transform back, she hadn't led him to the other dragons yet. The plan Isadora had to help her mother would work by the blood of a first-born descendant. When Isadora came back with her grandson, Aldabus was the only one who knew that this child was not the first born the spell was talking about, it was Isadora. He let Isadora continue with her plan because he knew if she followed through with the spell it would make Velatha a dragon permanently.

Velatha would spend more time flying around the tower than she did with her daughter whose hatred toward her father had turn her soul dark. Most of Velatha's time was spent with the other dragons. Since she would not show Aldabus where the other dragons were, he had her followed. Velatha was a clever dragon and could not be followed without her knowledge. When she spotted one of Aldabus's spies, she would burn them to a crisp. He would always send more but they stopped following Velatha because they didn't want to be burned by the dragon. When Aldabus found out that his spies betrayed him, he made their fate worse than burning. After a while, he stopped sending them because he was losing too many possible cannon fodders for his battle.

As Velatha arrived at the cave where the other dragons were hiding she looked in the directions of the tower. She was thinking about the young woman she saw there. Her face was familiar to her. She knows she had seen this face before, but where. As she walked past the glass waterfall in the cave and saw her reflection, it came to her. She remembers as a young girl roaming the halls of her father's castle, she came upon a room she was forbidden to go into. As she went to open the door, it was locked. Every day she went to that door and it was locked. One day she came to the door, turned the knob, and it opened. Inside was a large room with a big, beautiful canopy bed. There was a cradle next to the bed and by a large window was a rocking chair. Across the room from the bed was a large fireplace that she could almost stand in. As she looked up above the fireplace, there was a life size painting of a beautiful woman. That is who that young woman looked like; she was the perfect likeness to this beautiful woman.

The cave was in a mountain that was across the seas from Asimeritian. A dragon could get to these caves in minutes but took longer for anybody else to travel to them. These caves were also hard to find. The sea was vast and if you didn't know how to read the stars or sail, you could be lost for months, maybe even years. Many dragons lived in these caves, they kept treasures there. Treasures that were found on ships that had been long abandon. Velatha was the only dragon of her kind but they excepted her because she kept them safe. She told them where it was safe and where not to go. One young dragon got bold and went to a forbidden place. The great white dragon cared greatly for this young dragon and felt the need to rescue him. The youngster was rescued at the cost of the great white one.

Velatha knew that the young woman she saw could help them, she had to go to her somehow. Velatha was the only dragon who could wonder around Asimeritian because she was the daughter of Aldabus, the Darkheart. She had to try and approach Victoria and assure her she means her no harm. She knew this young mage had the power of speech; she needed Victoria to cast that spell on her. Even though Velatha was not like the other dragons, she was still connected to them. Once she obtains the power of speech the rest will obtain it too. She had to go back out there and find her.

First, she had to see who held the great white one hostage. The young dragon told her that he was captured by orcs. Even though the dragons did not have speech, they could understand each other with their snorts and growls. It was hard for Velatha to understand at times, but she remained patient until she understood. She had to help the great white one because he had faith in her and knew she was good for the pride of dragons. Dragons were already magical but with the connection they had with Velatha, their magic was even stronger. Magic and dragons had been around for nearly a thousand years. Not many people knew where this started from, only a few select in Aldabus's horde knew of the birth of magic. It had been around for a very long time and from a time that would devastate Victoria.

*****

Sitting behind Cullen, Victoria had her arms wrapped around him. All she could think of how good this felt. Every now and then Cullen would place his hand on hers checking to make sure she was still there. When they first got on the horse, he tried to tell her it would be better if she sat in front of him. She told him she felt like she was going to fall and that riding behind him she could hang onto something solid. He submitted to her plea but with insecurities that she would fall off.

They rode for several hours then arrived at Hamesbring; the same town that Claire had first met them. Cullen got off the horse and helped Victoria down. Grabbing her hand, he led her to a place where they could eat. He wanted Victoria to experience some of the peasantry food. It was much different and didn't have anything magically done to it. One of the things on the menu was mutton, which Clark was appalled by. Clark was obviously not a meat eater; he loved his fruits and vegetables. When they had the hot dogs and French fries, he ate the fries but left the hot dog.

Luckily for Clark, there were a lot of centaurs in this town. Centaurs were not meat eaters, so their meals were prepared without meat. The centaurs had their own menu that consisted of tubers, oats, molasses, and other grains. Clark loved eating at the centaur's stall. They made the best combinations of grains and vegetables he had ever eaten. His favorite meal was made with eggplant, lentils, salt, water, olive oil, onion, garlic, tomatoes, green chili, mint leaves, tomato paste, crushed peppers, and pomegranate molasses. The centaurs let the stew mellow for several hours before serving it. This process is what made the stew taste good. The stew that the other three were eating had to simmer for four to six hours before serving. The ingredients in their stew was; grape seed oil, onions, garlic, carrots, celery, rosemary, mutton, red wine, tomato paste, vegetable stock, salt, pepper, potatoes, and butter. All the preparations for the meals at these stalls were done in the early morning hours; this is what made the outside of the tower food taste so good. The bread was made in the big stone fireplace, which you could smell throughout the town.

The four got their meals with some bread and took it outside to eat in the fresh air. You didn't get much of that living in the tower, the fresh air, that is. Next to the food stalls were tables set up underneath pergolas. Some of the pergolas had a type of canvas on top of them in case it rained, and others had vines growing across the tops of them. As they sat there eating, a dragataur came up to them. He was a big man, bigger than the first dragataur that Victoria seen. When he came up to them, Victoria got a little scared. She still wasn't used to the fact that she had a lot of magic to protect herself with. He turned his back to them briefly and she noticed those slits in his back. The other dragataur had the same slits. These slits made her extremely curious and wanted to ask the man what they were from. But her fear of him took over her curiosity.

The dragataur looked at Claire and nodded, which caused Claire to come down closer to her bowl of stew as if she were trying to hide in it. Tilting his head at her reaction to him, the dragataur looked at Victoria and announced in a deep thundering voice, "I am Barroth. I was told you were looking for men to join your guild." With great confusion, Cullen replied, "Our guild? Who told you that we were looking for anybody?" With his big claw like hands, he pointed at Claire, "The little one there drowning in her stew."

Claire looked up from her bowl and chuckled saying, "What, don't be such a bunch of pus buckets. I thought we could use a draggy man like him. I mean look at that ass nut, who would say no to him. One kick in the dangle bags by him and you be down like a sack of shite." Clark covered his dangle bags and looked at Victoria, "He would be a nice addition to our little collection, not to mention some more eye candy to look at."

Barroth walked up to Clark and looked down at him. He smiled and said, "You couldn't handle the likes of me, goat boy."

Clark looked up at this man that stood about six feet six inches and had a shoulder span of four feet. On the top of his forehead grew horns like a dragon, which curved to the back then tip up to a point. He had long, black hair that was braided with cloth. His eyes were this brilliant yellowish green. They were deep-set almond shaped and slanted slightly up toward the temples. Around his eyes was black liner and eye shadow which made his eyes look more intense. His eyebrows were an exotic natural shape and were as black as his hair. His face was diamond shaped and he had an extended goatee stubble. He had a roman shaped nose that was just slightly over his full lips. His ears were different, kind of like elves, except for being pointy they bent over.

He wasn't wearing a shirt but had a harness on to carry his axe. The axe was a double blade with the head of a dragon on top and the body of a dragon was carved into the handle. With a big axe like that, you would have to have arms the size that he had. His skin looked tan but had a soft scaly look to it. He wore pants made of some kind of animal hide that fit him so snug you can just make out the shape and size of his man hood, which was bulky. On his feet, he wore something like moccasins that laced up to his knees.

Clark couldn't stop looking at Barroth's package, so Victoria slowly pulled him away and turned him around. Barroth looked down at Victoria and smiled. He had beautiful teeth for a man of his nature, they were very white and straight. His eye teeth were just a little sharper looking but not enough to make them look unnatural. Taking a deep breath in, Barroth could smell something different about this woman. Something powerful, but very good. Victoria thought he was a very handsome man, different, but handsome. She put her hand out to shake his and said, "Welcome to our, what did you call it, guild?" Barroth took Victoria's hand and kissed it. She turned and looked at Clark and tried to stifle her grin. Clark looked at Victoria, then quietly he teasingly said, "Bitch."

Cullen cut his eyes at Claire who was observing the interaction when she saw Cullen looking at her. She gave him a sheepish smile and chuckled a little. Claire was a beautiful elf with coal black hair. Her hair was thick, and it bumped up on the top then fell behind her. On one side, her hair was tucked behind her long-pointed elf ears. The rest of her hair flowed down to the middle of her back. She wore a head band that had six thorny looking points that made the band look like a crown. It also had some holes in it where she pulled some of her hair through to the front but brushed over to the left. The hair in front was just slightly long enough to shadow part of her left eye. She had big, violet, almond shaped eyes that had dark liner to show off their shape. Her eye shadow was a dark purple almost black that came out and up to the tip of her exotic shaped black eyebrows. She had a perfect shaped nose that was just slightly above her plump luscious lips. Her slender heart shaped face sat on her gracefully soft neck. The clothes she wore were sparse since being a wood elf they only wore enough clothes to cover up the essential parts.

She wore a light but strong looking armor across her small shoulders. It came up her neck a little for added protection. The color was a burgundy purple with gold trimmings. She wore a harness that buckled together with thin straps that were slightly to the side and above each side of her breast. The straps went under her arms then to her back which held her quiver of arrows. Underneath her collar armor hung a necklace made of a thin leather strap and a delicate piece of jade shaped like an oak leaf. On her arms, she wore gauntlets that starting at her wrist to her elbow and then above the elbow and ending just below her shoulders. They, too, were the same color and hard leather looking armor as the collar. Even her top was made of the same material and color and it just barely covered her breast. Her bottoms were of the same material, except for the part that went between her legs and up her butt. She wore boots that came up to her knees and had that same hard leather look. She was a very agile elf, so heels would not be part of her attire. The boots had no heels and were soft on the bottom but tough enough not to let something puncture through them.

Any man would love to be with this beautiful woman, but this was not the case for her. She had a thing for women, she loved the way they smelled and the way they looked. Whenever she made herself up, it was for other women. The way a woman felt when she touched them would excite her. They were so soft, and their lips tasted so good to her. The thought of a man's rugged face touching hers repulsed her. She could never lay with a man; it just wasn't in her to be that way. No man could ever touch her voluptuous breast or her tight rock-hard butt. They will never feel the smooth curves that shaped her narrow waist. She will never wrap her long slender legs around a man.

Claire was the only one that had sat down and was eating. After introducing Barroth to her little group, Victoria invited Barroth to sit and eat with them. She felt the best way to get to know each other was to sit and eat. A conversation always came up when they ate. They sat there for several hours getting to know Barroth. Claire made a good call when she invited him to their group. He was a major asset to this group and his great strength would come in handy if they ever encountered any orcs or ogres. The chances of them running into any of them were low. Orcs and ogres never wandered too far from the dark kingdom. They believe they would never have to travel to that territory.

Barroth was very good at coordinating quests, he had been on many in the past but was never happy with them. When he discovered how meager their supplies were, he told them to wait here while he congregated supplies that were fit for their journey. As they sat there waiting for their new member, Claire noticed an elf woman wondering around. She recognized the woman and walked up to her. It was her cousin that left the forest and joined up with Aldabus. She approached her and was about to strike when she saw an emptiness in her eyes. The elf looked at Claire smiled and said, "Do I know you? Do you know me?" Claire frowned and replied, "I wish I didn't know you, cousin, what's with this act."

"Act? What act?"

She reached up and put her fingers on Claire's lips and said, "So pretty." Claire grabbed the elf's arms, shook her and angrily said, "You slimy pus bucket, ass nut chewing bitch, what's wrong with you?" The elf just put her hand up to Claire's face again and smiled. Cullen had been watching and recognized the elf. It was the same elf spy that was at the tower. Ipion stopped her before she left the tower and placed a spell on her to slowly forget everything, even who she was. He went over to Claire and explained to her what had happened. At first, she was upset but then realized that she can now help her to start her life over. She took her to the edge of the forest and had a honey nabber and a couple of flitters to show her the way to her people's camp.

An hour had passed when they heard the thundering of horse hooves and the sound of wheels turning. They looked in the direction that Barroth had gone and saw that he had a wagon pulled by four Clydesdale sized horses. These horses were bigger than Thunder but had the same long mane, tail, and long hair down by their fetlock. The colors of these horses were different from Thunder, they were a pinto coloring of black and white. Inside the wagon were tents, cooking utensils and tools to repair weapons and armor. There was some bedding for the tents and toiletry for bathing. With their well-equipped wagon, Victoria's guild was ready to set off on their adventure of the land. He also invited his two friends Ryo and Fodgrel. Ryo was a handsome elf that carried swords on his back. He had a Hispanic accent and seemed self-absorb. Fodgrel was a tough looking dwarf that had a long scar starting from just above his right eyebrow down across his nose to his left cheek. He had a huge hammer that looked to weigh at least 20 pounds. His arms were huge, which they had to be to swing that hammer around. They made their introductions and proceeded on their journey.

Cullen was about to put Victoria on his horse when Barroth grabbed her and put her on the wagon. Cullen felt a tug on his heart strings but said nothing. Clark wasn't sure if Barroth could be trusted with Victoria, so he got on the wagon with them. Barroth almost objected until he saw that Clark pushed her closer to him. Clark wanted to ride in between the two but he knew that Barroth would object to that. He wanted to make sure that the big brute didn't take advantage of his best friend. Fodgrel rode in the back of the wagon, he didn't ride horses, he didn't like riding horses because they were so big. He said his feet were not meant to be that far off the ground. Ryo had a beautiful palomino horse that was not as big as Thunder but was a female and drove Thunder crazy at times. At one-point, Cullen had to calm Thunder with some magic and remind him who his true love was.

As they rode for several hours, Victoria started to fidget. Her butt was getting sore from sitting on the wood bench. Cullen could see that she was getting tired, and he had noticed several times that Barroth's hand would go around Victoria's shoulders. Even one time he put his hand on her leg, which Clark slapped. He hated to see her uncomfortable, so he walked his horse in front of the team and stopped them. Barroth looked a little angry from Cullen's gesture until Victoria got up, climbed over Clark, and jumped off the wagon. She rubbed her butt and gave Cullen an appreciated smile.

The sun was skulking down behind them, so Barroth thought it would be an innovative idea to set up camp. Victoria stood there and watched the six of them pitch the tents. They all made it seem so easy, except for Clark who had never set up a tent before. Several times, he got tangled up in it and Cullen thought for sure Clark would rip the canvas. Cullen had Clark stand over by Victoria and told him to let the others set up the tents. Claire was very good with the set-up, after all, she did live in the forest for most of her life. Moving and pitching was one of the first things she learned as a very young child. She was good at cooking too. Before they pitched the tents, she started a stew. She was even kind enough to Clark that she put a pot off to the side with just vegetables in it. While the stews simmered, they set up the tents and made a warm campfire. It was nice during the days but when the sun went down it got chilly at night.

When they were done with their meal, Clark grabbed up the dishes to clean them. He was O.C.D. about cleanliness. His mama always told him that cleanliness was next to godliness. Victoria went to help Clark because she was starting to feel useless. He welcomed her help with a smile and started to talk to her about the new brute in their assemblage.

"I think the brute has a thing for you."

Looking over at Barroth she saw that he was a very handsome man, dragon or whatever he was, "He is very handsome, but…"

"Not your type. You know, like Cullen," Clark looked at Victoria and smiled. He knew that Victoria had something going inside her heart for him.

"But he is a guardian."

"So," Clark stated shrugging his shoulders.

"But I thought guardian couldn't be with women."

"Well, they're not supposed to be, but it is obvious the man cares a great deal for you."

"Oh, I think he is just being nice to me."

"Oh honey, there is more to it than that. Didn't you see the look in his eyes when Barroth grabbed you and put you on the wagon."

Victoria looked at Cullen and he was looking at her. He gave her that side smile then looked away.

"Oh yeah, he has some feelings for you. And what's this look on your face? Can it be, no, dare I say, love?" Victoria felt a flush of heat go across her face and she placed her hand on her cheek. She looked at Clark and said, "What do I do."

"Well, the man obviously has never been with anybody before. He is not going to make the first move."

"I am not any more experienced than him," Clark looked at Victoria and was shocked to hear it. He understood why Cullen had not been with anybody, but Victoria? He had heard that women from her world were outgoing and really liked men or women. He recalled hearing a story about a woman that had been sucked into this world just last year. She has one child and is now pregnant with another man's child.

"Honey, you mean to tell me you have never jumped on the band wagon."

"No, I am not that easy," Victoria hissed at him and a sparked snapped from her hand. Clark slowly closed Victoria's hand and said, "Calm down, I didn't mean anything by it. It's just that I have met some women from your side, and they couldn't control their selves over some of the fine choice of men here." Victoria looked at Cullen and she began to submit to his innocence. She had never met a man such as him. He was handsome, loyal, honest, and respectful. She felt like she could trust him with her life and that meant something to her. Victoria was terrified to make the first move but knew she had to so that he would know she felt the same way he did. She was about to walked toward Cullen when she heard a rustling in the woods behind her. Both Clark and Victoria looked in the woods that fashioned a shape in the darkness.

Victoria stepped a little closer to the shape. Clark had better vision than Victoria and he grabbed her arm, yelling, "Dragon!" With the sound of the word exploding from his lips, Barroth and Cullen were up and running toward the shape. The dragon stepped into the moonlight and there stood Velatha. Barroth fell to one knee and bowed his head, while Cullen pulled out his sword and was about to strike the dragon. "Stop!" Victoria shouted and knocked the sword out of Cullen's hand with one flick of magic from her. Even though the dragon's size frightened her, she felt like she knew what the dragon wanted. Victoria slowly and gracefully walked up to the dragon. The dragon opened her mouth, which caused Cullen to scramble for his sword.

Victoria put her hand up to him, then a strange ball of magic formed in her other hand. It was a purple color and had a cool temperature to it. She had never formed this kind of magic before but somehow, she knew what she had to do with it. It was as if the dragon was talking to her, in her head. As the ball got bigger, the dragon opened her mouth as far as she could. Then suddenly Victoria heard the word *now* in her head. With great force, she threw the ball of energy into the dragon's mouth. The dragon reeled back and began to choke and sputter. Flames started to come out of the dragon and at first the flames were red hot. Then the flames changed, it had an ultraviolet color to it and wasn't as hot. She coughed a few more times and then the words, "Thank you," came out of her mouth.

Everybody was stunned to hear words come out of the dragon's mouth. They were not sure if that was a good thing or not.

"Victoria," the dragon uttered, "I knew you were the one to be able to perform that spell. Do not be afraid, I am here to help."

"Velatha, how do I know that you won't help Aldabus?"

"My father is an evil man; he did this to me," Velatha explain Aldabus's intent when he had Ipion change her into a dragon. He planned to use Velatha to show him where the other dragons were to enslave them. But there was one thing that Aldabus did not count on. When Velatha was turned into a dragon, it changed her. She didn't have her heart, but she had the heart of a dragon now. Ipion was the caretaker of this heart, who kept it safe.

Victoria was surprised to hear that Ipion had the dragon's heart. She had sensed Ipion was hiding something from her. She wanted to go back and confront him about it but Velatha encouraged her to continue forward with her quest, "What quest might that be?"

"You must venture into the dark forest. There, you will encounter a great creature that has been imprisoned by some stupid Orcs."

Looking at her group, she was a little nervous. Velatha sensed her insecurities and said, "Victoria, you are from great magic, once you believe in that, there will be nothing that could harm you."

"You know where I am from."

"Yes," Velatha opened her wings to take flight.

"Wait, tell me."

"Go, help the great white one. He will forever be in your debt."

With that, she flew off toward the other dragons. Victoria turned and looked at her followers and said, "Well, I guess we set off toward the dark forest." She was smiling, then the smile faded as she asked, "Does anybody know where that is?" They all looked at each other and made gestures that they knew which way to go. It was getting late, and they all figured they might as well turn in, with no thought of the day, they all walked to their tents to get some sleep. They knew the feat they had the next day would require much needed rest. Battling those orcs were not going to be easy. Orcs are not friendly and will fight to the death for their treasures. Like Velatha said, they were stupid and if it meant their deaths, they would fight hard for this great white creature.

Victoria did not want to be alone in her tent, so she went to Clark's. She knew she was safe with him and he invited her with open arms. They laid there and talked for a while. Clark had become her shoulder; he was always there for her. Victoria was glad she met Clark, he made things so much easier for her and he was a great informant. They pulled Lucy's book out and started reading things out of it. Some things were omitted but Clark could fill in the blanks. He still had the fear of his father creeping up on him. His father still wanted to kill him for his transgressions. Victoria promised Clark that she would not let Zorxox get to him.

Looking at the book, she began to study their calendar. From what she gathered in her head some of them were using the Celtic calendar and some the Celtic tree calendar, it was a bit confusing to her. Kind of like the Euro money, for some reason, she had a challenging time understanding it. It was strange how some things come so easy to her, but these things just go over her head. According to Lucy's book, she arrived here in the month of Elembiuos; which means claim time. It is now Edrinios; arbitration time. Clark reminded her it won't be long, and it will be Cantlos; song time. That is when their festivities start, and she could wear that beautiful dress. Clark told her they had plenty of time to help this great white one, then get back for the festivities. Clark really wanted to see the look on Cullen's face when he sees her in that dress.

They looked in the book for a little while longer than Victoria started to feel sleepy. She asked Clark to tell her a story. Clark told her a story about a guardian who left the tower for love. This didn't happen very often; most guardians were loyal to their calling. There were some hardships, but love would always triumph. Clark didn't like to tell stories that had bad or sad endings.

"So, did he cut his hair?"

"Yes, only because she wanted him to."

"I would never ask Cullen to cut his long, beautiful hair." Clark looked at her quizzically and said, "Do you know how long his hair is?" She shyly smiled and said, "Yes, he let me pull his hair out of his armor." Clark's mouth dropped open, and he said, "Such a flirt and for a guardian." Victoria smiled than said, "Wait, what? Are you talking about me or him?" Clark slapped her hand and said, "The both of you." He bumped her with his shoulder and they both smiled.

Clark's life had some sad ending at one point and he never wanted to feel that way ever again. He always wanted to surround himself with positive thinking people that helped him to get over losing his mother. She was the best thing that ever happened in his life. Always there for him and educating him on the goods and evils in this world was her goal. She knew she couldn't be around forever, so she wrote everything he needed to know in her books. Lucy knew that Zorxox was going to catch up with her one day. She might not be able to get away from him, but she knew Clark could. Every day, she always made him run. She wanted his speed to pick up and because she did that, he was the fastest Satyr in the world. Lucy would sacrifice her life for her child; he was the only thing important to her in this crazy magical world she had fallen into.

Chapter VIII

As the morning sun peeked over the horizon, it slipped through an opening in the tent. The wind was blowing a little, which caused the sunlight to dance around on Victoria's face. She quietly got up so not to wake Clark. As she slipped through the opening of the tent, Victoria took in a deep breath. The air was fresh and clean; it was not like this where she was from. Walking to her tent, she grabbed a solution that the alchemist gave to her, so she could swish around in her mouth to get rid of that morning taste. To Victoria, it was a magical solution that not only cleared up her morning breath, but it helped to keep her teeth clean.

As she looked up, she could see a beautiful pond in the distance. Walking over to the pond, she spotted Cullen squatting, admiring the beauty that fell before him. Victoria looked around and saw that they were the only two up. Taking in a nervous breath, she walked over to Cullen. Cullen stood up and turned around to see Victoria standing there. He looked at her, longing to be with her but felt he could do nothing about it. How he wanted to hold her in his arms and never let her go.

Victoria stood there looking at him with her arms crossed. She then stepped closer and was about to say something but instead grabbed his face and began to kiss him. Cullen put his arms around her small waist and affectionately kissed her back. Victoria reached up around his neck and his arms slid up her back and cradled her in this longing embrace. As they slowly parted their lips, they looked at each other and a sad look came over his face. Cullen then reached in his shirt and yanked something from his neck and handed it to Victoria. She looked down at a gold medallion charm with a dragon etched into it. As she looked back up at Cullen, he slowly walked away from her. A little confused Victoria held this charm close to her chest and closed her eyes. There was no doubt in her mind she was in love with him. Staring at the pond as Cullen walked away from her, she vowed that one day, they would be together, and nothing would stop them.

After breakfast, they gather up the tents and cooking gear then placed them in the wagon. As Victoria placed her belongings in the wagon, she looked over at Cullen who was harnessing Thunder. He gave her that side smile then continued what he was doing. When he was done, he walked over to Victoria and helped her up the wagon. He felt it would be best if she rode in the wagon. He then gestured to Clark with his eyes to get up there next to her. Clark looked sideways at Cullen, then smiled, "Don't worry, sweet cheeks, I will keep an eye on her." Cullen looked at Victoria, smiled than got on his horse. Clark sensed something had happened and said, "What did you do to that man." Victoria tried to hide her smile but couldn't and looked down. She swallowed hard and said, "I kissed him."

"No, you did not," Clark said, sounding sarcastically shocked.

"Yes, yes I did."

A flush of red came over her face and Clark squealed in excitement.

"Oh, you little nymph, you did. Oh, honey you need to tell me the whole juicy details."

"There is really nothing to tell, I just kissed him."

"Huh uh, honey, you are telling me everything."

Victoria smiled and glanced at Cullen, he looked so handsome on top of his horse. *How corny*, she thought, *My knight in shining armor*. She could not believe this was happening to her. She never really had a boyfriend, she was waiting for her knight, which she thought she would never meet. Victoria believed she would be alone forever because there was no such thing as a knight in shining armor anymore. Yet here he is, as real as life and he gave her, her first kiss.

"Hey, what's going on here, are you holding out on me?" Clark was trying to get Victoria's attention by blocking her view with his face, "Tell me, did he kiss you back?"

Her face became even redder, and Clark responded with, "Oh, he did, shame on that boy. Being a guardian and all."

Victoria looked at Clark and said, "But you said," before she could finish, Barroth jumped up onto the wagon. It startled Victoria and she looked at him red face and all.

106

"Why is your face all red? I know, don't tell me, I have that effect on women," Barroth belted as he snapped the reins to prompt the horses into moving, "Don't worry, I have a remedy for that." He placed one of his hands on her leg and Clark slapped his hand then smiling he said, "Stop," in a teasing way. Barroth grabbed the reins with both hands and began to laugh.

Fodgrel sat in the back of the wagon as he watched Ryo ride his horse up next to Claire. In his Spanish accent, he smiled at her. Claire wrinkled her nose and said, "What, what are you staring at, ass nut?"

"Tell me something, have you always been fighting?"

"What? What are you talking about?"

"Well, I ask because you must have been fighting all your life."

"Why do you say that?"

"Because you are so beautiful, you must have had to fight them off of you," Claire rolled her eyes and said, "Ugh, Ass Nut!" She kicked Thicket sides to get him to pass the wagon. As she passes the wagon, Fodgrel bellowed out a laugh that made her face turn a little red. Then he said to Ryo, "Give up, you fuckin' wanker, you don't have tits." Even Fodgrel knew that Claire was not interested, but Ryo was still going to keep trying.

Several hours had gone by and they were getting closer to the dark forest. They weren't kidding when they say dark. This place was so dark the sun could barely cut through it. They were traveling in the forest for what seemed like hours when something came bursting through the trees into their view. This startled Thicket and he reared up which caused Claire to lose her grip and she fell off. As she got up and started to brush herself off, an orc jumped her and started to molest her.

"Ugh, get off you, mother friggin' ass biscuit," Claire kicked the orc very hard in his dangle bags and he fell over groaning. As she scrambled to her feet, she grabbed her bow and pulled an arrow out of the quiver within seconds. She was about to release the arrow when the orc cried, "No kill Wadester."

"What?" Claire was surprised to hear an orc speak, they never speak, they just grunt, "Listen, you shite bag, ass nut, pus bucket. Give me a reason why I shouldn't kill you."

"Wadester only make humpy humpy."

"Not with me you don't."

Still hanging onto his wounded pride, Wadester slowly got up. "You no like humpy humpy?" Claire pulled the string on her bow harder. The others came over to see what was going on. Wadester saw Clark and ran to hide behind him, "Tell lady, humpy humpy is good."

"Why would I tell her that?" Clark tried to get away from the orc, but he continued to stay hidden behind him, "You satyr, satyr say women like humpy humpy."

"Step aside Clark, so I can put an arrow in this green shite bag."

Victoria felt kind of bad for the hideous creature and started to intervene. The Orc mistook her kindness for something else and started for her. Cullen jumped off Thunder, pulled his sword, and pierced the orc just enough to make him bleed a little. The Orc began to cry like a child and curled up into a ball. Claire could not believe what she was seeing and put her bow and arrow away. She walked up to the Orc and bent over him to see his cut, "It's just a little cut, you're fine." The orc looked up at Claire, his eyes were filled with tears and snot was coming out of his nose.

Claire whistled for Thicket and he slowly walked toward her. Looking at the deer with great frustration, she said, "Well, come on, you chicken shite, he ain't going to hurt you." The deer put his head down to show his antlers, "You better friggin' put those away before I kick you in the dangle bags." The deer brought his head up and walked up to Claire. Reaching in the bags, she had hanging on the deer she grabbed some ointment and a rag. She put the ointment on the rag and tried to put it on the orcs cut. The orc wriggled around and would not be still.

"Come on, I'm not gonna hurt you."

As she put the rag on the cut, the orc cried out like a child. "Maker's breath. Stop acting like a child, I am just cleaning it off," Claire responded with great frustration.

Victoria stepped closer and watching the action of the orc she couldn't help but conclude that maybe he was a child, "Claire?"

"What!"

"Claire, I think he is a child," Claire looked at the orc and wrinkled her nose, "I don't think so."

"Wadester," Victoria said in a very gentle voice, "Do you know how old you are?"

"Wadester old enough. Wadester see the snows on the mountains eight times."

"Oh, my god, he is just a child. Isn't he?" Victoria responded, looking at Cullen. Cullen put his sword away and said, "Eight? I am still trying to figure out how he can talk."

"Wadester can talk. Daddy Satyr learn me how," Clark pursed his lips and frowned, no Satyr would father an orc. Clark walked over to the orc and stomped is hoof next to his head. The orc grabbed his head and got up quick, "Wadester, sorry. Wadester not do again." Clark knew that this orc has been kicked in the head by a satyr before. He knows the reaction from what his mother put in her book. She had seen a male satyr train a young satyr before and knew she was not ever going to give her son up to his father.

"This is crazy, who would raise an Orc," Clark looked at Wadester and asked, "Did you hear the name of Daddy Satyr?"

Wadester covered his head and said, "No, no tell. Daddy Satyr said no tell."

Clark wanted to know the name of the Satyr who raised him. He began to stomp his hoof at the Orc again. The Orc got scared and fell to the ground. He continued to say, "No tell. No tell."

Stomping his hoof even closer Clark continued to ask, "Who!" Victoria had never seen Clark like this before and it started to scare her. "Clark," Victoria pleaded, but Clark continued until the Orc finally said, "Zorxox." Clark looked at Victoria with fear in his eyes.

"Daddy Satyr leave Wadester," the orc wiped the tears from his eyes and said, "Went tower. Look for real son." Clark breathed a great sigh of relief. They were nowhere near the tower.

"So, why don't you stay with the other orcs?" Victoria asked.

"Other orcs not like Wadester. Wadester not like them. Wadester all alone."

Victoria knelt next to Wadester, "If you behave yourself and not try to make humpy, you could come with us." Wadester got up and wrapped his cloth that barely cover his privates tighter, "Wadester keep it tight. No humpy. Wadester be good for nice lady." Claire wrinkled her nose and said, "Well, that didn't work very good, you can see the pus bucket's dangle bags hanging there."

Victoria thought one of the first things she would do for him was to use a blanket to cover him better. He couldn't go anywhere with them while his junk was hanging out. She went to the wagon and grabbed a blanket. Taking a knife, she cut a hole in the middle. Placing the hole over Wadester head she took the knife and cut a strip to use as a belt. It wasn't the best-looking attire for the orc, but it would have to do. Wadester smiled at his new clothes and began to jump around. He was so excited to have new clothes that he started swinging from branch to branch like a gorilla. Barroth said, "So are we going now, or are we going to watch the monkey play."

Victoria went to get on the wagon and Wadester noticed the direction they were facing. He ran in front of the horses and said, "No go that way. Mean brothers. Have white horsey." Victoria squinted her eyes at Wadester, "Did you say white horsey?"

"White horsey, big. Sharp mouth. Hot."

"Wadester, could you do me a big favor. I would be so happy with you if you do."

"What Wadester do for nice lady?"

"Take me to the white horsey," she saw the scared look on his face and continued, "I promise you, we will not let the mean brothers or the white horsey hurt you."

Wadester smiled, "Wadester show nice lady."

He started to walk away then turned to Victoria saying, "Not let horsey hurt Wadester."

"I promise you, I will not let anybody hurt you," With that, Wadester jumped into the tree and started swinging from branch to branch.

"Come. Wadester show."

So, the group followed the swinging talking green ape into the dark woods.

Traveling through the woods, Victoria felt this need of urgency. She didn't understand why she was feeling this. A voice was telling her to hurry and that she was getting close. She had that same feeling as she did when she came face to face with Velatha. The words "hurry, they want to eat me" kept pounding in her head. She could feel fear, anger, and perseverance all at once. Up ahead, they could see a glow of light and hear a lot of grunting. Then they could hear the roar of a dragon.

Victoria made Barroth stop the horses and she quietly climbed out of the wagon. She slowly peered over some bushes and she could see about five orcs fighting over a weapon and five more dumbfounded by the fight. Beyond the orcs was a massive white hill or mountain, but then it moved. She moved over to the left to get a better look. There it was, the great white one. A white dragon, he was bigger than Velatha. The orcs managed to tie the dragon down with these strange magical chains. When Victoria's eyes met with the dragon, she could hear what he was saying. For some reason, Victoria had a special connection with dragons. This was the second dragon she met, and she could read the minds of both. She could hear his voice thundering in her head. He had a Scottish accent with a calming tone. She listened to what the dragon said, then went back to her coterie.

"He said we could go behind him and free him of the chains while the dumb mongrels fight over who's going to kill him."

Clark looked at Victoria with great misperception, "He said, who's he?"

"The dragon."

"The dragon? What dragon?" Clark was looking at the orcs and could not see a dragon. Victoria grabbed his chin to raise his level of sight above the Orcs, "There's nothing there but a white—" Just then, he spotted the shape of the dragon when it raised his eyes at Clark, "Dragon!" Victoria shushed Clark and covered his mouth, but it was too late, the Orcs heard him and stopped fighting over the weapon the moment they saw the entourage. When Clark realized that the orcs were looking at them, he screamed. Barroth belted out, "Oh for the love." Then he raised his axe and charged after the orcs. Claire climbed a tree and started shooting arrows at the orcs. Victoria saw how scared Wadester was, so she magically lifted him up into a high tree. One of the orcs was in kicking distance of Clark so with great force, he kicked the orc and sent it flying into Cullen's blade. A bluish, green blood splattered on Cullen's face as the blade sliced through the Orcs stomach. Cullen pulled the sword out as the orc held his wound, then came at him. As Cullen spun around, his sword met the Orcs neck, which sliced the head clean off.

Claire had six arrows in one of the orcs and she said, "Come on, friggin' pus bucket, die already." The orc jumps up into the tree with Claire as she pulled an arrow out of her quiver. She didn't have time to place it in her bow, so she jammed the arrow up his chin and through the top of his head. "Friggin' ass nut, rot suck, mother friggin' pus bucket," she quickly let go of the arrow when she felt the gooey green blood touch her hand, "Ewwww, shite bag." She did a flip out of the tree and landed on her feet just as another Orc came at her. With great force, she kicked him between the legs, and she said, "Right in the dangle bag." She giggled, put her hands on the orc's shoulders, and flipped over him.

These orcs were stupid because the one she jumped over couldn't figure out where Claire went but his eye caught Victoria who was walking toward the dragon. The dragon saw the Orc coming and told Victoria to watch out. She turned, and a bolt of energy flew from her hands and hit the Orc. This sent him flying into another orc, which caused the two of them to start fighting. Victoria used the same bolt of energy to set the dragon free. While she was working on the chains Barroth was swinging his axe around in a kind of graceful dance. Pulling the axe up, sliced off an orc's arm, then bringing it down on the other side he took off the other arm. He spun around with great force and sliced the head and part of the neck off.

The two orcs that were fighting were fighting over a weapon, stopped fighting to see that Ryo and Fodgrel was watching them. The one let go of the weapon and lunged at Fodgrel. Fodgrel was ready for him; he swung his hammer at the orc that knocked him on his back. Running up to the orc, Fodgrel pulled his hammer up over his head and smashed it down on the orc's head. This splits the orc's head like a melon. Ryo had cut up the other orc's chest with his blades by the time Fodgrel got to it. Taking his hammer, he smashed it into the orc's chest. With another mighty swing of is hammer, he caught the orc under the chin, which separated his jaw from his head. This caused the orc to walk in the path of the dragon that open his mouth and a rush of flames burn the orc to ashes. The other five sees that the dragon was loose, and in a panic, they howled, ran into each other, and then tried to run away. One of the orcs pulled another one down then went for the trees. The one on the ground turned around just in time to see the dragon standing over him. The dragon opened his mouth, and an ultraviolet light came rushing out of it. It hit the orc who sat there for a few seconds before he imploded. There was no mess, it was as if the orc folded into himself and disappeared. The other four managed to get away in the trees.

The white dragon turned to Victoria and bowed, "Thank you, dragon protector, I am indebted to you." With the wind under his wings, he took flight and yelled down to her, "We will meet again." Watching the dragon fly away Victoria turn to see Claire and Cullen washing the orc blood off them at a nearby stream, while Barroth let out a sonic roar of victory. He raised his axe in the air and shouted, "That was a good battle. I will forever follow you. You pick great battles."

Cullen looked at Victoria as he wiped his face off with a rag and gave her a nice smile then placed his hand on the small of her back, "You did very good today Victoria, are you ready to explore some more of this land?" Victoria smiled at Cullen and replied, "Yes, I am ready. I am starting to understand this more. You can't deny what the eyes see, I believe in all this now, more than I did before. When we get back, I need Ipion to tell me everything, I am ready to hear it all." Clark was a little confused as he watched this huge dragon fly away. As he walked toward Victoria, he saw these strange piles of green dirt. Standing on this green dirt, he asked, "How did only ten orcs bring down a huge dragon like that?" Victoria looked at Clark's hooves then at Clark and replied, "I think there were more than ten of them." Clark kicked the dirt at his hooves and said, "How would you know? Can you see what happened here?" Victoria smiled and said, "No, but that green dirt you are standing in looks to be piles of orcs." Clark wrinkled his nose and said, "Gross!"

Cullen helped Victoria up onto the wagon then climbed onto Thunder. As they were about to leave, they heard this whining, "You leave Wadester?" Claire looked up and wrinkled her nose, "Come on, you chicken shite." Wadester jumped out of the tree and grabbed Claire. He groped her chest and started to air hump her. Claire knocked him down and repulsed said, "Mother friggin, pus bucket. Keep your banana hands off my buppies and keep your dangle bags away from my flower." Victoria glanced at Wadester, then he remembered, "Wadester be good." He grabbed his package and talking to it he said, "No, Wadester be good."

Cullen rode up next to the wagon, he gave Victoria a reassuring smile. She stood up, climbed over Clark, and jumped onto Thunder behind Cullen. As she put her arms around Cullen, he placed one of his hand on hers. He gave a side smile and headed the trek to their next adventure. Victoria was so happy to be sitting with him that she gave him a squeeze and laid her head on his back. Cullen was glad to have her on the horse with him again. He started thinking about the kiss, closing his eyes he took in a deep breath. He still wasn't sure how he was going to tell Ipion about his decision.

The adventures through parts of Asimeritian were very educational for Victoria. When they stopped in some of the little towns, Victoria would get her notebook out that she had bought at Stonehenge. She remembered all the names and faces of the missing people and would walk around to see if she could spot any of them. When she recognized them, she would ask them who they were and what they are called now. She didn't understand why they changed their names until she ran into Elizabeth now known as Eppiny. She was 16 when she went missing and is now 28. For 12 years, she spent her time in this place and a lot has happened to her. She had several scars on her from attacks she had suffered, one of the scars was across her face. She used to be a mouthy and ornery girl, but life here had changed her. She was a lot softer spoken and submissive. She never knew how to use a sword, so she had to rely on men to keep her safe. She was a pretty girl and she used that to find a strong man. Doing so landed her in a food vender waiting on tables. She now has five boys and another on the way. She feels that when the boys get older, they will keep her safe if they don't get killed. When Victoria asked her why she changed her name, she told her it wasn't her choice. Slavers will stand by the ring as they called it and wait for unsuspecting victims that come through the porthole. There were certain times of the year that people would get sucked through. It didn't matter what their year was they would always come through at these certain times. When they did the slavers would capture them and they would go through these kind of torture methods to make them submissive and give them a name. They were never allowed to use their names they were born with again. Victoria wanted to know if any of them had magic and she told them so far that she knew of anybody who came through the rings were not magical.

The journey back to the tower would take several days. Victoria loved every day and every minute that she had with Cullen. Unfortunately, because of Wadester they didn't get very much time to be alone, Wadester was very time consuming. He was almost like training a dog.

"We really need to cut that pus buckets dangle bags off."

Every time Claire threatened to do that to him, Wadester would go crying to Victoria. He felt safe with her, because she had so much magic. When he slept at night, it would be in front of Victoria's tent. He would curl up into a ball like a dog and sleep there. One-night Victoria almost tripped over him. She couldn't stand to see him shivering so she grabbed another blanket and covered him with it. He needed more training, especially when relieving himself. She had to tell him many times that he should go behind a bush. He didn't understand why but she would explain it to him several times. Finally, to her surprise, one time he went behind the bush. He wanted to do as Victoria told him, she was nice to him. When he woke up that morning with the blanket, he knew it was Victoria that gave it to him. He wanted to make her happy, so he would try very hard to do what she asked of him.

When they arrived at the tower, Clark froze in his steps and Wadester went running behind Cullen's horse. Victoria looked to see what the two were so afraid of. Standing, just at the bridge, was a very large satyr. He looked very angry with his arms crossed and his brow furrowed. From the looks of this creature, Victoria knew it had to be Zorxox. She jumped off the horse and ran up to Zorxox. Before she could get any closer to him, he rushed up to Clark. He ran past her so fast she barely even seen him. He had his hands around Clark's neck and was trying to choke the life out of him. Victoria panicked and threw her hand out in front of her, and a bolt of lightning zapped out of her hand and knocked Zorxox on his ass. This angered the satyr even more and turned to rush Victoria when Velatha just suddenly appeared and roared loudly at the Satyr. Zorxox fell back on his haunches, then quickly turned onto his knees, got up, and ran away from the dragon.

Victoria looked at Velatha with bewilderment, "How?"

"Erross, the great white dragon told us what you did for him," she replied in a sweet, English accent.

"So, his name is Erross."

"He apologizes for his rushed exit, but he had to return. Aldabus's lackey was clawing at his heels."

"He was out there with us," Victoria responded a little worried about the thought of their enemy so close.

"You have nothing to worry about Victoria, he does not know about you yet. But he will soon. He could not detect you or your company. You are magically undetected under his radar as your world calls it."

"How is it that I am undetected, can others do the same thing?"

"No, only you."

"Why?"

"Come with me, Victoria, Ipion waits for us on top of the tower."

Victoria glanced at the others, then at Cullen. "Go, I will be all right. Cullen, please help Wadester." Cullen groaned a little but assured her that he would be all right.

Velatha lay lower to the ground, so that Victoria could climb up on her back. Never in a million years did she think she would ever be riding on the back of a dragon. Velatha gracefully took off. She stretched her wings out to let the wind catch them. As she flapped them a few times to get up speed, she could fly higher. The view that Victoria had was amazing, she could almost see all Asimeritian. In the distance, she could see mountains of the dark forest that they had been in. She could even see the few towns she had been to scatter out around in the area. When they were up high enough Velatha slowly turned around and headed for the top of the tower. As they got closer, she could see Ipion standing there. He had his hands folded behind his back and he kept rocking on his heels. When they landed, Ipion walked up to Velatha, stroked her then helped Victoria off. He knew without her saying a word that it was time to let her know where she fits in all of this.

Long ago, Ipion fell in love with Velatha. She was smart, polite, beautiful, and kind. He couldn't understand how Aldabus could be her father. She was obviously more like her mother. None of that mattered to Ipion, he wanted to marry her. Aldabus only agreed because he had a plan and they fell right into it. When they had Isadora, something happened to Velatha, at the time, they didn't know it but Aldabus had cast a spell on Velatha. The spell caused her to act out in a way that Ipion had never seen in her before. Aldabus told Ipion he had to cast a spell on her that would cure her. It didn't cure her, it changed her into a dragon. When Ipion found out what Aldabus did to his own flesh and blood, he feared for their daughter. With a heavy heart, Ipion secreted her away into another world and tried to destroy the only way in. This is what caused the strange fluctuation with the ring.

Years went by when he heard that somebody came through the gateway and taken Isadora to Aldabus. Isadora had no idea what she was until Aldabus told her. He lied to her about her mother, he said that Ipion was jealous of the relationship Aldabus had with Velatha, so he changed her into a dragon. For years Isadora tried to find a way to change her back. When she left her world, she left a husband and child behind. But as she discovered the spell could only be broken with the blood of her child. She needed to get back through the porthole. Aldabus told her she could not use her child, but she could use her grandchild and never knew it was her that was the cure.

The only way this could work is with the first-born child of her child is what she was told. The child had to be fathered by somebody from this world. This is when she wanted to use her uncle but without her knowledge Aldabus had Zeddicus kill him. So Zeddicus became the chosen one for this task. Isadora was Hope's mother. Hope was Victoria's mother and she had already been told who her real father was. Victoria looked at Velatha and said, "So you are my great grandmother. And that makes you my great grandfather." Victoria responded as she turned toward Ipion. Victoria stood there pondering on all this information she just received. Then a look of horror came over her face, "So, this means that evil man who has my mother hostage is my great, great, grandfather."

"Don't fret, Victoria, you might share his blood but that doesn't mean you could end up like him."

"My grandmother did. Grandpa has been waiting for her all these years. How could she do that to him?" Velatha placed one of her huge claws gently on Victoria's shoulder and said, "Victoria, I can see your soul, it is good and pure." Victoria looked at the claw, patted it, then said, "I am from a world with assumptions. I don't believe in nature over nurture. I believe that you become what you are through the upbringing of your family and peers. My grandfather was a good man. He had faith in the great spirit, and he believed that we were guardians of the land. We are there for a brief time and we are to do our part in preserving and caring for the land that was lent to us. He believed that nobody truly owns the land because everything in the land has a spirit. He believed that a spirit could not be owned by anybody, spirits are free. Like people, they are free to choose their own path."

Victoria stood there and thought of her brother, "I remember him now, he is my twin, but we are not identical."

"No, and as you were told, you don't share the same father either. Saphon is your father and Zeddicus is Victor's father."

Ipion stepped in.

"Poor Victor, I remember him being so fragile. Mother kept telling me since I was his oldest sister, I must help her watch out for him."

They stood in silence then Victoria broke the silence, "Can I save him?"

"I don't know, Victoria; he has been raised around evil. Like you said about nature and nurture," Ipion replied, raising his eyebrows.

"I have to at least try to save him, and my mother too," Victoria replied with great sorrow.

"I know they are important to you, but neither can be saved if Aldabus succeeds in is nefarious plan to destroy your world. It is now time for you to retrieve *Le Bijou du Roi*," Ipion put his hand on Victoria's shoulder and guided her to the doorway that led down inside the tower.

Stealing the Hope diamond, that means she would have to go to Washington D.C. This will be interesting to say the least. How was she going to go to the Smithsonian, unnoticed? Surely, they would find Barroth a strange sort and Clark too. The last time she saw the Hope diamond it was in the Harry Winston gallery.

Chapter IX

As Victoria walked through the halls of the tower all she could think about was the Hope diamond. How was she even going to get back, she was told that the way she came in looked broken. Was there enough magic to open the porthole back to her world? Would she even do what was needed or would she just go back home and pretend none of this happened? She started to doubt herself until she laid eyes on one of the reasons. Just a couple feet ahead of her was the man she has been completely enamored by.

Cullen. He was strong and brave, yet gentle, and loving. She loved how he was very respectful to her and how he always tried to protect her. There was something about him that she had never seen in a man before. Men like that don't come into your life very often. They are few and far away. His eyes would light up when he spotted Victoria, it was like she was the only one in the room. What woman wouldn't want that in a man. It was almost like a storybook and seemed impossible for a man like him to be real.

While she was standing there in a trance, mesmerized by his looks and the way he carried himself, Victoria didn't notice Clark standing next to her. She nearly jumped out of her skin when he said hello to her. "Hello, Tori," Clark said, clapping his hands together, "Snap out of it."

"What, sorry."

"Oh honey, you got it bad."

All Victoria did was cracked a side smile and said, "Pinch me."

Clark obliged her and pinched her on the upper arm. She jumped, and a loud thunder crack came from her hands as she still did not quite have control of this magic. As she touched her arm where Clark pinched her, she lightly scolded him saying, "Owe, what did you do that for?"

"Well, you told me to pinch you," Clark stated, putting his hands on his hips.

"I did?" she replied gazing back at Cullen, "I don't remember..."

Clark grabbed her by the arm and led her to the stairs. As they passed Cullen, she looked at him and smiled. Cullen gave that sexy side smile that drove her nuts, then turned to continue his conversation with his crew. Clark practically had to drag her away from him and get her to climb down the stairs. The whole way down he was going on about how she must have some sexual aggression going on. He had never seen somebody so love stricken as she was. Then he asked her if she has ever had sex before. This broke her trance and she nearly screamed, "What!" Clark placed his hand gently over her mouth and responded to everybody that was now staring at them, "Everything is okay, nothing going on here. Go back to, to whatever you were doing."

Clark then gently led Victoria down the flight of stairs that ended at the dining area. He sat her down at one of the long tables to continue his conversation. Clark looked at her with a kind of gentleness that Victoria was not use to. He knew that this girl was innocent and had a kind of purity that he had never witness in his lifetime. Victoria was like the little sister he always wanted. Somebody he could protect and educate at the same time. He wanted to teach her all the things his mother taught him, "You really have never been with anybody before, have you?"

"No, I haven't. I know it may seem a little old maid-ish, but I feel that it has to be with that right guy."

Clark didn't understand the old maid part, but he assured her that there was nothing wrong in the way she felt. This was the first serious conversation she had with Clark and she was the only person he showed it to.

As they sat there in their secret discussion, a ruckus broke out in the kitchen area. There was screaming and the sounds of pans hitting the floor that echoed throughout the dining area. The two looked toward the kitchen just in time to see Wadester dodging the pans, being hurdled at him with great force. Running on all fours with fear in his eyes and a big onion in his mouth, Wadester ran for Victoria. Cullen was watching this fiasco engaging as he was descending the stairs and with instinct, he ran to protect Victoria. He did not trust this big green ape that she had trustfully and with open arms assimilated this wild beast into their fold.

Wadester got behind Victoria and started spouting out, "Wadester sorry, Wadester be good. Don't hurt Wadester." Clark stood there with a disgusted look on his face. Mainly because as Wadester talked, he still had the onion in his mouth which cause saliva to spray in Clark's face. Wiping his face of the spittle, Clark noticed a ruckus at another table.

Claire gracefully came walking out of the kitchen with an apple in her hand. As she sauntered toward Victoria's table, she caught the eyes of a few men in the room. One was taking a drink from his cup which spilt down the front of him. Another took a bite of his sandwich and the makings inside his sandwich fell into his lap. Claire had that effect on men because of the way she looked. She looked at them with a kiss it look on her face as she took a sexy bite of the apple and smiled. Pointing her finger with the apple in her hand at Wadester, she voiced, "You should have seen it. That pus bucket made off with the cook's best onion. But while they were shite firing their pans at him, I snatched this kick ass apple."

Cullen was near the end of his descent from the stairs because of the commotions. His sword was in his hand and as he got to the landing, he came to a skidding stop when he saw what it was all about. Placing his sword back in its sheath, he walked up to Claire. "Claire, I asked you to keep an eye on him," Claire took a bite of her apple and said, "I did, I watched him try to steal the onions from the cook. It was hilarious. He was swinging from those things that hang up the pans. Friggin' funny, they come crashing down. He was sliding all over the floor with an onion in his pie hole. They picked up the pans; started chucking them at him. He high tailed it out here with his ass and dangle bags in the air." Claire was laughing so hard until she noticed nobody else was laughing, "Oh, come on, you pus bucket, that was some funny shite." Cullen furrowed his brow and replied, "You're supposed to keep him out of trouble."

"Oh, well you didn't say that, you just told me to, keep an eye on him," she mockingly replied with a deeper voice and English accent. Cullen gave her an unappreciated look and said, "That is not what I meant."

Suddenly, a burst of men talking came into the room. Barroth's voice echoed throughout the dining area, "So, when's this party I have been hearing about." He clapped his hands and started rubbing them together, "I always like to party after a great fight." Clark looked at him confused and realized that he was talking about the dance. "Oh, you mean the dance," Clark said with excitement.

"Dance?" Barroth scoffed.

"Yes, a dance. It's tonight. You can dance, can't you?" Clark teased. Barroth raised one of his eyebrows at the challenge in Clark's voice. "Bring it on, goat boy," Clark smiled at Barroth and turned his head sideways, "I love it when you talk dirty, big boy." Barroth smile then all expression left his face, "Wait, what?" Clark wrapped his arm in Victoria's arm and said, "Come on, honey, let's go try on that pretty dress of yours." They walked to the back of the stairs and took the lift to her floor.

As they walked into her room, a couple of elf maids were drawing a bath for her. One pulled out the beautiful dress that Victoria had seen in the closet. She laid it on the bed and then proceeded to help the other maid finish the bath water. They were pouring skin softeners in the water that smelled like flowers. Victoria walked over to the bath and felt the water. It was warm and the fragrances coming from it smelt so good that she started to take her boots off. Looking at Clark, she queried, "Are you going to get ready, or would you rather stand there and watch me." Clark waved his hand at Victoria and said, "I'm going to leave you here with these ladies, but don't you worry, I will make sure your beloved Cullen looks really handsome." With that, he turned on his hooves and walked out the door.

Dropping her clothes to the floor, she walked over to the bath. The maids picked up her clothes and slipped out the door, leaving Victoria alone to relish in the heavenly scented bath water. She put one foot in and felt the soft warm water then climbed in. As she slowly sank into the tub made of brass and lined with linen, she took a deep breath. The only thing that came to her mind was an old commercial she had seen online. Calgon take me away. She had plenty of time to sit there and soak in this luxurious bath. As time went by the water started to get cold but all she had to do was heat it up with her hand and the refreshing smells and warm pleasure filled her senses.

When she was done the elves came back in. They helped Victoria with her long hair. It took a while to dry the long locks that came down just slightly above her but. They pulled her hair around to a side sweep up do so to show off the back of her dress. The dress was a rose pink that fit snug to her body. As it reached her knees, it flowed out and had a train behind her. The straps were thin that came up and over to her back where it made one big cross, then a few little criss-crosses just below her waist. Her shoes looked like crystal but felt soft, kind of like memory foam. There was a gold design that swirled and looped along the sides, then back and across the top of the shoe. On the top and heel of the shoe was a ruby. She had never seen a shoe that looked or felt like that. Standing in front of the mirror, she pulled her dress up enough to see the shoes, then slowly releasing it, she looked at the dress. It was beautiful, she felt like a princess in that dress. She then looked at her long caramel colored hair that was swooped over to one side with long loose curls. She was liking what she saw in the reflection.

Her very first dance. She wished her grandfather was here to see this. She could just imagine him doting over her. Telling her to be careful and to be sure to come home at a good hour. Victoria missed him so much that it made her sad. Seeing the sad expression on her face, she imagines him talking to her, "Don't be sad, my little princess, I will be okay. I want you to go and have fun. You look so beautiful, we will see each other again."

The ballroom was just one floor below her. It was at the front of the tower and it had a large balcony outside as well as inside. When the ballroom is not used, the glass doors that lead out to the balcony are protected by large sliding armored doors that the dwarfs run. When the armored doors are opened, the whole wall is entirely made of glass. The view from this wall and balcony is majestic. Many people will wonder out onto this balcony just for the view. When you first come into the room, the double wooden doors are opened revealing a large landing with stairways to the right and to the left that led up twenty steps. Comfortable seating is place throughout these balconies for those who wish to sit and gaze upon the dance floor below. Just beyond the landing is a wide staircase that descends twenty steps down to the dance floor. Under the balconies were pillars made of marble that stood twenty feet high which were bracers for holding up the upper balcony. The stairs and dance floor are made of marble as well. Seating is place under the balcony as well for the guest.

The kitchen will have brought drinks and refreshments to help keep the guest energized for a long night of mingling and dancing. An area close to the glass wall will be a place for the orchestra to play their music for the dance. In the center of the room is a huge chandelier that will light up the room as well as the floor. Cascade of crystals hung from this chandelier that caused the floor to sparkle with dancing lights. Black swirls ran through the white marbled floor which made it seem like the swirls were dancing gracefully in the wind. The walls were made of marble enlace with hints of gold. The framing was gold that reached to the celling. The room itself seemed magical with its beauty.

As people started pouring into the room, the atmosphere became enlighten with chatting and some graceful flirting. This was the moment when nothing else matter, no studies, testing or accidental singeing. They were talking, laughing, and enjoying this special moment in time. Some went out to the balcony to see the changing of the seasons, the leaves had turned and as far as you could see, there were golden, yellows, and reds stretching across the horizon. Some stayed out on the balcony for a fleeting time because the night skies were slowly gliding in and the air was a bit chilly.

Clark sauntered into the room, looking suave and debonair. He had a raven regal black and silver brocade jacket on. Underneath that, he wore a ruffled white cotton shirt. His pants were very snug and was accessorized with a black leather belt that was pulled through the loop then tied in a belt knot. He didn't wear boots but had some leather covers that gave the presence of boots. His goatee was neatly trimmed as usual, and his hair was braided in one long braid. Standing there, scanning the people in the room, he spotted Barroth.

Barroth was wearing a long leather coat with a black shirt. His cotton pants were black as well and snug to his form. He wore leather boots that would come over his knees but were folded down. Standing there, he pulled his coat back by placing his hands on his hips. Walking up to him, Clark asked, "What, you don't have anything—formal?"

Barroth looked at Clark and replied, "These are my formal clothes."

"Oh, and how are these particular clothes formal?" Clark enquired. Barroth adjusted his belt and said, "Because they are clean." Barroth looked at Clark, gave him a side smile, and walked over to the refreshment table.

At the bottom of the stairs stood Cullen. He was deck out in his formal guardian wear. It was very similar to the knights' templar tunics. The tunic was white with red trimmings on the bottom. In the center of the tunic was a big, red Pattee cross. He wore the tunic over his chain mail. Being a guardian, you must always be prepared for the unexpected. He wore black, cotton pants that tucked into is leather black boots. On his side, hung his sword that was safely tucked into its sheath.

Across the room was a beautiful woman getting attention she did not want. Claire. She was stunning, her hair was down and flowed in loose curls down her back. She had on an aquamarine dress that shimmered in the light. The top part of the dress was halter style that fit snuggly down her body, then came to an inverted v that started at the pelvic and came over her hips. It had a type of breast plate style that wrapped around her neck, came down between her breast, then laces out over the torso of her body. There were three turquoise jewels, one at the neck, between the breast, then a large one at her sternum. The dress flowed like silk and strains of sheer ribbons were layered across the bottom of the inverted v. She wore bracelets on her arms. One was above her elbow, one just below her elbow and one around her wrist.

Clark couldn't believe what he was seeing and had to tease her about her outfit. As he stood next to her, he gave her a sheepish smile and was about to say something, "Not one friggin' word comes out of that muzzle of yours."

"Well, you look really nice."

"Yeah, well get a good look, you won't see it again," Clark was looking at her and she cut her eyes at him and said, "What!"

"It's just that in this outfit we don't have to stare at your hoochie."

"Friggin pus bucket, ass biscuit, nut sack," she lifted her hand to punch him, but he took off running, "Run goat boy, when I get you, you won't see it coming." As she turned, she ran smack into Ryo, "So, my delicate flower, what are you doing later tonight." He responded in his Hispanic accent. Claire frowned at him and punched him in the shoulder. Fodgrel walked up next to Ryo and stated, "Trying to roll the oats," Fodgrel chuckled.

"What?" Ryo enquired.

"You know, tapping the midnight steal, forging the moaning statue, dawning the velvet hat."

"Is that what you call making love?"

"I don't think love has anything to do with it," Fodgrel declared as he chugged on his beer.

"Ah, that one will be mine by the end of the night. She won't be able to resist the charms of, the Ryo," Fodgrel sprayed his beer out of his mouth, bust out laughing, then ran his arm across his mouth and replied, "Well, you better pluck off your love rod for that one, she won't let anybody clean her pipes, unless it has tits." He walked off laughing and went to fill his mug with beer.

Cullen started to ascend the steps to see if Victoria was coming. He got halfway up the stairs when she elegantly walked through the doorway. How beautiful she looked; he couldn't take his eyes off her. As he finished his climb to the landing, he stops and took her all in. He gives her an elegant bow then stretched out his hand to take her arm and escort her down the steps. He felt like the luckiest man in the world to have such a rare beauty accompanying him. Everybody stopped to see this beautiful couple approached the dance floor. With the slightest movement, he had her in his arms and waltzed her across the floor. He looked deep into her eyes and gave that side smile that she loved so much. Not a word was spoken, and it was like they were the only ones on the floor.

Cullen breathed her in, and she smelt so good, "You look very beautiful tonight."

"Thank you. You look, very handsome."

As he spun her around on the floor, her dress flowed like the waves on the shore. Around the ballroom floor, they glided like a flower in a gentle whirlpool. Cullen danced her around the floor then stopped at the doors leading to the outside balcony. He escorted her out to the railing and gazed upon her beauty. He gave her that side smile which sent sparks throughout her body.

"Maker's breath, you are beautiful," Victoria smiled, and Cullen continued, "I don't mean to be so audacious. It's just that I have never been in this kind of situation."

"And what kind of situation might that be?" Victoria flirted gracefully. Cullen stepped in closer just as Ryo and Fodgrel stepped out onto the balcony. A little embarrassed for being caught out there Victoria started to play it off like nothing was happening but doing a poor job of it. Fodgrel bust out with, "So what are you two doing out here?" He was teasing, he could tell what was going on and wanted to see if Cullen would proceed. Cullen looked at Fodgrel than at Ryo with a stern glare. Ryo was a romantic and upon discovering what was going on, he pulled on Fodgrel to leave. Fodgrel boasted, "What!" Ryo replied, "Come, I heard tell of the best ale in these parts at the serving table." The word ale perked Fodgrel's attention and followed Ryo back inside. Upon entering inside, Ryo questioned, "What were you thinking? Did you not see what was happening out there?"

Fodgrel gruffed, "Yeah, I wanted to see if that prude was going to jump ship or follow through." He claimed with a sinister laugh, "Hey, there better be that ale you are talking about, or I am going back out there." Fodgrel headed for the door but Ryo grabbed him and reluctantly said, "There is." With that, he guided Fodgrel to the table that had casks of ale next to them.

Cullen turned and looked at Victoria who was red face and stammering, "I am sorry, if you need too—"

Before she could finish what she was saying, Cullen grabbed her and kissed her long and gently on the lips. When they slowly parted, Victoria was even more flushed but had a faint smile on her face.

126

"I have been wanting to do that since the day out there by the pond. Do you remember?" Victoria looked at him with unhindered love in her eyes and replied, "I do, I mean, yes, I remember it very well." Suddenly, she got a chill from the night air. It was beautiful outside, but she had nothing on her shoulders. Cullen felt her shiver and drew her closer to him. She wanted to wrap her arms around him but kept them inside the embrace to keep her warm. It felt so good in his embrace and he made her feel safe. She didn't want this moment to end but Cullen was concern about her being cold. He started to walk her to the door, but she stopped him for one last gaze into his eyes. Cullen looked down at her and gently kissed her again. As their lips parted, she smiled, and they walked back inside.

The night was filled with laughter, dancing and some heavy drinking. As it ended, Cullen walked Victoria to her room, he embraced her gently then sent her off with a good night kiss. Victoria watched him walk away but not before he turns and looked at her with his infamous smile. She smiled and turned to open her door. Just then, Clark skidded up next to her with exuberance to the tales that went on between her and Cullen.

"I saw you two out there in the balcony and I am crushed that you spent so little time with me."

"I am so sorry, Clark," with a sly look on her face, she said, "Would it help if I told you all about it." Clark smiled and interlocked their arms to guide her into the room, "If you tell me the whole juicy story, all will be forgiven." With that, they shut the door.

The next day, Cullen went to Ipion's office. He was regretting having to tell Ipion about his leaving the guardians. His decision to leave for Victoria was not regretful. This choice was the one thing he was sure of. He made a vow to the guardians but his love for Victoria was much stronger, he knew it was the right thing to do. He would have to appoint somebody else as commander but Ipion would have to approve of it first. Cullen didn't care about the consequences he could be faced with, Victoria was worth it. The only thing he feared was the fact that Ipion was her great grandfather, and he didn't know how he would react to this.

Cullen paced back and forth outside Ipion's office when the door opened on its own and Ipion encouragingly asked Cullen to come in. Ipion was sitting at his desk writing something on a piece of vellum. Without looking up from his work, he asked, "So, what brings you here this day, Commander Cullen?"

"Master mage, with great regret, I came to inform you that I will be leaving the guardians," Cullen pulled a little on his tunic at the neck. He did not want to disappoint Ipion or make him lose faith in him, "That is, unless you forbid it?"

Still looking down at his work Ipion responded, "Are you having doubts about your decision?"

"No, sir," Ipion looked up from his work and shot a glance at Cullen over the top of his glasses. He proceeded to get up and walk over to Cullen, "Has she captured your heart?"

"She? How..." Ipion smiled and said, "How do I know? I know many things." Cullen shook his head and looked down, "Of course, you know, you see all." He then looked up at Ipion and asked, "Then you must know who she is?"

"Yes, it doesn't take the power of foresight to see the love that has blossomed between you and my granddaughter," Ipion chuckled a little and said, "Whenever the two of you are in a room together, it is as if nobody else exists."

"So, you are okay with this?"

"On the contrary, it was meant to be. You and Victoria have set the course of your path the day you met. At first, I didn't want to follow through with the vision but realized that it was unavoidable. Your souls belong together," Ipion walked over to his desk and pick up the vellum he was working on. He handed it to Cullen, who proceeded to read it, "This is my acquiescence."

"Yes, but I still need you to go with her to get *Le Bijou du Roi*."

"Maybe I shouldn't, I'll be in the way."

"No, she gets her courage and strength from you, you must go."

"I am just a guardian and she a powerful mage, how can she draw strength and courage from that?" Ipion put his hand on Cullen shoulder, "It's your love that empowers her." Cullen closed his eyes and imagined Victoria's face. He opened his eyes and looked at Ipion, "I will always be at her side, nothing will harm her as long as I still carry breath in me." Ipion smiled and placed his hand on Cullen's shoulder, he believed she was safe with him. "You will keep your guardian powers," looking at Cullen over the top of his glasses, he stated, "You may need them still." They shook hands and Cullen walked out the door.

Walking to the lifts and after the ride down, Cullen found himself in the dining area. At one of the tables was his unorthodox group of warriors. Fodgrel

128

was nursing a mug of ale and making the vilest noises from his body which caused the others to react in half disgust and half laughter. Ryo was attempting his charms on Claire that were rejected with a few fowl words. Clark was flirting with Barroth by fluttering his eyes and receiving the traditional "You couldn't handle this goat boy." And sitting there was Victoria, trying so hard to teach Wadester how to sit properly at the table, using a napkin, and utensils to eat his food.

How he admired her strength and tenacity to help and teach the mongrel he considered as the green ape, Wadester. He saw no hope for the beast but maybe with Victoria's help Wadester might have a promising chance. As he stood there and looked at the group, he really didn't have much faith in their victory of getting *the Bijou du Roi*. Ipion gave him a map of the location to the diamond. This group would surely stick out, not just because of their looks, but how loud and obnoxious they could be.

When he stopped thinking about how they were going to pull this off, he realized that he had been staring at Victoria. She stopped what she was doing and walked over to him. Looking up at him she smiled and said, "A penny for your thoughts." Confused, Cullen replied, "A what?" Realizing that he probably didn't know what she meant, she said, "A penny. It's the smallest currency where I come from." Even more confused he questioned, "Currency?"

With a little chuckle, she explained, "It's money, coins, a token that we use to pay for things." A spark of recognition came to his face and he said, "Ah, you do not have to pay for my thoughts, I am willing to give them to you." She looked away to hide her smile at his innocence's then looked back at him, "It's actually just an expression we use to find out what is on one's mind, we don't really pay them anything." He gave her that side smile and said, "I see."

Placing his hand on the small of her back, he reluctantly guided her back to the group. It was time for him to explain to the group how they were going to get *Le Bijou du Roi*. Ipion had given Cullen some potions that the alchemist made to disguise the unusual parts of Victoria's party. When they get to her world, people will not see the pointed ears, the horns, goat hooves, and a green ape. Fodgrel didn't need a disguise, he would just be considered as one of the little people. He did not like to be called little people, he was a dwarf and proud of it. He assured them that he would be okay if he wasn't called that too many times. The clothes were not much of a concern because people wore what they wanted in her world. But they would have to conceal their weapons because weapons were not carried as openly there as they were here.

Victoria thought they were going to go in the way she came in here. Ipion said that way was not safe. The Honey Nabbers knew of another way to Victoria's world, and it came out a lot closer to Washington D.C. It's been some time since she was back in the states. She so desperately wanted to let her grandfather know she was there. She missed him so much but knew that she had to keep him from all of this. She would be constantly looking out for his safety.

Victoria was going to leave Wadester, but she was afraid he would get into trouble. Plus, she felt that he would be too scared to stay here without her or one of the others he knew well. After all, he was just a child and she felt responsible for him. Then there is the downside to him coming with them, it would be a strange world for him, and she feared he could get into just as much trouble if not more going with them. Victoria was going to have to make sure he doesn't start swinging on things or relieving himself in public.

Sitting at the table, Victoria wanted to finish the work she was doing in her journal. She had been writing down the names of the guardians that lived at the tower. A few of them were from her world and was given the power that all guardians have. They had the power of dispel and sleep and they all knew how to use a sword very well. As she was writing down the last couple of names down, Cullen asked, "What are you doing?"

"I am writing down the guardians' name. What they were called and what they are called now. I also wanted to know how long they have been here. See, I wrote your name down, but I still don't know what your full name was."

As he leaned over her, she could smell the leather he was wearing and the smell of his hair, "Let's see, it has been so long since I used it, but if it were not for my siblings, I would not remember it at all. It was Cullen Richard Msworth." Victoria looked at him and thought how strange, his name was very close to the Richard she knew. She shrugged it off and wrote the name down in the notebook and said, "There, I am done."

"Well, I can't be in the names of guardians because I am no longer one of them."

"What, why?"

"I have spoken with Master Ipion, I told him that my love for someone has broken my vow to the guardians."

Victoria looked at him with apologetic eyes and said, "I am so sorry."

"No, you don't have to be sorry, we have his blessings."

Victoria smile and ran a thick line through his name saying, "There, you are no longer a guardian." She looked at what she did and realized that she was the writer of that book found in that cave. She became very confused by it since the findings were dated over 2600 years. Was she 2600 years in the past? Was there magic in the past at one time? It was so hard to wrap her head around this that she decided not to think about it now, she would think about it another time. Then she quoted Scarlett and said, "After all, tomorrow is another day." Cullen looked at her and said, "What?"

"Oh, it's nothing. Come on, let's get started," she grabbed up her notebook and they all went to get packed for their trip. Barroth was already ahead of them and had his big wagon all packed and ready to go.

Chapter X

As the eight started off on their quest to retrieve *Le Bleu de France*, they were led by three Honey Nabbers. The adventure would be led miles away from Mage Mountain that could take a couple of days. Barroth made sure they had plenty of supplies in his wagon for the long journey. A few flitters curiously followed them, along with a few black skinned harpies that were secretly following them from above.

These Harpies belong to Aldabus, they were his eyes. When Aldabus saw that the group was being led by Honey Nabbers, he knew where they were headed. Sitting in his eerie throne room with one leg over the arm of the chair and a hand up to his head, he waited for Victor to enter the room. As Victor entered the room, he pushed both doors open and was followed by his father. Zeddicus was a frail gothic looking man. He lacked any handsome facial features; his hair was long and stringy and fell in his face. Victor, on the other hand, though pale and gothic looking, was a very handsome man. As they approached the chair that Aldabus was sitting in, they both bowed.

"Grandfather, you sent for us?" Aldabus looked through his fingers to see his grandson and Zeddicus standing before him. He raised his head and replied, "Yes, they have left the tower to retrieve *Le Bleu de France*." Victor knew that he was to follow them and steal the diamond from them, "How many of them are there?"

"There are eight, but one of them is magically hidden from me. How such meager mages can hide somebody from me is preposterous?"

"Surely they don't have more magic than you?" Zeddicus cowardly replied. As Aldabus angrily stood up, Zeddicus cringed at his power, "Incontestably, no one mage has more power than me you sniveling bag of bones, get out of my sight." Zeddicus bowed his head and walked backwards all the way to the door than shut them in front of him. Aldabus sneered as he watched Zeddicus leave, then in a detestable voice, he grumbled, "Why I ever

agreed that he fathered you is beyond me. I must have been having an off day."
He stepped down and walked up to Victor and placed a hand gently on his face
and sadly said, "How you end up with some of her features I will never
understand." Dropping his hand down to his side, Aldabus turned and sat back
on his throne. For a moment, Victor caught sight of something gentle in his
face, but the minute he was back in his chair that gentleness left. With anger in
his voice, he thundered, "Follow them, and find out who this person is that
they are hiding from me."

Victor left the room and gathered a party of men to bring with him. His
group consisted of elves, ogres, and a few evil mages. As they were heading
out of the castle Aldabus's alchemist, Maggart, came running up to them. He
handed Victor some potions and stated that he will need them for where they
are going. Victor asked, "What are these for?"

"You will know when to use them when the time comes," replied the
alchemist.

Victor raced through the dark forest with his macabre entourage. In his vial
belt held the potions to change the appearance of each horrifying creature he
had with him. At one point, some of these creatures such as the elves, humans,
and dwarfs were normal until evil touched their souls. As their souls became
darker, so did their appearance. It would take a strong potion to hide their evil
outward appearance.

When Victor got close to the group from the tower, he held back. He didn't
want to get too close and have them discover they were following them. A
strange feeling came over him and he knew he was close enough. The feeling
he got was strange, he had never felt that before. It gave him a feeling of
calmness and safety. This disturbed him enough that he had no problem
keeping his distance.

As Victoria and her group were traveling along, something strange came
over her. Sitting on Cullen's horse behind him, Victoria had this strange feeling
come over her. She couldn't shake the feeling that they were being followed.
The closer they got to their destination, the stronger the feeling she had. At one
point, she looked behind her, but couldn't see anything, she just had this feeling
something was behind them.

That night as they were sitting around the fire Victoria still could not shake
the feeling that they were being followed. The distressed look she had on her

face made Cullen concerned. He came over and sat next to her, "Are you alright?"

Putting a hand on the small of her back, he could feel something was bothering her. Victoria looked at him and smiled, "I'm fine, just a little tired and nervous." Cullen knew it was something else and a look of distress came over his face. Victoria put her hand on his and said, "What is wrong?" Cullen looked at her then stood up urging her to follow him. As he held her hand, she followed him willingly.

When Cullen saw that they were far enough out of the others ear reach, he said, "I wish you would have faith in me to tell me anything that is on your mind. Victoria, I am in love with you. I would do anything for you, please confide in me." Victoria put her arms around him, and her guard went down. She knew she could trust this man and decided to confide in him. "I just had this feeling that we are being followed," she looked at him with concern in her eyes, "And it is not just anybody. There's a pull, like the same pull I get from my father, grandfather Ipion and Velatha." She looked up with some sadness in her eyes and replied, "I think Victor is following us." Cullen put his hand on his sword and started to look around. Victoria placed her hand on his to retrieve it from the sword.

"I don't think he will come close to us, I feel confusion from him. I don't think he knows anything about me, I don't think he remembers me."

Cullen looked down into Victoria's eyes, they were blue as the morning sky. His love for her was true and strong. He gently embraced her and pressed his lips against hers.

Even though they were too far for Victor to hear what they were saying, he cringed at the sight of their kiss, a pang of jealousy ran through his veins that he couldn't understand. There was something about this girl that made him mad. He turned away but slowly looked back and a flash of recognition came to him. There was something very familiar about her. Then out loud, he said, "How does she have the power to shield herself from my grandfather?" An evil looking elf who called himself Gogan sauntered up to Victor and asked in a prim and proper but icy undertone, "What's the plan? Would you like to go in now and force them to take you to the stone?" The elf finished and started to walk toward Victoria and Cullen, but Victor stopped him and said, "No, we wait until they have the stone." The elf smiles and said, "And then we snatch it from them, then send them to their demise. How marvelous, that sounds like a better plan. And it should make your grandfather more appreciated toward you." Victor looked at Victoria and smiled, "Yes, that would please grandfather. Come, we settle in for the night and continue our trek in the morning." Victor patted the elf on the shoulder and led him toward their camp.

The next morning, Victoria decided to ride in the back of the wagon, mainly because her bum was getting sore from sitting on the horse. As she lay on the bundles of tents and blankets, she grabbed the book Clark lent her. Thumbing through the pages, she spied a picture of a dragataur. Just as she started to read about this strange but alluring creature, Clark jumped up into the wagon beside her. Clark looked at Victoria and smiled, "Quite the men aren't they." Victoria was mystified by these creatures, she has never even heard of them or seen anything like them, "How did your mother know so much about the creatures of this world when she was from mine?" Clark took the book and settled next to her. As he turned the pages, he began the tale that he read so many times in the past, "My mama was, what did you call it the other day? A social butterfly?" Victoria shook her head *yes* and continued to listen to Clark's story.

"A dragataur on the outside is a brazen and boastful creature, but on the inside, lays a heart of gold. She would pick a creature to learn about and observe them from afar. She followed this one dragataur when I was young. We followed them for at least a month. She watched how love blossom between the two, they usually mate with each other but the handsome dragataur fell for a beautiful woman with golden blonde hair, and blue eyes, I believe she came from your world. That is what attracted him to her. He felt like she needed him, because she seemed so helpless and fragile. She captured his heart and when a dragataur falls in love with somebody, it is forever. There is only one way you know when it is true love for a male dragataur and that is when their wings open for a woman. They could be with a woman for years and if their wings didn't open, they knew they had to move on. One day, mama witnessed the dragataur open his wings." Pointing at the slits on Barroth's back he said, "See those slits on his back, you can tell the slits are still sealed shut, so he has not found his true love. I feel sorry for him."

Victoria looked concerned and said, "Why?" Clark turned a page and showed a drawn picture of a dragataur kneeling and wings coming out, there was so much pain on his face. "Mama said it is very painful for them when the wings finally come out. The pain is a reminder of how strong that love is."

Victoria stroked the picture, and a sad look came over her face, "That is sad but beautiful at the same time." She smiled and said, "So what happened to the couple, did they live happily ever after?" With sadness Clark shook his head *no,* "Mama watched him fly her all over the place, she had a hard time keeping up with them. As strong as dragataurs are his beloved died, she was killed and from what Mama said that when a dragataur can't be with the one they love, it slowly kills them. At least, that is the way it was for that couple."

"Oh, how sad," Victoria exclaimed, "Well, what about the females, is it the same for them?" Clark turned the page to a female dragataur. Victoria leaned in and got a closer look at the female and saw what looked like specks of gold. She pointed at the picture and said, "Is that gold?" Clark shook his head and said, "Yes. When a female becomes of age, flakes of gold start to appear on their skin. Then shortly after, their wings gently break through the skin. This all happens around adolescents. They need their wings to have a fast get away. Their skin is coveted and if caught they are slain for their skin. This all happened years ago in their home world, Ipion found them in one of the portals and brought some of them here, (Clark kind of cringed when he said that and hoped that Victoria didn't catch on to what he said, he wasn't supposed to tell her about the portals.) but he couldn't save them all. There weren't very many female dragataurs and because of this the males try to look to other species. My mama and I once witness a dragataur meet a woman for the first time then instantly drop to his knees. He started yelling in pain as we watched his wings rip through his back. It looked so painful, and it seemed like it took forever for them to break through. It doesn't always work out that way, only a few are lucky enough to find their true love."

"That has to be so lonely," Victoria responded, Clark looked at Barroth and said, "They might not find their true love but that doesn't stop them from seeking love. Some of them just mate to bring up the count of dragataur. They don't stay with each other very long, only long enough to plant the seed. They all do it except one, our dear friend here is waiting for his true love, what a romantic." Looking up at Barroth, Victoria said, "He is such a handsome man, I hope he finds his true love and never loses her." Victoria looked back at Barroth, she could see the side of his face and he appeared to be smiling.

They stopped only twice to prepare food; everybody was getting tired of one of the members complaining about being hungry. Victoria half expected Wadester to be the one complaining but it was Clark. When they set off again,

Victoria rode with Cullen. She loved the way he smelled, he had a leather and musky smell to him. A few times she thought about the stories Clark told her and she would look over at Barroth. He would just wink at her and smile.

As darkness shrouded the entourage the Honey Nabbers gestured that they had arrived at their destination. It was a very thick wooded area. A part of the trees looked strange like they were moving but not by wind. It was suggested that the horses and wagons stay behind; they would be walking the rest of the way. Before they entered the area, Cullen had the more conspicuous members drink a potion to change their outwardly appearance. The spell would not last very long, so they had to hurry. As they walked through the trees, they came out in Ash woods that were near the Washington Monument. It was dark there too except for the streetlights. Wadester saw the reflective pool and started to run for it but Victoria stopped him, "No, Wadester, you can't go in there. You have to listen to me, this is my world, and they will arrest you, (thinking he wouldn't understand what she said,) you know, lock you up, put you in a cage."

Wadester understood and said, "Wadester be good, Wadester listen to the pretty lady."

He was not very good with names, only his own, because he heard it so much.

As they walked past the monument, they noticed that it was surrounded by scaffolding. They all looked at the contraption around the monument which gave them pause, then they continued to their destination to the museum. Walking along, some people spotted them and one of them said, "Oh look, it's one of the little people." Fodgrel looked at the man and sneered, then he reached up, and punched the man in the face knocking him out. Hovering over the unconscious man, he said, "I'm a dwarf." He kicked him in the side and Victoria grabbed him and apologized to the unconscious man's friend. As they walked off, Victoria said, "I thought you said it would take a couple of times before it made you mad." Fodgrel frowned and said, "I lied." Then walked off past the group.

Behind them, in the distance, was Victor and his group, which just emerged through Ash woods. Victor upon watching Cullen pass out potions understood what the potions he had were for and had them drink it. It took some of the darkness away, but now they just look like scary hoodlums. They continued to follow the group but from a safe distance. It was late, but people were still out walking around. When the unconscious man woke up, he saw Victor's group and got up without saying a word. Then the two of them crossed the street to avoid another encounter. Watching from a distance, Victor could see the group sneaking around to the side of a building. He kept his distance when he saw that a few of them stayed behind by the doors while the others went inside.

Victoria found an employee's entrance but before entering, she made Wadester, Claire, and Ryo stay behind to watch the entrance. With a wave of her hand, she disarmed the door and as she entered, she disarmed the cameras. She was still nervous about getting caught, she wasn't sure if her magic would work here, but it did. As they were walking quietly through the corridors, a guard came around the corner, she raised her hands mostly in fear and the guard froze. She smiled and said, "Humph, just like Piper, cool." They entered the area where the huge bush African elephant was on display. Victoria knew the Hope diamond was on the second floor but was slowed down by the group mesmerized by the displays. Clark dismayed said, "Why aren't these creatures moving? Is there magic involved here?" Victoria smiled and chuckled a little and responded with, "No, there is no magic here, at least not that I know of." Peaking around a corner, she found the stairs that lead up to the second floor. At the top of the stairs, she went left and there along the wall was the entry way to the Hope diamond.

Disarming the alarms and locks, Victoria walked up to the case that held the Hope diamond. How beautiful it was shimmering in the lights, the way it sparkled like the stars in the sky was very enchanting.

"I feel so bad taking this, it's the Hope diamond, people look forward to see this precious gem. They come from all over the world."

Cullen walked up to her and put his hand on her shoulder, "This means a lot to you doesn't it." Victoria just nodded and continued looking at the gem. Cullen turned her toward him then placed his hand in his bag. He pulled out a flawless duplicate of the Hope diamond. "We will be replacing it with this. No one will never know the difference," Victoria put it in her hand and looked at it, it looked exactly like it, "Why take the diamond at all if they are the same thing." Cullen place his hand over the fake gem and said, "Not quite, there is a substance in that diamond that is not in this one. Don't worry, they will never notice the difference."

Victoria placed her hands on the case and slowly went through it. As she reached for the Hope diamond, she replaced it with the fake one. Stepping away from the case, she saw that it looked the same, Cullen was right, they would not notice the difference. She started to hand the gem to Cullen, but he folded her fingers around the diamond and told her to carry it. As she looked around, she noticed that the others were not with them. Alarm bells started ringing in her head when she realized that there were alarms going off in the Live Butterfly Pavilion area. Clark had gone in there and was eating some of the plants when he heard the alarms go off, he came screaming out of that area, followed by Fodgrel carrying a large bone. Victoria yelled at Clark to spit that out which he did and told Fodgrel to put the dinosaur bone down. All at the same time running toward the stairs and looking to see where Barroth was. At the bottom of the stairs was Barroth staring at the elephant with three guards down by his feet, "Oh my God, they're not dead, are they?" Barroth smiled and said, "No, they took one look at me and I believe they fainted." Pointing at his horns, he continued saying, "Potion wore out." Victoria's eyes got big with fear and said, "Oh shit, Claire, Ryo, oh no, Wadester."

They all ran out the front doors and were met by Claire and Ryo. Scanning the area, Victoria spotted Wadester heading toward the monument, he still had the desire to jump into the reflective pool. They all ran toward the monument when they were stopped by the police. Cullen told Victoria to keep running while the rest of them butt heads with the police. Barroth spied Victor out of the corner of his eye and saw he was going toward Victoria. He yelled at Cullen, "Look, it's Victor. You got this I am going to help her." Cullen drew his sword and pursued toward the police. They were so shocked by the look of this group, they couldn't even get their guns out. When they did, Clark came running toward them with the speed of light and snatched all their guns away from them.

Victoria almost made it to Wadester when she was stopped by Victor. He grabbed her arm and spun her around to meet her face to face, "Who are you? How do you possess the power to shield yourself from my grandfather?" Looking him in the eyes. she responded, "Victor?"

Anger swept over his face and he said, "And that, how do you know who I am? I don't know you."

Suddenly, Barroth came running up to Victor. Victor put his hand up and Barroth fell to his knees, "Stop, what are you doing to him?" Victor turned at Victoria and snapped, "I have done nothing to him." With a loud whistle, Victor called for his black skin harpy. The harpy grabbed Victor and Victor grabbed Victoria. They flew to the top of the scaffolding that was incasing the monument. The harpy place Victor on the top scaffolding that was at least 555 feet high, then continue to circle around them. Victoria went to place her hand on Victor, but he slapped it away, "Victor, don't you know me? It's me, Victoria." Victor flinched from her presences of being so close to him, he hissed, "How would I know you?" Perplexed by his action, Victoria retreated and said, "They have not told you?"

"Told me what?"

"She must have told you, don't they know?"

"Would I be asking you these questions because I enjoy your presence?"

"Victor, I am your sister, Victoria."

His face softened a little and responded, "My sister?"

"Yes, your twin," she went to touch his face and almost saw a trace of humanity in it when it glazed over, and he yelled, "You lie!" With that, he shoved her so hard she went over the guard rail.

Down below, Barroth was writhing in pain. The slits on his back were ripping open and wings were trying to break through. The sounds of his roar echoed across the reflective pool. Even with the pain, he was going through he had to see where Victoria went. As he looked up, he could just barely see the harpy flying them both up the scaffolding. He watched as the pain flowed to his heart and he roared again. Just then, he saw Victoria falling to the ground and with all his might, he forced the wings out which felt like razors cutting him open. He flexed his wings and flew up to Victoria before she could get any closer to the ground. Scooping her up in his arms that were dripping with blood he flew her over to the Ash woods. He gently landed then placed her carefully on the ground. Still in pain, he fell to his knees. Victoria realized what just happened and she said, "Oh, Barroth."

Victoria tried to help Barroth through the trees back to Asimeritian. Draping his arm around her shoulders, she urged him toward the part of the woods that had a shimmering look to it. He was such a big man, and she was having a hard time getting to their destination. She was only a foot away when she heard somebody clapping, "Look, the dumb beast went and fell in love with a woman that has already given her heart to somebody else." Barroth tried to defend her but he was too weak. Victoria gently lowered him to the ground and advanced toward Victor. "How could you do that?" She started hitting him on the chest and he grabbed her arms, "You're a feisty little strumpet, aren't you?" He pulled her arms behind her and brought her face closer to his,

"You're very pretty too, I should take you for myself." Victoria tried to free herself from his grasp when she kicked him hard in the shins. He back handed her and threw her to the ground. He was about to run her through with his sword when Cullen and the rest came running. Victor did not have time to fight with them and he did a side smile, threw the diamond in the air, caught it, and said, "Thank you for this." He spun on his heels and escaped through the forest.

Victoria went to run after him when Cullen grabbed her and told her she was not ready to fight him yet, "But he has the diamond!" Cullen looked in the direction that Victor disappeared through, squinted his eyes, and said, "Yes, he does, but they can't use it." Victoria stopped trying to escape his grasp and looked at him quizzically. Cullen did his side smile and said, "That's the good thing about the diamond. Evil cannot use it. And, I don't think Victor knew that, because if he did, he would have taken you with him."

When Victor got back to Death Mountain, he went looking for his grandmother. He found her sitting at the long dining table. His grandfather and Zeddicus was sitting there too. They had just finished eating, "Ah, my grandson, come sit and have something to eat." Isadora waved her hand over the food that was still on the table. Victor came up to the table, threw the diamond across it and shoved a good portion of the food onto the floor and yelled, "Why didn't you tell me, why didn't you tell me that I had a sister?" Isadora stood up and shouted back, "A sister, what are you rambling on about, you don't have a sister." Isadora had never seen him this angry before and was a little startled by his actions. Victor grabbed Isadora by the throat and repeated what he said. Isadora used her powers to get him off her and said, "Don't you dare lay your hands on me like that again." Victor through a fireball at her and she stopped it with ice. Aldabus had just about enough and shouted with a voice that echoed throughout the castle.

"Enough!"

They both stopped and looked at Aldabus.

"What is this nonsense about a sister?" Still angry, Victor said, "Yes, and not just a sister, a twin. How is this possible?" Aldabus and Isadora looked at each, other than toward the tower where Victor's mother is. With haste, they both ran up toward the tower followed by Victor. As they reached the door, Aldabus blasted the door open with his power and yelled, "Hope!" Hope came around the bend with her hands folded in front of her. "Is something wrong?" Isadora briskly walked up to Hope and grabbed her face.

"Why does my grandson think he has a sister, a twin sister?"

Fear fell onto Hope's face when she heard the words twin sister, "Why would you think that?" Victor walked up to his mother and slapped her across the face, "I don't think it, I know it. I was confronted by her just mere hours ago. Voron, come, show her."

A dark elf entered the room holding his hands together. He had the ability to show pictures. As he entered the room, he slowly opened his hands and a picture of Victoria appeared in them. Hope gasped in fear when she saw her precious daughter appear in the elf's hand. Aldabus stated with anger and said, "So it's true, there is a twin. Was she born first?" Hope did not want to answer but with his booming voice, he asked again, "Was she born first!" She answered behind her sobs that Victoria was born first.

"You should not have kept this from me, she—" he turned and looked at the girl and he could not believe the strong resemblance she had of, "Shadowmoon," Aldabus whispered then disappeared and transported himself to the locked room. In the room was a large canopy bed with a cradle next to it. On the far wall was a large fireplace that had not been use for years. Above the fireplace was a painting of a woman that looked a lot like Victoria. They had the same eyes, nose, and lips. Their hands were the same and their build. They only thing that was different were their ears. Shadowmoon was a beautiful elf and had died shortly after giving birth to Velatha.

Shadowmoon was the only person he loved more than himself. When she was alive, he was a kinder person. The image of the day echoed through his head and he yelled, "Why! Why must this girl portray your image, am I to be tortured by her presence?" Anger filled his veins and he picked up the cradle and smashed it against the painting.

Aldabus stayed in the room for hours, staring at the painting, then he made a decision that needed to be done. Appearing back in Hope's room, he waved his hands and chains appeared on her wrist, "Don't worry, you will soon have company. I will bring your precious daughter to you and she will be my prisoner, just like you are." Walking out of the room, Hope ran toward him but came to a jolting stop, "No, please, leave her alone. She is new to this, she doesn't know anything about her powers."

"You should have told me about her, but instead, you kept her a secret."

"She won't be a part of your plan, she does not have evil in her."

"I am counting on that," he raised the diamond and said, "Only good can make this thing work."

"She won't help you," she replied snidely.

"Oh, she will, when she sees her mother as a prisoner." Hope began screaming and crying, she pulled on her chain and fell to the floor sobbing. Aldabus walked up to her and lifted her face toward his, "We can't have your daughter seeing you with puffy red eyes. There is nothing you can do, so there is no need for crying, it doesn't work on me." Hope screamed and threw her hands at him as if she were throwing something at him. Aldabus looked at her and smirked, he believes he was going to win this battle.

Chapter XI

The trek back to Magic Mountain was long and quiet. Victoria rode in the back of the wagon with Barroth and tended to his back and arms. When the feathers first come out, they are razor sharp. Barroth had cuts on his arms from protecting Victoria from them. Since he forced the wings out and flew so soon, it didn't give the slits time to coagulate, so he wouldn't bleed which is needed so the wings can retract and extend. It was amazing that he was even able to fly with the feathers like that. But because of his unconditional love for Victoria, he wouldn't be able to use his wings for at least a week. For now, he needed to rest. Wetting a rag and dabbing his back and arms Victoria was sadden by the deep cuts. She wished that she could heal him but, because these wings are special no magic can heal his back, only time. After a long silence, she mustards up the courage to say, "Barroth, I am so sorry." He turns on his side and looked at Victoria, he reached up and caressed her face, "This is not your fault my little Eppiny bird." With a puzzled look on her face, she asks, "Eppiny bird?"

"Yes, it is a bird from my homeland. It's feathers shimmer in the sun like diamonds. Such a beautiful bird but with such great sorrow because it knows its destiny. Coveted by all and yet, it knows the length of its life could be short," he winced from the pain and put his hand down. Victoria dabbed the rag on his back and continued to listen about this bird.

"The Eppiny bird longs to fly in the sun and shimmer across the water. He has only one chance to find his mate that would spot him in the crossing. He takes a chance flying so low which could cause him to be snatched up by a fish. His true love must spot him and guide him away from the dangers. This must be done before the gauntlet of fish spring out of the water to taste their sweet nectar. It is the male that must decide if he is ready to risk his life or stay hidden in safety. My people see great honor in these birds as their love is stronger than their needs. We try to live our lives like that of the Eppiny bird, but we don't always achieve that goal. We have the blood of dragons running through our veins and the fiery temper that runs within." Victoria looked over at Cullen then back at Barroth, "I still feel like I am to blame for this." Looking at her with his aquamarine eyes, he said, "I tell you this is not your fault. It could not be helped. It happened the moment I laid eyes on you, I felt something I have never felt before. I tried everything to make it go away and not surface. But that is not how we are, we cannot fight it, it is a force that cannot be contained. There was nothing you did that stirred this in me, it just happens. I know your heart belongs to someone else and I do not have any ill will toward him. The only thing that matters to me is that you are happy. Do not worry about me, I will be okay." Barroth looked at Cullen and back at Victoria and replied, "And if he hurts you, I will crush every bone in his body." He smiled and winked at Victoria then closed his eyes to rest.

His remarkable personality made him what he is, and she smiled at him as he laid there resting. He is such an amazing and talented man. In her world, he would have to fight the women off him. They wouldn't care that he had horns or skin of a dragon. He has what most women want and that is a man who could protect them and keep them safe. He was handsome and resourceful; he took care of things. But her heart completely and unconditionally belonged to Cullen. Cullen was just as protective and resourceful as Barroth. He was strong and handsome not to mention a great kisser. His kisses were filled with passion and sent a spark through her that she couldn't explain. She had never lay with a man before but this one, Cullen she believes is the one, her soul mate. She met him or at least his soul at the hospital, Richard. They even look a bit alike. She sat there and wondered how he was doing, his child and run-a-way wife. Then she thought of her grandfather and turned her face away from everybody just in time for a single tear to glide down her cheek.

Clark brought the wagon to a stop as Victoria woke to the sounds of the mechanical doors opening to Mage Mountain. She had fallen asleep thinking about her grandfather, and she felt a loving hand caress her face. Opening her eyes was Cullen's handsome face, "I am sorry, I did not mean to wake you." It had grown dark, and Cullen did not want to fully waken her, so he gently grabbed her up in his arms and carried her inside. All the lights inside were dimmed but there was just enough light to see their way. Victoria looked back just as a couple of men were helping Barroth inside, then she laid her head on Cullen's shoulder. She could feel the strength in his arms as he carried her to the lift. Walking to her door, she could hear him hum a beautiful song. It was soothing and was lulling her back to sleep. His voice was pleasant and in tune. She had never heard him sing or hum before and she liked the way he sounds.

There was an elf in her room about to turn the light up, Cullen shook his head no and gesture her to leave. The bedding had been pulled down and he gently laid her on the bed. He caressed her hair and kissed her on the forehead. He continues humming and proceeded to take her boots off. Placing them gently on the floor, he grabbed the bedding and slowly pulled them up to her shoulders. Seeing that she was asleep, he leaned over and gave her a gentle kiss then whispered in her ear, "I love you." This moment was all he cared about, he stood there and watched her sleep for a few moments then slowly walked out the door. Before he closes the door, he looked at her and a sad expression came over his face. He thought he should let her try a relationship with Barroth since she spent all that time in the wagon with him. He didn't want to interfere, so he decided that he should stay away from her.

The next morning Victoria woke up with that song in her head. She climbed out of her bed and could smell a sweet aroma coming from her bathing area. When she saw that the tub was full of warm water, she could see flower petals floating around inside. Removing her clothes, she slowly glided into the water an enveloped herself in the sweet fragrance. She couldn't get that humming out of her head and found herself humming this song. When she finished her bath, she draped a towel around her. She walked over to her wardrobe and sifted through the many clothes that Ipion got for her. She came across a pair of black soft leather pants that just came halfway up to her hips exposing her hip bones. The shirt she put on came just down above her navel. The sleeves came down over her wrists and there was a hole for her thumb to go through. There were holes for her shoulders to be visible and the collar came just up but low enough to show her collar bone. She sat on her bed and proceeded to put on her boots when Clark came bursting through the door. He was so excited that he could barely contain himself. He saw Cullen carry her up the lift to her room and he wanted to know every little juicy detail, "You have to tell be everything that happened last night, was it good? Of course it was, I have seen his magnificent man hood." He looked at Victoria smiling and then he heard her humming.

"Wha…what's that you are humming?" Clark recognized the song and his mouth dropped, "He did not!"

"What? What is that look for?"

"Where did you learn that song?"

"Cullen. He was humming it to me last night. It was the last thing I heard. Why? What is that song it's beautiful. Are there any words to it?" Clark plopped down on the bed and questioned, "Why would he do that and especially him?"

"Do what? What are you talking about?" Clark gestured for Victoria to come sit next to him, "That song is the song that the guardians sing to invoke sleep on the mages. It puts them to sleep." He raised his eyebrows and continued, "And Cullen is known to put them to sleep by just humming. He has that special voice, and he is the one that starts it off."

"I don't doubt that; his voice is magnificent. Are there words to it?" Clark rolled his eyes and began to sing the song:

"Nightfall has taken the suns radiant blaze,

and coolness of the night leaves a mystical haze.

Let the sleep come through with promising dreams,

they will swim over your mind like a flowing stream.

Mage Mountain slumbers deeply, the winds are humming, and the moon is high.

Mage Mountain slumbers deeply, watchful dragons fly through the sky.

The paths lays to rest, the trees sway to the sounds,

of the humming guardians that walk the grounds.

Rest come upon you in the stillness of the night,

until the sun comes out to shine it's light.

Mage Mountain slumbers deeply, the winds are humming, and the moon is high.

Mage Mountain slumbers deeply, watchful dragons fly through the sky."

Clark rolled his eyes and looked at Victoria who was pretending to be asleep. Clark nudged her with his arm and said, "Stop."

"What? I was sleeping," she said with laughter in her voice.

"Oh, come on, only guardians can put you to sleep. I don't have the voice to do that."

"Well, you do have a voice, it sounded beautiful," she winked at him and said, "Come on, let's go get some breakfast, I'm starving."

She grabbed her long jacket that was resting on the chair and they both hurried out of the room.

Victoria grabbed a plate of bacon, eggs, and toasted bread with butter and black raspberry jam. She grabbed a cup of coffee with her free hand and glanced at Clark's plate. It was more like a huge bowl filled with strawberries, grapes, blueberries, sweet honey melon, peaches, apple, banana, and a few kiwis. "What? I'm a growing boy, I need my strength," he smiled looking over at Ryo. Victoria saw that glance and her mouth dropped. "No, you and Ryo?" Clark tucked his chin in and smile saying, "Well, at least one of us got some manmuck."

"Manmuck?" Clark hustled in front of her and said, "Shh, we don't need the whole mountain to hear." With her eyes big and a confused look on her face, she interrogated, "Manmuck, what is that?" Clark looked down gesturing with his eyes in a concealing way, "Yeah, you know." Victoria rolled her eyes and said, "Clark, really, some of the words you use here, they can be so confusing." Clark turned his head sideways, tucked his chin in and smiled, "Yeah, but it was a lot of fun, who would have thought…" She stopped him before he could finish, "Please, I would like to eat my breakfast without the thought of you and Ryo dancing around in my head."

"Oh yeah, there was dancing but not in the way you are thinking," Victoria looked at him and pretended to be shocked, then sat at the table with the group. She didn't know if she could look at Ryo without smiling because of what she knows. "Good morning, everybody," she glanced at Ryo and said, "Ryo." Ryo was a smart elf and very observant, "Ah, I see that Clark has told you of our nightly escapade." Victoria opened her mouth, but nothing came out. "No matter, all is good," he leaned over and plucked a grape from Clark's bowl and popped it into his mouth, winked and continued tasting the sweet nectar of the grape.

Victoria smile and placed her plate on the table. She took a drink of her coffee when she spotted Cullen. He was sitting at the table next to them and she gestured for him to come sit with them. He looked down at his cup and didn't move. A little confused as she looked at the others at her table, then back at Clark. He shrugged his shoulders and was just as confused as she was. Ryo saw the confusion on her face and stated, "Oh, you don't know."

"Know what?"

"It is Barroth," Suddenly Victoria got really confused and said, "What about Barroth, is he okay."

"Yes, yes, he is how you say, ah, better," even more confused Victoria questioned, "Then what is it? I don't understand." Clark straightened up and said, "Yeah, what's going on, I usually know everything, how is it that I don't know what you are talking about?"

"Well, word has it that your beloved Cullen has heard about you and Barroth."

"Me and Barroth? What about me and Barroth?"

"Well, his wings came out for you and Cullen believes that you and him..." Victoria stood up and thunder cracked from her hand. Everybody in the room heard it and looked her way. Embarrassed by the sound she made, she took off toward the outside doors, she yelled, "Open the doors," and the sounds of the mechanical doors and the dwarfs swearing at each other proceeded.

Cullen stopped at her table of friends and asked what happened. When they told him, he looked toward the door and ran yelling, "Keep the doors open." Running out the doors, Cullen saw Victoria climb onto a horse and rode off. He yelled at the stable boy, "Saddle my horse." The boy stood there watching Victoria leave, then glanced at Cullen. "Now!" while the boy was saddling Thunder, Cullen looked at the ground than in the direction that Victoria was going. Another little magical talent that the guardians have was being able to track mages. Especially if they took one of their horses. Each of the horses had special shoes made by the dwarfs but enchanted by Ipion. They left a trail so that a guardian can follow no matter how far ahead the mage got. Victoria got a big head start ahead of Cullen and she had no idea the danger she was in. Since Aldabus had the stone, Victoria was safer staying inside Mage Mountain. Flying above her was a black skinned harpy, which spotted her and flew in the direction of Death Mountain.

Cullen followed Victoria's trail and by the looks of it, she was wonder aimlessly and dangerously close to Death Mountain. She left in such a state that she didn't see where she was going or which way she came from. There were a couple of times that she went around in a circle. Cullen grew very worried about her and knew he had to find her soon. It started to grow dark, but not because dawn was approaching but because there was a big storm brewing. As it started to rain, Cullen could see Victoria just ahead of him, he spurred Thunder and caught up with her.

149

"Where are you going?" Soaked, Victoria looked at him with this face of a child that had lost its mother. Crying, she said, "Home." Looking at Cullen, she broke down and said, "But I can't find my way. I got lost." He looked off to the left and saw an empty cottage lit up by flitters flying around in the distance. They carried small jars of lightning bugs to see their way. The rain usually brought small animals out that needed their help. The glow of their lights gave the cottage a warm and enchanting look. He took the reins of her horse and led them to the cottage. He got off Thunder and help Victoria off her horse. She held onto him tight and began crying, "Please, please don't cry, I can handle anything but see you crying." Victoria looked up at Cullen with streams of tears mingling with the rain. He put his hands on her shoulder and looked down at her. Seeing that she was drenched, he guided her to the cottage. He couldn't stand the thought of her getting sick from being out in this cold rain because of him. Opening the door, he could see that there hasn't been anybody here for quite some time. He spotted a pile of wood next to the fireplace and proceeded on making a fire. He found some hides and blankets and laid them on the floor and encouraged her to rest there.

"Cullen, why would you think I wanted to be with Barroth?" She quietly said looking up at him. He put his hand on her shoulder and with the other hand he gently wiped a strand of wet hair away from her face, "Cullen, I love you." He looked down at her and pulled her close to him. He put his hand on her chin and gently kissed her. Looking at her, he pulled her closer to him and she wrapped her arms around him. He held her tight and said, "I love you."

Standing in the middle of the floor, dripping wet, Cullen started to take his armor off. It looked heavy but to him it was light, "Come on, we need to get these wet clothes off." They slowly took all but the under clothes off. Victoria felt a little shy and crossed her arms and rubbed her shoulders. She started to shiver a little and Cullen saw this and brought her closer to the fire. He started rubbing her arms and as she looked at him, she could see the muscles in his arms. Then she looked at his chest that was lightly covered with dark hair. The hair spread across his chest and grew narrow down to his navel. A line of hair trailed down below his navel and disappeared in his braies. His long hair was exposed, and she could see how far down his back it went. It was a beautiful golden blonde and it had a little bit of wave. Since most of it was tucked in his armor, his hair was dry. Cullen's armor always concealed his shape and Victoria, seeing him for the first time, was aghast by the muscles that rippled

150

across his stomach. She touches his stomach to feel how firm the muscles were. She looked at him and asked, "Have you ever been with a woman before?" Cullen placed his hands in hers and pulled her closer, he looked down at her and replied, "No."

"Neither have I. I mean I haven't been with a man, or a woman. I mean..."

He could tell she was getting nervous, and he slowly brought her face closer to his, "Shh, I understand." He leaned over and wrapped both of her legs around his waist and carried her to the blankets on the floor. As he kneeled, he placed her on the blankets. Standing back up he took off his braies and she could now see what Clark was talking about. She quietly pushed Clark out of her head for fear of spoiling her view. Crawling down on his knees, he gently pulled off her undergarment, then poised over her body, he slowly took off her breast coverings. He took in the pleasant view before him and began kissing her. He kissed her neck and breast and became aroused by her reactions. Laying on her but using one arm to keep from crushing her little frame, he asked, "I'm not hurting you, am I?" She put her arms as far around him as she could and said, "No." Entering her, he watched her face as it glowed with pleasure and he kissed her on the lips. The only sounds they could hear was the crackling of the fire and the rain dropping on the leaves of the trees that hovered over the cottage. This moment would be something Victoria would treasure for the rest of her life. He was now forever in her heart, a bond that was unbreakable. They both shared this pleasure throughout the storm. They laid there close to each other, holding on to the love that fervently blossomed that day.

High above the cottage was the black skinned harpy. It was circling the area below him to show Victor's men, where Victoria was, but as the weather got worse, it seeks shelter in the huge trees in the forest. Victor didn't go with the small horde to fetch his sister. He was too busy sulking. He was mad at his mother for not telling him about his sister. He was also mad at himself for not thinking to take her when he had the chance. If they would have let him in on the details of their plans more often, he would not have made that mistake in the first place. He was so mad at them all he started throwing things around, like some spoiled child. Aldabus could hardly blame him for being angry; if it were him, he would have been just as angry.

While Aldabus had been in the locked room, he had time to think about what he needed to do. He knew he had to get this doppelganger if he was to succeed with his plans. He had to put aside his feelings that came through when he saw the apparition that had the likeness of his beloved Shadowmoon. Understanding Victor's anger, he told him to retire to his room and he would send somebody else to retrieve the girl. Putting his arm around the boy's shoulder, he said, "And when we have her in our grasp, she will be ours." Victor still looked mad and Aldabus saw a spark of jealousy in his eyes, "Or maybe she will be just," he paused a moment and looked at Victor, "Yours." Victor liked the thought of that, having his own plaything. He liked the idea of that and gave his grandfather an evil side smile. Most evil creatures in Death Mountain bestowed a horrid outwardly image, but no matter how evil Victor might seem, he was still very handsome. His long dark hair and shockingly blue eyes masked the atrocity that he could look like. His skin was pale, but his lips were blood red that now and again they would expose his white teeth when something pleased him.

As he sauntered into his room, he shut the door behind him. Walking past his huge bed cover with a blanket that was made from a hundred minks, he peeled his shirt off and through it on the floor. His skin-tight pants he wore came down a couple of inches below his navel. You could see a line of black hair below his navel and disappearing in his pants. The massive bulge that protruded in his hosen indicated the size of his manhood. The slave girls would swoon over him when they helped him with his bath. As he walks to the balcony, the muscles in his stomach rippled with every step. The thought of having her excited him and he raised his arms and strands of lightning bolts came out of his hands, "She will be mine, I will have her. It is a good match, after all, she is my sister." The world Victor was raised in saw nothing wrong with incest; it was not frowned upon here like it was in Victoria's world. They encouraged it to make the magic stronger. It was good to keep the strong blood running in the family. The only one who would oppose it was his mother, she still went by the rules in their world. Not to mention that Victoria would be against by it, that excited Victor even more.

Victoria lay next to Cullen with her head on his chest, she could hear the soothing beat of his heart. She ran her fingers through his chest hair and said, "Sing it to me."

"What?"

"The song you sing to put the mages to sleep. Clark told me that you are the one to start it, only I never heard it."

"That's because you are always already asleep. You know most mages have a hard time sleeping but you. Why do you suppose that is?"

Victoria took in a deep breath and squeezed him tight, "That's because I love to dream."

"What do you dream about?"

"My knight in shining armor," she looked at Cullen and smiled, "You." He put his hand on her face and drew it closer to him, then gently kissed her on the lips. She smiled and laid her head back on his chest, "Go on, sing it, I want to see if it really works." Cullen started to get up and she said, "Where are you going?"

"I have to stand up, it won't work with me laying down." He stood up and put his braises on, then he had her put her undergarments on, "It might be best if you put these on."

"Why?"

"It would be much more proper if you woke with something on."

She smiled at him and put her undergarments on. She then ran her fingers through her long hair that dropped past her waist. He looked at her and smiled, "Maker's breath, you are so beautiful." He helped her fluff up the hides and blankets to make it comfortable and then he kissed her and had her lay down. He grabs his shirt and put it on as he started out humming, "You are going to sing the words?"

"Yes, it starts out with humming, that helps them to get settled."

"Will I get to hear all the words?" he smiled and said, "Probably not." She laid there listening to him humming, then he began singing the song. His voice was so magnificent and soothing. Her eyes started to get heavy when he got to the verse, then her head started to swim, and she slipped silently asleep. He finished the song, then kneeled next to her, and kissed her. It was so quiet all you could hear was the crackling of the fire, even the rain had stopped but water dripped from the leaves.

There wasn't a sound outside the cottage, but there was a pair of evil eyes peering through the dirty glass windows. What Gorgon witnesses during that storm gave him an evil idea, one that will tear apart the heart of this guardian of Mage Mountain. He gestures for the harpy to fly back to Death Mountain and let the others know he will be coming. The package will be delivered, and his master will be very pleased with him. As he divulged the plan to the others and had them standing by and wait. He had all the time he needed for this plan to work. Getting the rope ready, Gorgon peered in the window to see what was going on. He could see her falling asleep, he smiled and said, "It won't be long now." He gave an evil smile to the others and slowly rubbed his hands together as he waited for Cullen to make that fatal mistake.

As Cullen got off his knees, he grabbed his pants and put them on. He needed to go outside to relieve himself. This would be the perfect time for him to do that since she was asleep. Singing the song over a thousand times before he knew that song would keep her asleep for eight hours, nothing will wake her. Opening the door and stepping outside as he took in a deep breath; he could smell the fresh rain. He walked over to a bush a few steps away from the cottage. A strange feeling came over him and he finished up. As he started to walk back toward the cottage, something hit him on the back of the head, and he fell to the ground. When he woke up, he was tied and gagged and standing in front of him was Gorgon and an ogre with Victoria draped over his shoulders. He tried to yell no, but it was muffled by the gag. Gorgon walked up to Cullen and grabbed a hand full of hair and made Cullen looked at him, "What a naughty guardian you turned out to be. A mage and a guardian, oh how the people will talk." Cullen tried to pull his head away from the Gorgon's grasp, but he let go anyway, "You tell Ipion, we have the key now."

Cullen struggled and tried to yell through the gag, but all he could do is watch them leave with Victoria. He rolled and crawled until he could get inside the cottage. There, up against the chair, was his sword. He inched his way toward the sword and managed to position it so that he might free himself from the ropes. When he finally freed himself, he grabbed up his armor and ran outside. Looking to the left, he could see that Thunder and the horse that Victoria rode were still under the large tree where he left them. If only they took one of the horses, he could follow them, but he didn't need a guide or trail, he knew where they were taking her. Going after her alone would surely get him killed and there would be no saving her. He had to go back to Mage Mountain and get help.

By the time Cullen returned, it was dark, he jumped off his horse and yelled at them to open the doors. They had already seen him coming and the doors were already opening but not fast enough for Cullen. He stormed through the tower in a rage, calling all his men to come now. He wanted to get them going now, there was no time to waste. Barroth wanted to go but Ipion told him no, he wasn't well enough to go, he would only make it harder for them to rescue her. He thought about it and believed he was right. Saphon was interrogating Cullen, how she got captured? What was going on? When Cullen told him that she wanted him to sing the song to her he yelled, "Why would you do that, you made her completely vulnerable."

"I know, I shouldn't have agreed to it, but she wanted to hear it. I saw no harm at the time."

"You should have never sung that to her, she could have waited until you got back."

"You don't think I thought of that, I keep beating myself over and over for what I have done," Ipion came over and put his hands up, "Enough, Saphon, Cullen would never purposely put her in danger, he loves her too much for that."

"It should have made him a lot more careful. He knew that Aldabus would want to get her so that they can open the gateway."

"Maker's breath, I wish I could take it back, but I would not trade the time we had together back there for anything. My love for her is bonded and unbreakable, I will not stop until she is safe here again."

Ipion understood what Cullen was going through and only he knew that this was supposed to happen. He had no choice but to let it happen. Now the events that are supposed to take place have been put into action. Someday, they will understand but now is not the time to let them know what is to happen. He had faith in Cullen's love for Victoria, that he will accomplish his need to rescue her. Things will happen to Victoria that he hopes she will forgive him for. He will help guide her to understanding what had to be done. Nobody knew of this circle of events save one. As Ipion quietly left the group, he teleported himself to the top of the tower where he met the save one, Velatha. He sadly sauntered over to her and put his head down, "It has begun." These were their children, their grandchildren and they both hated to put them through this. "You must wait until after he opens the gate before you can rescue her," Velatha knew and sadly flew away. Her job was to get the one dragon who trusted her more than anybody captured. They needed him for this to start. War was coming to Victoria's world, it had to happen this way, it was the only way to save at least, most of them.

Chapter XII

Hope was standing in front of her balcony; she couldn't quite touch the rails because of the chains that were magically bound on her. As she watched the rain lightly fall from the sky, she heard a noise behind her. Suddenly, her door burst open and the ogre carrying Victoria came through. He uncaringly threw her on the bed, snarled at Hope and walked out the door. She was about to run to the bed to see who it was when Gorgon came in the room. He had an evil grin on his face, and he was rubbing his hands. She looked back at the woman on the bed and knew instantly that it was her daughter. She ran to go by her side when Gorgon grabbed her, "Yes, it is your obscured daughter. She has quite the likeness of, Shadowmoon." Tightening the grip, he had on Hope he announced, "Her likeness will not stop the master. He will go through with his plans, and your beautiful world will be his." He came up closer and put his other hand around her waist. Smelling her hair, he licked her face. Discussed that he was even touching her, she wiped her face off.

"I should have been the one to father Victor, my semen would have killed Saphon's."

Hope looked at him with surprise, "How did I know it was Saphon's?" He released her and walked over to Victoria. He picked up her arm and exposed the mark, "She has Saphon's mark." With that, he through her arm down and left the room locking the door behind him.

Hope ran by Victoria's side and brushed her hair away from her face. She did look a lot like Shadowmoon, Hope had gazed upon the portrait in the locked room. The door might have been locked but Hope knew how to get into locked rooms. She was not as magically regressive as they thought she was. Looking down at her daughter and not noticing a cool wind blowing in from behind her, she couldn't figure out what was wrong with her daughter, why won't she wake up. "She has the guardian sleep on her," a pleasant but quiet voice answered. Shocked at hearing a voice coming from her balcony, she spun around to see Velatha, "You can speak now?"

"Yes, she is as powerful as we thought she would be."

Hope looked back at Victoria then proceeded to come out as far as she could to the balcony.

"Chains! Why have they bound you?" appalled by the thought of her granddaughter being chained like an animal angered Velatha and with a rebellious act toward her father, she blew on Hope's hands. The chains suddenly slip off and she was free to come all the way out to the large balcony.

Hope rubbed her wrist and hugged her grandmother's snout. She was glad to see her and that there had been no harm done to her. She had heard some disturbing stories from the slaves that would come up to clean her room. They were saying that Velatha was capture and chained in the dungeon. She was so afraid that she was being tortured into giving them Dragon tears. When she told Velatha these stories, she responded, "Really, Hope, the gull of them stating such rubbish. When I see them, I will show them how free I really am."

"Grandmother, please, they are poorly influenced and have not a speck of intelligence in them."

"Well, it wouldn't hurt them to learn the truth a little," she turned from Hope than looked back; as she flew away, she said, "I won't harm them, much. Maybe singe their bums a little." Hope put her hand up to her mouth to stifle the laughter she hadn't felt in years. Turning back to Victoria, she grabbed a chair and placed it next to the bed, "The guardian sleep." She leaned over and kissed her forehead than sat on the chair. It would be a while before she woke up. As she sat there, she wondered why a guardian would put her to sleep, was he not aware of the dangers he put her in.

Standing in Victoria's room Cullen thoughtlessly grabbed a shirt that she had been wearing earlier that week. He brought it up to his face and he could smell her on it. Placing it on her bed, he walked to the balcony. There were two chairs and a table between them with some pretty figurines and a vase of flowers sitting on it. Angry with himself, he yelled and flipped the table over. He walked to the railing and looked across the vast country. As he stood there, he thought of that day he spent with her. A memory that will stay in his head forever. The soft glow of light that was emanating from the fire caressed the soft curves of her face. She was so beautiful, and at first all he wanted to do was hold her. Cullen was a strong man but thinking about her brought a tear to his eye. He stood there thinking what they could be doing to her. He couldn't bear the thought of them hurting her. He had to get her back, he didn't care what happened to him just as long as she was safe; that was all that mattered. Ipion had assured him that Velatha will keep an eye on her, she will keep her safe.

Velatha still angry with her father flew over to the balcony where the dining hall was. She knew that Isadora would be skulking there. As she landed, she blew a flame of fire into the room yelling Isadora's name. Isadora was about to take a drink of her wine when she heard her name being announced along with a stream of fire that singed a tapestry that Velatha detested when she lived there. Isadora jumped out of her chair, spilling the wine all over herself, she replied, "Really, mother," trying to wipe the wine off her with a napkin, "Was that necessary?"

"It is when you chain my granddaughter like an animal."

"That was Aldabus's idea, and he always gets what he wants," Still trying to wipe the wine off.

"My father will hear from me when I am done with you," Isadora looked at Velatha's eyes and saw the tears. She quickly grabbed her vial and walked up to her. Velatha let her place the tears in the vial, then took another stab at the tapestry that the cleaning slaves were trying to put out. Isadora upset with the burning of the tapestry, said, "Really, mother, that is my favorite tapestry." Velatha came closer to her and said, "I detested that one." She turned away and was about to fly away when Isadora asked, "Why the sudden change?" She ran up to Isadora and made the whole floor shake, the slaves were so frightened they began to run. Velatha knew they were the ones that cleaned Hope's room and she shot a flame at their bums, just enough for them to feel it. Then she looked at Isadora and said, "You have Victoria. No harm had better come to her." Turning to fly away, she looked back and said, "I don't ever want to see either of them chained up." With that, she flew away toward the cave of dragons.

Velatha hated what she had to do next. She had to convince the great white one that what had to be done was not just for the good of all dragons, but for the country. Things had to happen this way, or it will never be. She had to convince him that being chained up in the dungeon was protecting the other dragons, even if it seemed like it wasn't. The potion they had to take would only last for a little while and that it will wear off. She promised him that she

158

alone would free him from the chains. Aldabus will have his battle but he will not enslave the dragons for long. They will be free again, they will be able to escape to other places, places where others could not follow them. Velatha had seen this place, Ipion showed it to her, she could even go there too if she wanted to. Away from her father and Isadora. Even away from her beloved Ipion, which the thought of that sadden her. She knew when this was over, she would have to leave, so that she would never again be forced by Isadora to extract tears from her.

Now that Isadora had the dragon tears, she could have the potion made that will enslave the dragons for their army. She went to the alchemist dorm and showed him the tears. He clapped his hands together and grabbed a huge book from the shelf. Opening it up, he started running around the room gathering ingredients for the potion. As he was placing some ingredients in his mortar and grinding them with his pestle, he looked up and told her that he will need some of the enchanter's hair, the one that gave them the ability of speech. She checked to see if her knife was sharp enough by cutting a strand of her hair, then placed it in a pouch she had hanging on her belt. She left the alchemist dorm and began walking quickly down the corridor. Dressed in her black pants that fit snug to her nicely formed body for her age, she picked up her pace. Even with her six-inch boots she wore, she had great balance. Her white hair flowed down to the middle of her back. Wearing a jacket that was snug to her arms and waist it flared out and dragged on the floor. With the speed of her walk, it made the jacket flow out like a horse's mane. As she rounded the corner to the stairs that led to Hope's tower prison, she ran into Zeddicus. A bit startled by his unexpected appearance Isadora let out an exasperating sigh.

"Must you always appear like that."

"I am sorry, your majesty, but I heard that you have the girl."

Not wanting to confide with Zeddicus, she released another exasperating sigh, "If you must know, yes, we have Victoria." He squinted his eyes at her and said, "You call her by her name?" Not understanding what he was getting at she asked, "What are you getting at?" Zeddicus turned his back to her and smiled, then he turned back around and stated, "You called her by her name."

"So, what is your point Zeddicus, I don't have all day."

"Well, calling her by her name demonstrates signs of, how do I want to put it, you care about the girl."

Now he had pissed her off, she grabbed his jacket and pulled her knife out and brought it up to his neck. Just as she was about to pierce his skin, Victor came around the corner, "What's going on here?"

Zeddicus might be a worm, but he was still Victor's father, and because of that he was safe to do as he pleased. He knew what he was doing when he was found as the favor to be the father of the mage that would help start the war that Aldabus needed or wanted. He was always good to Victor, treated him well, taught him things, and was always there for him. Not just for protection, but he really cared about the boy. He always made sure that Aldabus saw favor in the boy even if it led to his beating. He might not have much respect with those in the castle, but he made sure that the boy always knew he did everything for him. As much as he wanted Victor to lash out at Isadora, she would find a way to make it look like it was his fault, "Just a little misunderstanding son, no harm done." Isadora slowly released him, and he wiped his neck and showed Victor the little spot of blood, "See, just a little scratch, no harm done." Isadora furrowed her brow at Zeddicus, then turned to Victor. Patting Zeddicus shoulder, she replied, "Yes, no harm done, just a little misunderstanding." With that said, she flicked her jacket and headed up the stairs.

Victor was intrigued by her urgency that he followed her. Not knowing that she was being followed, she felt a hand grab her shoulder. She spun around with her knife in her hand just to see that it was Victor. "Oh, it's you," Isadora witnessing Victor's new-found steam gave her pause. He became a little more frightening to her. If she would have known that deception was the light that put the fire under him, she would have done it a long time ago. That night, he was out on his balcony and he expelled thunderous lightning out of his hands was witnessed by her. She had never seen him with such power. The girl must have brought it out in him or maybe the deception. Either way, he doesn't hold back as much and now he shows no emotions when he crushes something with his hands.

"Did you want something?"

"Yes, I want to know why you are in such a hurry to mothers' room?"

"What makes you think I am going there?" Victor moved in closer and had her plastered against the stair well walls. He put one hand on her shoulder and gestured up the stairs with the other, "Because these stairs lead right up to her room." Isadora tried to advert his attention to what she was up to and said, "I was just going to check on her, Mother was just here, and I think she released her."

"But why are you going up there?" she looked away and that was his sign when he knew she was trying to keep something from him. He looked up the stairs then back at her. His eyes got big, and he released her and headed up the stairs.

"Now Victor, you mustn't…"

"Mustn't what grandmother? See what you are hiding from me again? She's here isn't she?" Victor ran up the stairs, skipping some of them to get to the room. When he walked down the corridor, Isadora was trying to keep up with him, she didn't want him to do anything rash, "Victor, Victor, slow down I have to get my keys." Victor looked at his grandmother with this insane wild look then back at the door, "I don't need any keys." He raised his hands and with a powerful thrust lightning crack and the door flew open.

On the other side of the door Hope ran to the other side of the bed to protect Victoria. Victor shoved his mother out of the way and went after Victoria. Just as he was about to put his hands on her, Aldabus appeared in the room and with a gesture of his hands, he through Victor a few feet away from Victoria. He scrambled up to his feet in a rage, "Why do you need her, I can open the gate." Aldabus calmly said, "No, you can't, only something pure and good can open the gate. The first born, the magic was given to the first born. She has been sheltered from this world and is unknowing. Her intention will be for good," and with a scowl he continued, "And for love. That is why we need her." He looked at Isadora and asked, "Did you get it?" Isadora sauntered in the room and smiled saying, "Maggart is making the potion as we speak." Aldabus smiled and clapped his hands together. Then he looked at Victoria and his smile faded. In a whispered voice, he said, "Shadowmoon." He hovered over her face and breathed her in. He sharply glanced at Isadora and asked, "What is wrong with her, why does she sleep." Isadora smiled and said, "It's the guardian sleep." With laughter in his voice, he said, "Splendid, when she awakes, we will go. How soon will Maggart be done? We have to be there before the winter solstice starts." Isadora walked over to Victoria and pulled her knife out. Reaching for a strand of her hair, she cut it and replied, "All he needs is this." Aldabus grabbed the hair and asked, "What about the dragons?"

"Mother is on her way, she should be doing her part as we speak."

"What made her agree?" Isadora pointed at Victoria and said, "Because we have her." With joyous laughter in his voice, he shouted "Splendid, Splendid." He spun around and disappeared. Isadora turned to see Victor sitting on the bed next to Victoria, he leaned over and picked up some of her hair to smell it. Then he looked down at her small frame and ran his hand across her chest than down her stomach. He continued down her body, between her legs and that is when Hope yelled at him, "Stop, what are you doing? She is your sister." He picked up the arm and revealed that mark, "She's only my half-sister. She carries the mark of Saphon." Hope didn't care, to her it was still wrong. She ran over and pulled Victor away from her and shielded her with her own body. Victor just smiled and said, "I can wait, after the gate has been open, grandfather promised her to me."

Hope was disgusted by Victor's idea of being with his own sister that she pushed him away from her and continued to push him out of the room. She couldn't believe that her own mother would be okay with the idea and made Isadora follow him. They looked at each other than at Hope, they began to smile because there was no door. Hope raised her hands, and the broken door came flying up toward them, this made them jumped backwards in surprise. They looked at each other and Isadora said, "She's been holding out on us."

On the other side of the door, Hope went to Victoria's side. She took a brush and began to brush her hair the way she used to when she was a little girl. What a beautiful woman she turned out to be. She wondered how the man she knew as her father was and if he was still alive. Was Carver even alive? He must be because she turned out beautiful. Then Saphon came to her mind. Have they told her that he was her real father? How did she take it, if so? Does she know what the birthmark on her arm was? She remembered how when Victoria was young, she questioned the mark. Hope lied to her and told her it was just a birthmark; most people get them. Then she started to remember the many days he came to her. She was still very much in love with him. He was so handsome and gentle, the soft tones of his voice putting her to sleep. Then that horrible night that her mother and Zeddicus came to her. Why would she let such a horrible man as he violate her the way he did? She would never let any man force himself on her little girl. Her sweet, kind, beautiful Victoria. As she sat there humming, suddenly Victoria began to wake up. Hope stopped brushing her hair and place the brush on the nightstand as she sat there watching her daughter wake.

Victoria was a bit startled by where she was. She jumped out of bed and began to look around. She was not in a familiar place. Where was Cullen? She than saw a woman sitting on the bed then got up and walked toward her. Victoria put her hands up and they began to crackle in fear. Hope put her hands up to assure her that she was safe for now, "Victoria, it's okay, you are safe with me." A stir of recognition came to her and her heart nearly leaped out of her throat, "Mother?" Hope pleaded with her hands in hopes that Victoria remembers her, "Yes Victoria, don't be frighten, it is me." She put her arms out and Victoria ran into them, crying, "Mother, it really is you." They hugged each other in a tearful reunion. A gust of wind came from the balcony as they both looked to see Velatha landing. Hope grabbed up her dress and ran to her with Victoria following behind her, "Grandmother, quickly take her away from here." Velatha looked down and said, "I can't, it is too late. Forgive us for what must be done. The wheels are already in motion and there is no stopping it now." She flapped her wings and flew away. Hope turned to Victoria and said, "She will be telling Mother what she has done, they will be coming up here for you. I am so sorry Victoria, I don't have the power to protect you." She wrapped her arms around Victoria and held her until they came bursting through the door to get her.

Hope tried to shield Victoria from them, "No, mother, I can stop them." She went to raise her hands and Aldabus swirled his hands around and bindings appeared around Victoria's hands and arms. She struggled to get free but was met with words of wisdom from Aldabus, "You cannot free yourself of my bindings and even if you could this is what will happen to your mother." Sharp wired bindings appear on Hope, they started to cut through her arms and legs as she screamed in pain. Victoria ran by her side and pleaded with Aldabus to stop, "Please, stop." Tears came to her eyes and she bowed her head, "I will do anything, just don't hurt her." Aldabus smiled and said, "I thought as much." He released the bindings from Hope and grabbed Victoria, "Come, we go to the gate."

They all met at the bottom of Death Mountain. At the entrance was a horde of evil elves, mages, dwarfs, ogres, harpies, and orcs. There had to be at least 10,000 or more and at the head of them was Aldabus carrying Victoria with him. His horse was massive, bigger than Thunder and black as the night. It would stomp the ground and made it shake. The harpies took flight and behind them were the dragons. Their eyes were not normal; they were red from the spell they were under. Over 1000 of them were there covering the sky, all but one. The great white one, he was chained in the dungeon. This was just the scouting party, there were others for the final battle, tens of thousands of orcs and goblin like creatures that Aldabus will use as cannon fodder. When the gate opens, he and his horde will go to England while Gorgon's horde will go to the States, by way of the passage that was sought out by Victoria's guild earlier.

There was nothing Victoria could do, she was not good with her magic yet. It only comes to her with her emotions. It took them nearly all day to reach the stones like those in England. The stones appeared weathered and didn't seem like they were much help for what Aldabus had planned. When they arrived, it was early, and the sun had not peaked yet. Seeing the cromlech, Victoria recognized where they were. She had been here earlier this summer, when she first met Cullen. The stones still seemed unstable but Aldabus raised his hands and calm the spinning. Victoria freed herself from Aldabus's bindings and jumped off the horse. She ran up to Aldabus and stated, "I will not help you into my world, I don't care what you do." Aldabus looked at her and smiled, he ran his hand across her face than through her hair, "So beautiful, you have Shadowmoon's likeness. But how blissfully ignorant you are." Victoria furrowed her brow, she detests the thought of him thinking she was ignorant, "Oh, this does not please you. I am merely stating the obvious. I don't need your help getting in. It's what is on the other side I need you for."

"I still will not help you," this angered him, and he grabbed her and faced her toward the stones, "You know what is on the other side of these stones. This is merely a gateway to your world that has always been easy to get to. It's what needs to be done to that world that will open the gate to other places here."

"I don't care, I still won't help you," Aldabus grabbed Victoria's arm and pulled her through to her world. As they reached the other side, Victoria saw them. Richard and her grandfather. The horde slowly followed through after them.

Richard and Hawke were confused by what was going on. When they spotted Victoria, they began to run toward her. Aldabus raise his hand and sent Richard to the ground staggering in pain. "Stop!" Victoria cried trying to free herself from Aldabus's grip. Aldabus turned to the horde and gestured them to grab Richard and Hawke. Richard realized that Victoria was being forced to do something she did not want to do. He tried to free himself from the grip of these creatures, "Don't do it Victoria, they will not harm me." Richard was so sure that there was a logical explanation for what was going on. He believed that they would not do him any harm. Just as he was about to say something, Aldabus lifted his head at the creature that had Richard. The creature then brought his hands up and snapped Richard's neck. Victoria screamed as she helplessly watched Richard's limp body fall to the ground, "That is what will happen to your grandfather if you do not do as I tell you." Victoria looked surprised at Aldabus's knowledge of her grandfather. Seeing her surprise, he said, "Yes, I know who he is, you think I would come her without knowing what I can use to sway you into doing as I want. Are you forgetting that Isadora was here?" Victoria began to cry as Aldabus dragged her past Richard's dead body. "Enough!" Aldabus bellowed, "He meant nothing to you. He only has the likeness of the man that you are truly in love with." The thought of him knowing who she cared about sent sparks of fear through her. She began to fear for her grandfather's life.

As they reached the heel stone, Aldabus place her next to it. He had her face Stonehenge and placed the diamond in her hands. He then raised her arms up and waited for the sun to come up. The sun slowly came up and hit the Hope diamond. The magic that flowed through her body began to pulse like blood running through veins. Soon sparks came from her hands and the diamond shot a violet color beam of light toward the alter stone. The alter lit up and a panel appeared. Suddenly, the ground began to shake as the stones started to fall into place. Stones that were lying down came up off the ground and slowly floated up to the top where they belong. Stones started coming out of the ground and filled in the empty spots. Aldabus quickly walked up to the alter and touched the panel. Now he could bring the rest of the horde in to begin the battle that no one has ever witnessed before.

Victoria ran toward her grandfather, the elf that had him began to panic when he saw her coming toward them. He looked at Aldabus then back at Victoria. Pulling out his knife he warned Victoria to stay away. She was just inches away when the elf looked at Aldabus again. This time, Aldabus looked at him and gave him an evil side smile, only because he was achieving what he set out to do. The elf took that as a sign and plunged the knife into Hawke's heart. Victoria screamed, "No!" She grabbed him before he could hit the ground. With her free hand she shot a fireball at the elf that stabbed him.

Engulfed in flames the elf ran around screaming helplessly. Turning back to her grandfather, she slowly lowered him to the ground and asked, "Why were you here?" Hawke grabbed a note from his pocket and gave it to her, "Somebody left this note on my nightstand. I called Richard and we both hurried out here." Victoria cradled him in her arms and started to heal him. Hawke stopped her and said, "No, he will always use me to make you do things you don't want to." Victoria didn't understand how he knew that would happen. "How…" Hawke caressed her face and said, "He is an evil man. I can look at him and see that he is evil." Victoria regretfully understood that what her grandfather was saying was true. She could see that he was in pain and did not want him to suffer. Placing her hand on his chest, she helped him to die without pain. She held him tight in her arms crying as he slowly slipped away.

Aldabus did not want him to die, he needed him. He couldn't leave the alter until he finished its cycle. He yelled for Maggart to go save him. Victoria saw what was to transpire and used her magic to keep them away. Surely, they cannot bring back the dead. Laying his head down, she got up and started shooting fireballs at him. He stopped them by placing a wall of water in front of him. Victoria kept hurdling fireballs at him; she did not want them to bring him back. Aldabus yelled at him to hurry before it is too late. Maggart stated that it already was. Then he saw Victor who had stolen his way into this world. A bit angry with his sudden appearance, Aldabus said, "Get her, take her back to her mother." Victor walked toward her with an evil smile on his face. She could not bring herself to harm him, and that was what he expected. He learned something about her in the short time he had been with her. Family was important to her. The people that she loved was her weakness.

Standing in front of her he smiled, with a gesture of his hands he had her in magical bindings. He picked her up and threw her over his shoulder. She wriggled around in hopes of freeing herself from his grip. He smacked her on the butt and said, "Behave, my sister, or I will have to find your band of friends and kill them all."

"You wouldn't."

"Oh, but that is what makes us different, because I would. You should never show your weakness sister, because now I can beat you every time," he looked down at Hawke's dead body and a spark of recognition came to him. He remembered as a little boy this man taught him about the animals of the forest, how you should be good to them, they could help you. He looked at

Aldabus then back at Hawke. He set Victoria down and cast a strange light at their grandfather. Suddenly, he turned into an eagle and flew away. Victoria shock at this gesture of good faith said, "Why did you do that?" Victor scowled and said pointing his face at Aldabus, "Because I don't want him to try and bring him back. It's the least I could do for the old man."

"Careful, Victor, you are showing your weaknesses," he angrily looked to see the direction the bird took then looked back at Victoria. He then picked her up again and threw her over his shoulder. He whistles for his horse and got on it. As he ran toward the gateway that was showing the way to his world, he looked at Aldabus. What was he planning now? What could he possibly do with this world? The people of this world had no magic. There was no use for them except as slaves. He gave a glance back as he led his horse through the gateway and headed toward Death Mountain.

On the ride back, flashes of that place kept coming back to him. Some of it seemed familiar, not just because he was there when he was younger. There was something else, he just couldn't quite put his finger on it. He knew things were still being kept from him, it was just a feeling that he would get. When she was near him, he felt stronger. She made him feel whole, like all these years a piece was missing from him. He started to get this feeling that he needed to protect her, but why, she was only his half-sister. But they were still twins, they shared the same place for over nine months. His thoughts of being with her were starting to get cloudy. Something else was coming through, he had to push that away. He was evil, the goodness that was trying to shadow his mind caused great anger in him. He kept saying to himself that he was evil. Evil will prevail, he will not let her get to him. He had to stay away from her. As soon as he got back, he ran up the stairs to their mothers' room. Forcing the door open, he walked over to the bed and threw her on it. Then he began to walk away as he reached the doors he turned and removed the bindings. A spark of sadness came over his face, but he quickly turned away from them, so they could not see it.

As the door shut Victoria turned to her mother and began to cry, "Mother, I had to kill him." She began to cry harder, "Who, Victoria who did you have to kill."

"Grandfather, I had to, he was dying in such a painful way," Hope cradled her daughter and tried to comfort her. She remembered how much Victoria loved him when she was a little girl, "Don't agonize over it, they would have used him against you." That is what Grandfather had told her, but still, to have to kill somebody you have been saving all your life was something she would not get over easily.

She then looked up at her mother and a strange thought came over her, "Victor?"

"Victor? What about Victor?" Hope asked.

"Grandfather was gone, I am sure of it, but Victor? Victor turned him into an eagle. How is that possible?" Hope did not know how Victor did this. He has been showing great power since he learned of Victoria. He could not have turned Hawke into an eagle if he was dead. You can only change somebody's form only if they are alive. Things were unclear to Hope, she was not sure of what was really going on. Were there things that Velatha was not telling her? Why this sudden change in Victor? Was his knowledge of Victoria the reason for his power? She will talk to Velatha when she comes back, and she will make her take Victoria out of here.

Chapter XIII

Cullen was standing outside the tower adjusting the straps on his horse. He was determined to liberate Victoria from the clutches of Aldabus the Darkheart. He would get her out of there even if it meant dying. He could not bear the thought of anything happening to her because of his carelessness. When he had her back, he vowed to keep her safe even if that meant putting her to sleep in her room. He would never sing that song to her out of the tower again, "How could I have been so foolish?"

"Love makes you blind, and careless," Cullen turned to see Barroth standing there. He looked much better. All his strength had returned, and he was ready to set out and help Cullen, "I had the stable boy load my wagon, we are all ready."

"We? No! I will not put anybody else's life in danger," he turned away and continued adjusting the straps.

"Well, it looks to me you could use some help," walking up behind him was Clark, Ryo, Claire, Fodgrel, and even Wadester. When Cullen saw Wadester he shook his head and said, "No! Not him, we don't have time to keep an eye on that, that, child." A sad look came over Wadester and he replied, "You go without Wadester?" Claire felt bad for him and said, "Oh come on, Cullen, we could use him, his brute force that he has when it comes to Victoria is immeasurable."

Cullen did not want any of them going with him, but he knew he could not stop them. They all seem to have a strong connection with Victoria, strangely enough even Fodgrel. Clark walked up to Cullen, put his hand on his shoulder and said, "Looks like you are stuck with us. You can't do this alone." Cullen looked at the group, shook his head and said, "Fine, but I am not watching over the child." Wadester was so happy that he got to go he went up behind Cullen and gave him a big squeeze. The strength of that orc was amazingly forceful that it nearly made Cullen pass out, "I admit we can use his strength. I don't know how you talked me into this, but I would do anything to bring Victoria home safe." He then looked at Barroth and said, "I am sorry, Barroth. I know how much she means to you. If I could…" Barroth put his hand up and said, "Say no more, I only wish for her to be happy. This happens sometimes, and like I told her, it is nobody's fault." Just as they were walking away, a voice said, "You can't go into the dark forest without a mage." Walking up to them was Saphon, "Do you really think I would let you go without me, she is my daughter."

He turned toward the stables and whistled. The group looked in the direction of the sound of hooves pounding the ground. Gracefully, trotting up toward them was a magnificent white horse. This horse was just as big as Thunder and her mane was just as long. It flowed elegantly down to her shoulder and past her withers. Her knees down to her pasterns were cover in long flowing hair and her tail nearly touched the ground. Cullen groaned a little because Thunder fancied this horse. Whenever she came around, he thought he had to show off. Rearing up Cullen had to let go his reins or he might jerk his shoulder out again. The horses were whinnying and snorting. As Lightning trotted up to Thunder, she gave him a little nibble, a sign of her affections toward him, but as she saw her master, she quickly came to his side. Saphon petted her and gave her something he had in his hand. It was some sort of treat that Saphon had created that she eats with enthusiasm, it was like candy to her. While she was still chewing on this tasty morsel, Saphon climbed onto the saddle and started toward the bridge. With haste, the others followed suit and joined Saphon toward the bridge.

Ipion stood on top of the tower and watched the entourage exit the tower's grounds. He was joined by Velatha who felt apprehensive about what was to unfold. They both knew they had no choice but to let these things happen. They were all for the survival of this world. These things had to come to pass, or this world would not exist. There were still places that Ipion had to send Victoria. He had to keep her in the dark for fear of Aldabus getting ahold of this information. Only Velatha and Ipion truly knew what was going on. The tricky part was making Aldabus believe that it was not easy getting what he has gotten so far. If Ipion made this easy, Aldabus would become suspicious and this world could become dark as Aldabus wanted it to or even worse, be destroyed. He could not tell Victoria these things when Aldabus had so many things

170

hanging over her head that he could use against her. He will threaten her with everybody that she loves.

Cullen wondered if Wadester understood what they were about to do. Does he understand why he does the things that he does. Orcs have not been known for their intelligence, but this one could talk. He must have a higher understanding about things, more than the others. Or he could have just possibly been mimicking the teachings of a cruel Satyr. If you put enough fear in something, they could learn. While he watched Wadester swing from tree branch to tree branch, he hadn't noticed that Barroth had pulled his wagon up next to him.

"What's on your mind commander?"

"I was just wondering; how does he know what we are doing. I mean does he even understand?" Cullen stated as he pointed at Wadester. Barroth smiled and said, "All he knows is that the one person that noticed him and was nice and gentle to him is now in danger. Wouldn't you want to help the person, the only person in your life that cared about you?"

"Yes, but he is an orc, they are not supposed to have that kind of understanding."

"Tell me something, commander, if you were injured and somebody who spoke a foreign language helped you. Even though you could not understand them, you could since their kindness toward you, couldn't you. That is what Wadester understood, her kindness."

What Barroth said did make since to Cullen, maybe there was a higher intelligence in Wadester, "Wadester, do you know what we are doing?"

Wadester stopped swinging and dropped down to the ground. He walked over to Cullen and a spark of enlightenment came across his face. He looked and pointed in the direction that they were all heading and said, "Vic-tor-ia." He looked back at Cullen and a smile came across his child like face. That was all he needed to say for everybody to understand what he was doing. This creature had so much love for the woman who was very kind to him. He had been trying so hard to learn the things that Victoria was trying to teach him. He had come a long way in the short time that he joined this group of individuals. Each of them having their own personalities, faults, likes, and dislikes. He was learning from each of them. And they were all teaching him bits of their own traits. Barroth was teaching him how to roar. Fodgrel thought it amusing to teach him how to belch and fart. Claire showed him how to sneak away with the kitchen's prized onions and Ryo tried to teach him about love. Clark felt sorry for him because of the way his father taught him with fear, he didn't want Wadester to fear him, especially his father. Clark was trying to teach him how to be brave. Even Cullen was trying to teach him manners. Wadester took all of this in and was slowly learning from everybody.

But the one he has learned the most from was Victoria. She taught him that there is kindness and beauty in this world. That is what he was trying to save, the nice lady who gave him a blanket when it was cold out. The gift of that blanket met a lot to him. He still has it and uses it at night when he sleeps. She also was the one to make him clothes. They had a hard time getting him to stop wearing the other blanket she used to cover him up with. There were times he would go find it and put it on. He always thought it weird that he would find it in the place where a lot of clothes smell nice and were hanging up.

Cullen knew they would be going into dangerous territory, so he brought some potions that Uwrick brewed up for him. He had a potion that would counter act with the poisonous plants they would encounter in the dark forest. Some other potions, he brought with him were made with agents that acted like fireballs, lightning bolts, and the power to freeze. He didn't figure Saphon joining them otherwise he would not have gotten them. It was good to have a mage with them on their journey through the dark forest especially this one. Most creatures in the dark forest knew of Saphon and were terrified of him. Not only was he an excellent mage but he was deadly with a staff. His staff looked light, but the spin he could put on it would give a powerful blow that could knock somebody across the room. Or better yet it could knock them out. It was made of a kind of ironwood that only the elves could craft.

Cullen felt having Saphon with them gave them the upper hand. All though Saphon was not powerful enough to take on Aldabus, Ipion assured them that Aldabus would not be there. He had already traveled to the other world, Victoria's world. The only ones they would have to contend with were a few guards. Ipion knew that Victor will disobey Aldabus by making his way back to join the battle. This was the perfect time to rescue Victoria from the evil clutches of Aldabus's lackeys. Ipion knew that they could get her out of there before Aldabus even discovers that she was not heavily guarded.

Victor didn't care if Victoria was there when he got back. He didn't even care if this angered Aldabus. With his new-found powers, he felt he could deal with Aldabus. Even the strongest lion in the den can lose to a younger much stronger lion. Those words rang through his head as he ventured his way through the castle. His mother would always say this to him. He never understood what she was trying to tell him until now. Even his own mother kept things from him. He was feeling alone and betrayed. Victoria could have her, he didn't need his mother or his sister. He would make his stand and chop off the dragon's head and that dragon's name was Aldabus.

He was feeling sure of himself now. When he had gotten back after leaving Victoria to her mother, he decided to check out what they were hiding in the dungeon. As he opened the doors, there he was, the great white dragon, Eros. Furious, he yelled Maggart's name, and the alchemist appeared. Seeing where he was, he asked, "What are you doing down here?" Pointing at the dragon, Victor asked, "I think you need to tell me what Eros is doing here?"

"That is none of your business but the business only for my master," Victor grabbed Maggart by the neck and heat started to emanate through his hands, "I will not ask you again Maggart!" As he squeezed a little harder and radiated more heat from his hands. Maggart was caught off guard with Victor's strength and power. He had no idea that Victor could generate such magic. He had always been under the misconception that Victor was weak. Frighten of his strength Maggart said, "Forgive, my master, I did not mean to speak with such unruliness." Victor squinted his eyes and slowly released the alchemist. Maggart carefully took Victor's arm and led him toward the dragon, "His capture helped control the other dragons Aldabus has. But you can take control of those dragons with this." Maggart revealed a vial from the sleeve of his robe, "Master, did not think I could come up with a potion strong enough to control this one."

Victor took the vial and examined it. Inside the vial was a swirling green potion that looked alive. Why wouldn't Aldabus want control of this dragon, did he really think that this dragon could not be controlled. He was a lot bigger than the others and seemed to have more fury in him. If he could have control of this dragon, he could overpower Aldabus and take control of all that was dark. The horde would be his, he would have control, and nothing would be kept from him. Maggart liked the idea of a new power, one that would let him experiment more. He could sense something different in Victor, someone that would let him advance with his experiences. Aldabus was getting too old and had no imagination, not like he used to. The girl, it was the girl, when he saw her that was when he softened. She looked too much like Shadowmoon. He got rid of Shadowmoon because she softened him and now it was time to be rid of Aldabus, "Come, let us take control of this dragon, so you may fly him into the gateway."

Victor took the potion and threw it at the dragon. He watched as the dragon reeled in pain, fighting, resisting the chains that would control his mind. As he watched, he saw the color of the dragon's blue eyes turn to red. It shot a hot stream of fire at the gates that led to the outside where he had been taunted with as he watched his fellow dragons fly by. Maggart yelled, "Quickly, jump on him, and ride the dragon to the gate. You have the control, he will only obey you." Victor hesitated at first but then took a giant leap onto the back of the dragon. Maggart watched as they flew through the iron gates that led out of Death Mountain.

Gaining altitude, he flew up above the mountain past Hope's balcony. Hope and Victoria ran to the railings just in time to see this magnificent dragon fly by them. Victoria recognized the dragon. It was the one she rescued from that band of orcs. Why was he carrying Victor? She got a closer look at the dragons' eyes and she could see that they were red. She knew he had that dragon under a spell. Victoria knew that had to be dangerous, because that dragon had the ability to make things implode. Victor now had control of a very dangerous dragon and he was headed in the direction of the gate. At that moment, Victoria knew her world was in danger. He could decimate everyone and everything with that dragon. Her world did not stand a chance with that dragon in the hands of a confused and angry man. Victoria had to get out of there and find a way to stop Victor.

Victoria grabbed her mothers' hand and headed for the door. She tried to open it, but it was locked. She could not let Victor destroy her world, the thought of what he could do to them scared her and made her angry at the same time. Releasing her mothers' hand, she made a forceful gesture and the door explode in front of them. They both shielded their face and waited for the smoke to clear. As they ran out to the corridor, Victoria spotted the only way out of this prison and that was the stairs. Running down the stairs she stopped to help her mother. When they got to the end of the stairs all Victoria could see was a long corridor with multiple doors. She figured she had to find more stairs, there only way out was down. Hope grabbed Victoria's hand and began to lead her around. At one time, she used to be able to roam the castle freely without any supervision. The castle was like a maze, they ran from one end of a corridor to another one, each time finding another flight of stairs. Victoria wished she knew how to astral project like Ipion, she could get them out of there faster that way.

Victoria was surprised that they had not encountered any kinds of resistance. But she thought too soon, just as they were rounding a corridor, there were the four resistance. The sudden appearance of these ghoulish looking creatures startled her and Hope that they both screamed, and Victoria brought her hands up and they all froze. "Very good, Victoria," Hope proudly said, "Yeah, I would have to say not so bad myself." Just than ten more came running down the corridor. Victoria was not startled by them and she couldn't find the right motion to freeze them. Hope through a fireball at them but it wasn't as effective as Victoria's freezing power, "Quick, Victoria do something. Your powers are connected to your emotions." Hope had to think fast and started saying things that would make Victoria angry. Victoria just looked at her and said, "That's not working."

"Think of what Victor can do to your world with that dragon."

The thought of what could happen filled her mind enough that several bolts of lightning came flying out of her hands. These guards were all wearing some sort of metal and because they were standing in formation, the bolts hit them all and sent them all crashing into the wall. One of them even went flying out the window, and another crashed through a door that led to more stairs. Hope patted her daughter and said, "Most effective, I was trying to remember where that staircase was."

They both ran to the stairs and climbed over the guard that fell to the bottom. Stepping over him, he grabbed Victoria by the ankle causing her to release something she had never done before. It was some sort of blue flame, just like the dragon. The same flame that caused the orc to implode. Hope turned back just in time to witness this power.

"The dragon's breath, how did you do that?"

"I don't know, let's just keep going."

Nobody was able to produce the dragon's breath, not even Aldabus. That was why he was keeping the white dragon in the dungeon, he wanted to find a way to learn this power.

Hope and Victoria were getting closer to the main floor, it wouldn't be long before they came to the large staircase that led to the castle's entrance. Unlike the tower, the large staircase was in the middle of the room. There were at least thirty steps from the landing to the main floor and the stairs were fifteen feet across. These stairs were Aldabus's weakness for Shadowmoon. He loved seeing her make an entrance. Gliding down these magnificent stairs with her dresses flowing down behind her was something Aldabus loved to see. As big as this staircase was, nobody was allowed to come down these stairs when she was coming down them. One time, an elf slave came down behind her to bring her comb to her. Aldabus had her stripped naked, had half of her skin peeled off, and hung outside the entrance of the castle as a warning to all. That was the only time Aldabus punished someone with Shadowmoon's knowledge. She thought what he did was horrifying and would not speak to him for months. When she finally forgave him, he made sure when he punished somebody, it would be without Shadowmoon's knowledge.

Coming around into the corridor they could see the great staircase. Both Hope and Victoria stopped when they saw Saphon fighting the guards on the staircase. His staff spun around with a whooping sound as it came to a blowing stop across an orcs head. Behind him was Cullen, swinging his sword that found the nape of and elves neck. His sword was so sharp that if severed the head of the elf like a knife through butter, smooth and clean. Claire was at the bottom of the stairs shooting arrows, while Wadester was swing around a pole and his big orc feet met with an ogre's face. Sending the ogre flying down the stairs, Wadester looked up and spotted Victoria. He was so excited to see her that he came galloping up the stairs toward her. Hope, not knowing that this creature was a friend of Victoria's, brought her hands up and sent the orc flying across the floor. Victoria stopped her mother before she could do him anymore harm and helped him up off the floor. Then Hope witnessed this orc hugging Victoria with great love and compassion. It was obvious to Hope that this creature cared very deeply for her daughter.

Running up the stairs as fast as he could, Cullen was relieved to see that Victoria was unharmed. Seeing Cullen running up the stairs, Victoria gently released Wadester grip from her and ran to Cullen. She jumped into his arms and he swung her around. Holding her as if he would never let her go, he said, "Maker's breath, you are safe. I was so worried about you." He kissed her passionately than set her down. He ran his hands through her hair and turned her face up toward his. Kissing her again then hugging her, a feeling of relief came over him. With an arm still around her, he let the others embrace her. When Saphon came up to her, Cullen put his arm down and let Saphon embrace

176

Victoria fully. When he pulled her away, he looked over her shoulder and saw her, Hope.

Saphon released his staff and strangely enough it stood in place, he cautiously and slowly walked up to Hope. She was still as beautiful as the first day he met her. He stood there in front of her for only a few seconds before he held her in his arms. He kissed her hair and the side of her face, then pulled her back, so he could get another good look at her. She smiled at him and reached up and gave him a kiss on the lips, "You are just as handsome as I remembered."

"And you are just as beautiful as the first day I met you. It has been a long time my love."

Hope smiled, looked at Victoria and started to cry. She walked him over to Victoria and held them both in her arms, "I never thought I would ever see this day. The two of you here with me." Cullen began to get a little antsy and thought they should hurry on out of there, "I hate to be the one to break up this family reunion, but I don't know how much longer we can afford to stay here." Victoria put her hand on Cullen's arm and said, "I don't think they will be here for several days, maybe longer."

"Why is that, I was looking forward to putting my hammer up Aldabus's ass," Fodgrel replied, disappointed.

"Aldabus forced me to use the diamond to open the gateway. I am sorry he tricked my grandfather into being there. When he pulled me through, Richard and Grandfather were waiting on the other side."

Victoria broke down seeing the images in her head again. She told them how Aldabus snapped the life out of Richard with no effort. How he threatened her with her grandfather's life, just to see one of his elves plunge a knife through his heart. The thought of them over there terrified her, she had to do something about it. She told them that Aldabus had two groups of war bands. One went through the gate that led to England and the others went through the forest where they came through to Washington D.C. She didn't know if she should go to England or save the states, either way, both places will surely have suffered some great losses. "We have to try and help, we must have as many people to help as Aldabus has," Saphon looked at Victoria and said, "Aldabus has a large horde of grimlocks and ghouls."

"What are those?"

"They are demon like creatures that don't have a language. They know nothing but fighting and death. They carry a sickness with them that would kill people, or worse, change them into one of them. Once that sickness gets into their blood stream, they would be like walking dead, they could become like them. Even Aldabus won't let them near him."

"If there were so many of them, where have they been?"

"The horde live underground, in the deep crevasse. There are many tunnels deep underneath us." All Victoria could think of were zombies, she asked, "So is their bite deadly."

"Not just their bite, but if any of their blood or ooze from them get in your eyes, mouth, a cut you could die or become one of them."

Frighten at the thought of that, Victoria asked, "Will he use them to kill everybody?"

"It wouldn't matter, they just kill unless Aldabus has found a way to control them. If so, he will mainly go after the generals of your world, leaders, the ones who command," Fodgrel stroke his beard and said, "That is smart, he is taking away their leadership, the ones that guide them. Without them the people will feel helpless, nobody around to tell them how to fight."

"The ones in the states won't have any magic protecting them, not even evil magic. There must be many men there that know how to fight," Victoria looked up at Saphon and responded to his verdict, "The states have large armed forces, Marines, Army, Air Force, Navy, and the National Guards."

"Do these, what do you call it, armored forces, do they have magic?" Ryo questioned. Worried, Victoria responded, "No, but they have guns, big guns."

"Guns, what are those?" Ryo questioned as he came closer.

"They're these weapons that shoot out pieces of exploding metal, they are not magical, but they are fast and can be very destructive."

"That might help, but those creatures will be wearing armor and can jump pretty high. Not to mention that there will be very many of them. That place of Dizz Cee will need some magic."

Victoria felt responsible for what was about to happen, she knew she couldn't stand around and do nothing. She needed to decide where she was to go. At first, she thought the worst would be in England, where Aldabus was and she believed that Victor was headed that way, too. But from what Ryo was saying the states might not have any survivors, at least with Aldabus, some could survive and become his slaves. That horde, it would mean sure death.

Going to the states would take longer, but she needed to help them. The states were her home, she was raised there. It was the land of her grandfathers. She could not stand by and let that horde strike them down. From the sounds of it, people will be thinking they were being attacked by zombies. Some of those gun slinging citizens will think they can fight them like the zombies in the movies. But with these creatures, you can't just chop off their head, they are fast and come at you with a vengeance. From what they were telling her to interact with them would be your demise. Whatever they were doing, they had to act soon, time is of the essence.

Saphon suggested that they head back to the tower. They could gather up their war party and split them up in two groups. Half would go to England while the other half went to the states. He could send messages across the great waters and get help from them. There should be gateways there. Saphon couldn't decide which of the two were more dangerous for Victoria. He did not want to send his daughter to her death. What he really wanted to do is make her stay here, she would be much safer, here, with her mother. But he knew she would not stand for that, she was a fighter and he knew she could not live with herself if she was made to stay behind.

Gathering the people and getting ready took some precious time, Saphon got word back from across the great waters. Apparently Aldabus had already had people there going through gateways on his behalf. People who were evil and conspired with Aldabus for many years. This message gave Saphon reasons to believe that Aldabus had many people throughout the world. With that thought, he sent out messages all over the world to let them know what was happening. It was not safe anywhere but here. He tried to reason with Victoria that her magic was not ready for this battle. She needed more time to practice and understand her capabilities. But Victoria would not here of it, she felt that this was her fault, if she hadn't given into to Aldabus, this would have not been possible. Her grandfather ended up dying anyway and now it seemed like nothing will stop Aldabus. She was going to try to stop him, even if it meant her death, she would stop him and Victor.

Victor was going to meet with Aldabus, but then he believed that Aldabus would try to tell him what to do. So, he turned the dragon around and headed to the only place he knew of that would bring him to the other side. Over there, he could be the ruler, master of the slaves. He would meet up with Gorgon and reveal his plan to be master of that world. He would make Gorgon his general with choices of his own. This was something that Gorgon would not refuse, especially if he was given free reign. Aldabus would never let Gorgon do as he pleased, he would always have to okay his plans with Aldabus. Once he tried to carry out one of his plans without Aldabus's okay, he believed that Aldabus would never find out. But somehow Aldabus always knew what was going on. He had spies everywhere. Spies who wanted to get just as ahead as Gorgon, like frogs jumping over other frogs to escape their demise. The world was a big place and he only wanted his small piece to do as he pleased, knowing that he had to start small to grow big.

As Victor approached the area that led to the other side, he didn't know if he had to make the dragon crawl on the ground, or if they could fly through. As he was contemplating that he flew above the area and found himself on the other side. The horde had done much damage already, alarms were going off, fires were everywhere. He could see the horde spreading throughout the entire city. He saw machines called helicopters flying around and other dragons shoot fire at them and making them explode. When he spotted Gorgon, he landed next to him. All the men that were with him were terrified of this great white beast, he was much bigger than the other dragons. They were told that this dragon was not going to be in the war, that it would be chained up in the dungeon. They all started to flee when they saw Victor jump off the dragon. Victor took Gorgon aside and told him of his plans. He needed Gorgon to send word to the others throughout this world that have come over from the other side their new plans. That Victor was the master, and they were to follow him or be destroyed by Erross, the great white dragon.

Chapter XIV

The decision was made to where each group would go. Saphon would go to England with his group and Ipion would take Victoria and her group to the states. Ipion knew that those who went to England would be safe and that the states had the greater threat. It would take many days to get to the passage that led to D.C. and Victoria had to come to terms that there could be some damage. She knew the president would be safe, there was always a plan to keep the president safe. The vice president would be taken in the opposite direction. The world needs to keep them both safe but separated.

Mike Pence was ushered out of the states in Air Force One. President Trump wanted to take buses. He wanted to save as many people as he could. He didn't care what their status was, he was going to save them. Hollering at people to get into the buses they all started to file in. There were several secret service men hovering over the president to ensure his safety, but Trump figured it was not his life in danger. This was a new threat, and everybody's life was in danger. He pushed through his protectors, so that he could encourage people to get on the buses. Producing this type of action did not make the secret services men job very easy. As people filled up the buses, the men ushered Trump into his bus and sat around him. As the buses were leaving, Trump could see the people that were left behind being attacked by these horrible creatures. Trump places his face in his hands and stated, "I never saw anything like this coming." Devastated by the lost, all he could do was to watch through the windows. All he could save was 30 bus loads of people, out of over 100 buses, he could only get 30 of them.

Walking through the strange forest Victoria passed through into D.C., she could not believe what she saw. Total devastation was everywhere, there were fires, and the civil defense sirens were blaring throughout the city. There was no sound of people, it was eerily quiet except for the sounds of the sirens. It was like a horror movie unfolding right before her eyes. How was this possible, where were the people? There was no sign of life anywhere, even Aldabus's people were gone. As she was walking toward the monument that was still standing even with its scaffolding around it, Victoria remembered Victor pushing her off the top. What had happened to that shy timid boy that she had begun to remember? What have they done to him? Had that sweet little boy disappeared for good or could she bring him back.

Victoria spotted a car with some people in it. As she approached the car, she could see that they were dead. The keys were in the ignition, so she pushed the driver over to see if she could utilize the vehicles left in the town. Using these cars could get them to their destination faster. She was about to turn the key when she noticed that it was already engaged. She looked at the gas gage and it read empty. There was a long line of cars behind this one with dead people in them. She ran to the next car just to find that it too had ran out of gas. All these cars had run out of gas, the people were killed but the cars kept running until the gas ran out. All she could think of was they were trying to escape. The horde didn't care if they wouldn't or couldn't fight, they just killed them. It sickened her because there were young children in some of those cars. Looking down the road, she could see that none of the traffic lights were working. From the looks of the place, the officials must have had the city evacuated; this gave her hope for the people. It started to get dark and none of the lights were coming on. She thought of the hospitals, they ran on generators when the electric wasn't working. Climbing onto the back of Cullen's horse, Victoria led them to the hospital. It was getting darker, and torches were lit to see their way. When Victoria saw that they were in front of the hospital, she got off the horse and walked toward the front doors. Nothing, no lights, no people, just nothing.

Falling to her knees, she placed her face in her hands and started to cry, "This is all my fault, all these people, gone." Cullen jumped off his horse and walked up to Victoria. He grabbed her in his arms and cradled her, "You had no idea." He stroked her hair and said, "Victoria, please don't cry, you can't blame yourself. Aldabus is an evil man and he used somebody that you shared your entire life with, to make you open that gateway. Anybody who had a loving heart as yours would have done the same thing."

He pulled her away to face him and said, "If somebody used you to get me to do something so relentless, I would do it. I could not bear the thought of somebody hurting you."

She placed her head on his chest to try to compose herself. She had to make this right; she couldn't sit here and cry, that would not help anybody. Ipion walked up with sadness in his eyes. He hated to see her go through this, but he knew this had to be. In time, he would show her why this was to be.

"Come, it is late. We will stay here for the night and head out in the morning." Victoria looked at Ipion and said, "No, we have to keep moving. We need to catch up with them if we are to stop them."

"We will follow them, but we need to be able to see our way."

"We have torches, and the mages can generate light," Victoria responded.

"Yes, we could do that, but generating light for long periods of time can drain a mages magic. They would need that magic if they had to fight," Victoria realized that what Ipion said made sense and she agreed with him to stay the night.

The timing was rather unexpected, from the looks of the trees and the cool air of the night and burning Christmas decoration hanging, it had to be December. She began to believe that Aldabus pick this time because of the cold. People would not be able to survive the cold. Taking a deep breath, she could smell the air, it smelt like snow. Victoria believed that by morning there would be snow on the ground. Her only fear was that a blizzard could be in store for them. As she started for the door, a snowflake landed on her eyelashes. When she looked behind her and with the glow of the torches, she could see that it was starting to snow. Seeing the snow through the light of the torches made her think of a Thomas Kinkade painting of lights. The soft glow of the torches as the snow hit the light, gave the scene an ominous look. That bad and unpleasant feeling she got was if the snow grew in strength throughout the night, they could have a hard time making their way to helping others.

Victoria walked in the lobby of the hospital and found it strange to see fires being made. The hospital had gotten cold without the power, so they had to make fires to keep warm. The only thing she could think of why the power was out is that they shut off the grid for that area. What was strange to her was to see the horses in the hospital. I suppose they had to bring them inside if there was a blizzard. Some of the mages had the ability to forecast the weather, which Victoria had no doubt that they could. They were the ones to have the animals be brought inside. She decided to go through the nurse's stations and pharmacy to obtain medicines and bandages. Then she thought the medicines were redundant, they had potions that could be administered for pain and many ailments. She even had the ability to heal if need be. So, instead, she went to the cafeteria in search for food. It should all be good since it was so cold in there. She thought about the time of year and how strangely cold it was. Was this because of the clashing of worlds or was it the types of forces inflicted in this world that cause it to be so cold. Either way, it was unusually colder for this time of year. Could this be the work of some of the dragons?

Not all the dragons blew fire, some had this icy blue flame that froze things. The dragons were to destroy as many power plants as they could. Their magic not only burned or froze but it could disable all source of power. Some of the dragons flew around destroying cellular towers. With these down, people had no way to contact each other, they were on their own. Being connected to the internet made it easier for the dragons to be able to hinder the power throughout the states. Not having power made it hard for some people, but there were some people who were ready for something like this and helped as many people as they could. Some still carried their phones out of habit or hoping that they would suddenly come on. How could this be happening? Why were there no fail-safe plans in case of things like this?

Victoria was looking out the windows of the George Washington University hospital and watch the snow pick up outside. It was as she predicted it would be, it was turning into a blizzard. It worried her how long this could last. She remembered a blizzard a long time ago when she was a little girl. She was so excited when the snow came mainly because this would mean she would not have to go to school. Blizzards were common in South Dakota and she had gotten to the point of knowing when one was developing. She remembered that they had a blizzard lasting for three days before the sun broke through. It took them weeks to shovel people out. Victoria didn't care, she got to play out in the snow, but her grandfather would not let her stay out very long. He had a hard time getting her inside, she was always telling him she was not cold. She didn't even think of it when she was younger, but now as she thinks of it, her magic was able to generate heat, so she would have longer lengths of time outside. Standing by the window, looking outside, she thought of her grandfather and how he had to bribe her into coming inside. He always had hot cocoa with lots of marshmallows waiting for her. She smiled thinking about those moments when a voice broke the silence.

"Sorry to bother you, I got worried and came looking for you," Victoria turned around and saw Cullen standing there. She was glad to have him with her. She missed him dearly when Aldabus had her as his captive. She wondered if he knew that she and her mother were gone. Surely, he knew this by now. Walking up to Cullen, she put her arms around him and held on, "Cullen, I am so glad to be with you. I had missed you so." She looked up at him and kissed him. She took in a deep breath smelling him, laying her head against his chest, she closed her eyes, "Oh, I had missed you, too. You could have been... I will not let the events that took place back there to ever happen again. You have my word." He stroked her soft hair and picked some up to smell it, "You smell so good. I missed the smell of your hair when you laid your head on my chest." She held him tighter and smiled, she never wanted to let go. All this planning and traveling took away time she wanted to spend with him. But she didn't want to think of her own selfish needs when people were in trouble. It was nice to have this moment even though it might not come as often as she would like.

Cullen was curious to what she was thinking when he found her standing there all alone looking out the window, "What were you thinking when you were standing here?"

"I was thinking about the time when I was very young and didn't have to go to school because of the blizzard."

"You liked the snow?"

"I loved the snow, I would always go outside and play in it as a little girl."

"Were there others?"

"No, I was alone except for grandfather. Only because we lived so far from town. Grandfather owned a lot of land, handed down to him by his father and so on."

"I am sorry you had to be alone as a child," Cullen responded as he stroked her hair.

"No, it was okay, I got used to it. Besides, I got to have all the marshmallows I wanted in my hot chocolate."

"Marshmallows? What are those?"

Victoria pulled back and looked at Cullen, she smiled and said, "What, you have never had marshmallows before? I will make sure I grab some from a store. I will not let you live your whole life without having to experience hot chocolate with marshmallow."

Cullen looked down at her and did his side smile, "I am looking forward to the experience."

There was something on his mind that he wanted to ask her, but he didn't think this was a good time, so he decided not to mention it. He walked Victoria to a tent he had set up for her. Odd that there were tents inside the hospital. Inside her tent were several hides laying down on the hard floor. Cullen had never seen floors such as these before. The tower was chiseled out by dwarves and elves many years ago. So, the texture was different. It was smoother, like ice. It was amazing how some of the things in this world differed so much more compared to his world. Even though there was no magic here, some of the things they had seemed magical. The power they had to make things run was amazing, but they were to easily disable. There was no back-up in case their power was taken away. He wondered if people knew how to make fire without their magic devices.

For several days the snows fell, making it impossible for them to travel. Cullen would find Victoria standing at the windows many times watching the snow. He knew the more it snowed the more she felt responsible for the people of her world. He had her show him around the hospital telling him how things worked. She wasn't a doctor, but her education gave her some of the knowledge that was needed in a hospital. There were moments when she remembered her time in the hospital in England, she wondered what came of that hospital. Then she worried about Richard's son, what had come of him. What did happen to the babies? There were no signs of babies in this hospital. The only thing she could think of was the parents took them or maybe the nurses might have taken them. Either way, they were gone. It saddened her to see some people lying dead in their hospital beds. Things must have happened so fast that the evacuations were in turmoil.

There were some hospital employees lying dead on the floor, some looked burned or frozen and some had suffered wounds made by swords. She couldn't imagine the fear that went through them when they were attacked. These were people that were always going out of their way to help others, now some of them lay dead on the floor. Victoria felt like she should do something for them, but there was nothing she could do except maybe placing bodies on beds. She couldn't stand the thought of anybody stumbling or stepping on these people. Even though they were dead and couldn't feel anything, it just didn't seem right to leave them like that. It was the way her grandfather raised her, to respect the dead, they were just as important as the living. As Cullen was helping her with the dead, he asked her, "Do you have an idea of where they might be?" Victoria had time to think about this and she replied, "I believe they would have gone to New York from here."

"Why this place, New York?"

"New York is the hub of the states, everything centralizes around there," she stood there and thought about it some more, "I figured the only way they would be able to tear this world down would be to strike at the most prominent places. Like New York, Chicago, Dallas, Miami, and most of the western coast."

Cullen scratched his head and said, "But, how would they know to go to these places?"

"Well, we do have unscrupulous people in the world. They would have weaseled their way to the top with advice," Victoria said, making quotation marks with her fingers when she said the word advice.

"And those type of people would make their selves convenient as to be spared," Cullen questioned.

"Yes. They are the Lex Luther's of the world," she replied as she thought of the old movie superman.

"Lex Luther's? What is a Lex Luther?"

Victoria chuckled a little at his response and replied, "Lex Luther is a who, not a what."

Cullen frowned not understanding what she was saying. She smiled and said, "Lex Luther was a villain in the movie Superman. When villains came to the world that were worse than him, he sided with them to gain acceptance and privileges."

"Oh, so something like this has happened before."

"No, it was a movie, a play, like a live story book."

"Oh, so because of these story books, some people become like the ones in the books."

Victoria kind of smiled and said, "I never thought of it that way. But, yes, I suppose you could say that, where else would people get some of their ideas."

"So, people here cannot think for their selves? They read these story books to become like them in order to gain favor," Cullen asked, Victoria gave an unsettling smile, thinking she would not have thought of that. Her naivety only saw the good in people. She never really believed that people thought this way, maybe she really did belong in Cullen's world.

It snowed for three and a half days or at least it seemed like it did. The blizzard created high winds that blew the snow around. But finally, the sun broke through the storm. While they were waiting for the storm to let up, they used that time to gather up materials to make sleighs for the horses to pull. It probably would have been faster to find some big trucks but that would do no good, she was the only one who knew how to drive and there was no time to teach them how to drive. She wondered how they were going to pull these sleds when there could be snow drift that would be almost as high as the horses themselves. A snowplow would be good to have but the problem of somebody driving was still there. A person could probably wear snowshoes and walk on top, but horses were too heavy, they would sink. Then she remembered they have magic, what couldn't they do when they have magic. Victoria was curious on how they were going to do this that she went to the front doors to see how they were going to make their path. When she got to the lobby, she saw a group of people heading out the door. Victoria asked Cullen, "Are we leaving now?"

"No, they will be going ahead to make a path," Victoria tried to work it out in her head how they were going to do that. Cullen smiled as he watched her, whenever she was thinking about something or trying to work things out in her head her hand would go up as if she were rifling through some papers. She had told him that it was as if she were going through books or pages that she had seen before. Everything she read stayed in her head, but no scenario would come to her on how they would do this. She hadn't read through very many books on magic yet and there was a lot of them, she had only briefly looked through Clark's book. So many things were happening that she never had time to check out all the books. Most of her time was spent on learning how to use the magic, Ipion thought that would be more important. He underestimated her though, because she could learn faster by reading about it. Images and written words stay in her head, all she had to do was pull them out.

"Look, those mages will melt the snow a little, then freeze it, making it easier to walk on. Then those elves, the ones carting bales of hay will spread the hay on the ice to keep it from being so slippery. That way the horse can walk on top of it, see, it won't be slippery for them."

He had her watch the process that proceeded in front of them.

"While they are doing that the rest of us will finish getting ready and follow behind them."

"But won't that make them vulnerable? What if they encounter trouble? The magic they use could wear them out, like what Ipion said about lighting the way."

"Lighting the way uses constant power, melting the snow use brief power, see it doesn't take much power. Besides, they will be followed by some mages and warriors, so they will not be so vulnerable."

Cullen smile at Victoria. "What?"

He put his hand on her face, "You are such a caring person, that is what I love about you. That is what made me fall in love with you."

Victoria put her hand on Cullen's and smiled, "I am not always so caring, I can be selfish at times."

Cullen laughed and drew her closer to him, "That is what makes us all normal, sometimes, we have to be a little selfish." Victoria's jaw dropped and she cracked a little smile. He smiled and grabbed her up in his arms and walked over to the group of people.

Barroth was preparing his wagon and he was getting help from Ryo and Fodgrel. Clark and Claire were trying to put more clothes on Wadester who at first couldn't understand why he had to wear so many clothes until he had run outside and discovered how cold it was. Wadester had never been in a place that was so cold. It did snow and got cold back home but there were trees to block the frigid wind. Wadester found some toilet paper and started to unroll it and wrapped it around his neck. When Victoria saw that she began to laugh, she had to show Wadester what happened to toilet paper when it got wet. She grabbed a blanket and cut it into two long strips, she then tied them together and made a scarf for him. He was so excited on how warm he was going to be he ran across the wet floor and slid across it smashing into a group of men. They all went falling down on top of each other, like bowling pins being hit by a ball.

Looking at his feet, she had to find a way to keep them warm. His feet were much too wide for boots, so she had to think of a way to make boots just for him. The only thing she could think of was wrapping them up with strips of blankets, then cover that with the plastic from a hospital mattress. The mattresses were made to stay dry, so she figured this would keep his feet warm and dry. Wadester liked his new-found boots and walked around looking at them. He wasn't watching where he was going and smacked right into a wall. When he recovered from that, he continued walking but every now and then he would look up. Victoria was getting a kick out of watching Wadester, she hopes that the new clothes and makeshift shoes would not change his innocent ways. She liked the way he was and hoped that he would never change. But he is a child, and all children grow up and mature.

A ruckus ensued at the front doors that caught her attention. A scout that came running through the doors was very glad to see them. He was telling them what had happened before they got there. The others gathered around to hear what was going on, "Thank the maker you are here, I didn't think anybody would show up. I saw the mages making a path in the snow and followed it back here." He continued to tell them that Victor had broken through with the great white dragon. He caused all this. When asked where they went, he pointed in the direction of New York. Victoria was right about where they were heading. He told them that they were being led by some filthy man from this world. Cullen looked at Victoria and said, "Your Lex Luther." Sadly, she looked down and said, "Yes, I was hoping I was wrong about that. I didn't want to believe that there were people like that." He told them that the chief of this world led a lot of people out in long carriages that ran on wheels. He wasn't sure how far they got because by the end of the day, all power was taken away. Nothing worked for them, he saw people carrying biscuit like objects to their faces and started yelling at them. Some of them threw them while others just kept them in pouches in their pants. He said that Victor was giving the orders and there were arguments among some of them. From what he overheard, Victor was acting on his own. He was not following Aldabus's plan. He had an agenda of his own.

Victoria was a little relieved to know that Victor was here, even though he was up to no good, he still provided some safety for others from the horde. She found out that the horde was given orders to kill people who would not follow Victor. The scout discovered that there were gateways which had opened all over the world. Apparently, whatever Aldabus did at Stonehenge, made this possible. Hearing this made Victoria angry as she was walking away lightning shot out of her hands and hit the lights above her. They turned on but pop and crackling before exploding through the entire floor. When the power was released from her hands, she screamed in fear and dropped to her knees while covering her ears. Ipion put his hand up to stop Cullen from running to her side. She needed to get control of this power of hers and not be coddled whenever something went wrong. Sitting on her knees, Victoria looked at her hands. She stood up, pushed her hands forward, and yelled fire. A stream of fire shot out of her hands. She was going to get control of this now. Out stretching her hands, she yelled lightning and lightning shot out of her hands. Looking at the fire, she started with her magic, she yelled freeze and the fire froze. She looked at her hands and smiled, "I did it, I controlled it." She turned toward everybody with her hands still out and they all ducked except Cullen. He stood there and smiled at her. He started to walk toward her but gave an approving glance toward Ipion. He shook his head yes and gestured for Cullen to approach her.

He grabbed her and hugged her, "You did it, you found your control."

"Yes, I only thought about it for a second, but within that second, I was flooded with many thoughts."

"I knew you could find that within you. I always had faith in you. But I think you frighten your friends."

She looked over at them and saw them getting up and coming out from behind wagons and other objects for protection. She put her hand up to apologize and realized that maybe she should keep her hands down around them. At least, until they got use to the fact that maybe she does have control after all.

They all gather their belongings and packed them up in their wagons. The wagons had even been brought inside to make their packing easier. Besides, the building was so big they saw no reason not to bring them inside. They filed out the door one wagon at a time, Victoria had to show them how the doors worked without power. They had loaded the wagons with the blankets and food that was left behind. Wadester had found his way into the gift shop and took a large fluffy teddy bear. He walked out of the doors cuddling this bear as if it were real. Victoria spotted Wadester with the bear and said, "Oh look, you found a Teddy bear."

Wadester looked at the bear and said, "Teddy, him called Teddy?"

"Well sort of."

Watching Wadester cuddling the bear, she agreed, "Yes Wadester, his name is Teddy." Holding onto the bear, he loved the way it smelled and how soft it was. He was happier than he ever has been, with his new clothes, shoes, and fluffy friend. As they continued walking the path it led them past the reflective pool. Wadester remembered that place and he still wanted to jump into the water. As he ran toward the water, Victoria tried to stop him, but it was too late, he was already sliding across the water that had frozen solid. He got up and a little disappointed that he couldn't jump into the water, he stomped it with his feet. Hanging on to his Teddy, he sadly walked back across the water and lost his footing, down he went. Not being able to get up and walk across this slippery water, he crawled most of the way back with his Teddy in his mouth.

The sun was warm that day and the path they made became packed, making it firmer and at times, a little sloshy. They were 225 miles from New York, it would take them a little over three days to get there. The scout got word that Victor was still in New York; he conquered the city he wanted and left Gorgon to continue with his plan. He said that Victor was angry that he couldn't find their leader, he had escaped Victor's grasps. His plans were to find this leader and show the people of this world who the leader was now. But if the president was still at large, Victor could not get the control that he wanted. If people knew that he was still out there it gave them hope. They still had their leader and that gave them their reason to fight.

On their travels, they picked people up that were of this world and had the fire in them to fight. Seeing what they were up against gave them pause but only briefly. This was their country, and they were not going to let somebody else take it from them. They had discovered that their weapons were useless because the magical beings that were brought before them were able to shield their selves from their bullets. The blacksmith that came with Victoria made them some armor and weapons they could use. The alchemist showed them how to use the potions. They told them how quickly some of their armed forces were shot down, they didn't stand a chance. They only fired at the magical creatures just long enough to give the people a chance to escape. The heroes of Victoria's world were relentless, they would not stop even when the enemy was upon them. The only thing that mattered to them was to get the people to safety, to serve and protect, even to their death.

Cullen was amazed at them men in this world, they had courage and honor. They cared and that gave them strength to hold out. Some thought of using nukes but others did not think that would be a good idea. It was bad enough they had to deal with this magical fall out, let alone a nuclear one. For some of the authorities that stayed on the back burners as a last result. A lot of the power that people were dependent on was gone and could take weeks to bring them back. They would have to try and learn how to live without these things for a while. Some men tried to show them how to use swords and other forms of weapons. They had to be taught while they walked toward New York, there was no time to stop. Victoria had faith in them because they had the heart of the land. Ipion met with Victoria and told her that he had to help Saphon in England. They had to close the gateways that Aldabus had opened. He told her not to worry, she will be okay and to watch the skies for him.

Three days had pass and they were still fifty miles away. The unexpected would happen which slowed them down. At least, the closer they got to New York the less snow they came across, but this became a problem because now they had to put the wheels back on the wagons. But they picked up many people along the way willing to fight. Some couldn't fight but found other ways to be useful. They stopped at empty farmhouses that horses and other animals were left behind. The livestock mages summon up food from the ground, so they may eat. Clark couldn't stand the thought of these poor creatures; being left behind, he told Cullen that some of the people they picked up along the way were spared and brought with them, so why not these creatures. Cullen did not want to debate this with him, so he made Clark responsible for these animals. The horses were useful, and some of places they stopped at had wagons, which were needed to carry some of the people that they picked up along the way. The war party grew bigger as they made their way to New York. Victoria was beginning to feel a little assured in their conquest. She felt like she could beat her brother now with this new-found confidence. The only thing is she didn't want to hurt Victor, she was hoping she could talk to him, convince him he is not the evil man they turned him into.

From a distance, she could make out the outline of New York. The skyline looked different; it wasn't as tall as she remembered. Fear began to rise inside her when she could see dragons flying in the distance. She had forgotten about them, how was she going to fight dragons. She was hoping Erross would remember her, but she was told that Victor had him under a spell. Uwrick had been trying to come up with a potion that would counter act what Maggart had done.

Maggart, how Uwrick detested that alchemist. How was he able to come up with the potion to get control of the dragons? If only he could get ahold of some of those spells that Aldabus had in his library. When Ipion left so did Uwrick, he knew that death mountain would have very few guards. He could astral project to the library and find the book he needed. With that book, he could defeat Maggart's efforts of controlling the dragons. He had to work fast before Ipion closed the gates.

Uwrick found himself in Aldabus's library, he searched the shelves for the book "Control of Magical Creatures." As he looked through this large library, he had to figure out the filing system that was used here. He knew there was one because all libraries had a system, even theirs. Once he figured out what the sections were, he came across a section that had bars and was magically sealed, "Probably sealed, my Maggart," Uwrick whispered to himself. He stretched his arms out in front of him, laced his fingers together and cracked his knuckles. Shaking them out, he raised his hands and said, "*Abra ca dabra*." He chuckled and said, "I always wanted to say that." He knew saying that wasn't the spell that broke the spell on the bars, he just wanted to say it.

Looking through the shelves, his eye caught something on the desk. There it was, the book that he long to have in his grasp. He knew he didn't have time to look through the whole book, so he turned it to the potion, "Oh, how did he get that? Velatha?" Looking through the ingredients, he knew what he had to get. A lot of the ingredients he had but two of the ingredients might be hard for him to get. He had to have the hair that was used to cast it along with the dragon tears from the same dragon. He looked at the very bottom of the page and in small writing was a foot note that you will need the hair of the person who obtain the hair and dragon tears, "Well that might not be easy to do, especially if the obtainer was Isadora." Just as he spoke her name, Isadora came walking through the library doors. Startled at first at the sight of Uwrick in the library, Isadora's first move was to place her hand on the pouch she had on her hip. Seeing this Uwrick's eyes grew big, and he thrust his hand forward and said, "*Ut eni pera!*" Before Isadora, could act Uwrick had the pouch in his hands. He looked in the pouch, smiled and waved goodbye to Isadora, and in a flash, he was gone.

Chapter XV

Among the rubble of buildings that use to tower in the skies of New York city, Victor sat in a chair in a building that still stood. He smiled at his glorious victory that was shattered all around him. Sitting in that chair was a young reflection of Aldabus, Victor's new-found maturity showed signs that he was truly Aldabus's grandson. Not only was he beginning to look like him, but he was also thinking and acting like him as well. For an evil old man, Aldabus was very handsome, that is where Victor got his masculine looks. Better to have Aldabus's looks and not Zeddicus. Sitting among some of the rubble behind Victor's building was Erross. Aldabus made the mistake of leaving this amazing beast in the dungeon for him to conquer. The dragon did most of the work, he destroyed many tall buildings on their way to New York. Leaving a path of destruction was the first thing you could see. Centuries of building and planning were demolished in a matter of days. People were trapped in some of these buildings, but Victor made no attempt in getting them out. He was tired and wanted to rest. He sent Gorgon out with many dragons, so that he could level other structures such as these. He didn't like them, he thought they were hideous, and you could easily see inside them. There were too many windows, you could see what was going on inside. Why would they build such revealing structures as these?

The building he sat in had a large window, which Victor used to see the destruction that he released onto this city. He had sat a large comfortable chair in the middle of the room, so that he could watch for Victoria. Victor used his magic to start up the magical rooms that climbed up to the many floors, so he wouldn't have to climb the stairs. When he got to the top, he just sat there and waited. He was told that Victoria was on her way and that she was not alone. While he sat there, waiting, Victor relished at the thought of beating his sister. He was told several times that day he found out about her, that she was the first born and was given the power. He didn't believe them, he worked so hard to get where he was, and he was not about to let an upstarter take his place. He didn't care if she was his sister, she will not be as powerful as him.

Victor came out of his happy thoughts when a harpy flew into the window and slowly slid down to the bottom. A balcony was on the other side of the window, so the harpy laid there on the balcony stunned. Victor placed his hand on his forehead and shook his head. How did he get surrounded by imbeciles? He yelled at one of his men to bring the harpy in. They went out the glass door and brought the harpy inside and laid it on the floor. The harpy was Victor's informant on Victoria's whereabouts. When the harpy showed up, Victor knew she was approaching.

Victor stood up and put his hands behind his back. He slowly walked up to the window and he could see Victoria coming. He was surprised to see how many people she had with her.

"My, my sister has become very resourceful."

Nevertheless, he would be victorious, he was the powerful one. He ordered his people to prepare for a final battle, "Wake the dragons and go deep below and bring up the horde." The horde had buried their selves deep under the grounds of New York City. There were many left since the armed forces of this world did not know how to fight these creatures. They had never seen beast like these that were fast and wore strong armor. Victor had magically sealed the armor, so that their metal pieces could not penetrate them.

Victor believed that the people of New York had been beaten and were scattered with the wind. Some were able to travel far enough away from the city while others stayed to fight. Since the power station and cellular towers were destroyed by the dragons, people had to adjust without electricity, internet, and cell phone. Before, if they needed to know something, all they had to do was get on their phone and get their answers. Now they had to turn to others that knew how to survive this new kind of living. Many of the rich figured they could buy their way into keeping their way of living. But when they tried to hand these creatures money, all they got was a sword in the belly and they were the lucky ones. Some were transformed into the hideous mindless creatures that they were trying to bribe.

Coming out of the sewers of New York clamored the horde, they gave pause when the people they were encountering were mages. Some of them scattered but many of them pressed forward. The mages shot fireballs and lightning at the pack of hordes while Cullen's men drew their swords and charged after the ones trying to flee. Claire ran up and shoved arrows in the ground and plucked them out one at a time shooting with accuracy at some of the fleeing grimlocks. Her arrow flew with great speed and plunged into the head of a grimlock, "Right in the brain pan. You ass buckets weren't using that anyways."

Fodgrel ran through a group of grimlocks, swinging his hammer, sending massive blows to the armor they were wearing. The armor split as the hammer smashed into it giving Ryo access to run his sword through them. Fodgrel could barely keep up with Ryo's little dance, he went into as he swung his swords. He would stab one in the chest then gracefully pull it out, spin around, and sever off the grimlocks head, "Ha, you fucking wankers, you don't stand a chance with Fodgrel the fierce." Swinging his hammer up, he caught the chin of a grimlock and busted his jaw completely away from his face. The jaw went flying toward Ryo who hit it with his sword like a batter hitting a ball, "Oh, good one my ferocious dwarf friend." Fodgrel and Ryo work well together, between the two of them many grimlocks met with their departure.

Not too far from them was Barroth, now that he had his wings, he could pick up a grimlock and fly it up high, then letting it drop to the ground as it's body splatter at the sudden impact. He used his roar to knock down a group of grimlocks heading toward him. Then with his mighty axe he could sever the top of its shoulder down across to under their chest making a diagonal slice to the top part of their body, triggering it, to slide off. Barroth had massive strength, like that of a dragon, slicing through these creatures was like a hot knife through butter. He had to chase some of the grimlocks down because they were afraid of him.

Wadester and Clark were afraid of the grimlock, so they stayed in the wagon. Wadester was clinging onto his teddy bear, when a grimlock came up to the wagon and snatched the bear away from him tearing it into pieces. Clark screamed and Wadester stood there for a moment with his mouth dropped opened and tears swelled up in his eyes, "That my teddy, you kill him." This reaction surprised the grimlock at first, but he was even more surprised when Wadester lurched toward him and began tearing him apart. There was a strength in him he did not know he had. All he cared about was that this mean creature killed his fluffy bear. Clark went up to Wadester and patted him on the shoulder, "It's okay, we will find you another one." Wadester looked at Clark with urgency and said, "Where find one?" Clark looked around and in the window of a building just across from them was a Teddy Bear twice the size of the one Wadester had. Wadester smiled and galloped toward the window. Smashing through the window, Wadester grabbed the bear and hugged it tight, "Don't worry, Teddy, Wadester keep safe."

Victoria would have been worried about her people getting sick from these grimlocks, but before Uwrick left, he administered potions that would keep them from getting the sickness. The battle was becoming bloody, she had never seen so much blood and body pieces. She had stumbled several times over a torso or a leg. Tripping over a dead grimlock, she was faced with a huge troll like creature. It was a massive beast that stood at least eight feet tall, and his arms and body was busting at the seams with muscles. When it opened its mouth to roar, you could see huge tiger like teeth in its mouth. Trying to get up, it slowly ran toward her. Cullen saw this thing going after Victoria, without haste, he ran at the creature plunging his sword in to its stomach. With his free hand, he grabbed a long dagger from his belt and plunged that into its sternum. He pulled the sword out and plunged that into its upper chest than plunged the dagger into its throat. The troll gurgled out a deathly roar and fell back on the ground. Cullen pulled the sword and dagger out of the troll and ran to Victoria, "Are you okay?" Victoria shook her head *yes* as he helped her up, "Come on, follow me. I found out where Victor is." He pointed up at a building 50 feet in front of them, "He is up there, but heavily guarded. We must make our way up there if we are to bring him back. Ipion will be opening a gateway around here soon. A scout informed me that we must make haste, something is about to happen, and we all need to leave through the gateway as soon as Ipion opens it."

Ipion met up with Saphon who was fighting around Stonehenge. Aldabus tried to maintain control of the alter but was led away by the fighting. Saphon went to fight Aldabus but was stopped by the voice of Ipion. Surprised to see him there, Saphon ran up to Ipion, "How is Victoria, is she here with you?"

"No."

"Then we must go back and help her," Ipion put his hand up to calm Saphon down, "That is why I am here. I must open a gateway for them to come through."

"Here, I do not want her here."

"She will not come here. I will transfer the power of the alter stone from here to the one in our world. She will come through that way."

198

"How are you going to do that with all this fighting around here?"

"Well, you must do your best to keep them off me while I do this. I only need a little time."

"I will do my best, you will have your little time," Saphon started to leave when Ipion grabbed him by the shoulder and said, "Wait, you must stay away from Aldabus, no harm must come to him. I know this seems trivial to you, but I need you to stay away from him."

"Yes, Master Ipion," Saphon responded in a reluctant voice. Ipion did not release him yet and said, "Promise me."

Saphon frowned and with hesitation, he responded, "I promise." In the magical world, a promise between two people is a bond that cannot be broken. Once you promise something, the magic makes you follow through with it.

Ipion released Saphon as he walked toward the stones. As he approached the alter, he generated a protective shield around him. Aldabus was furious that Ipion knew how to do this, not even he knew the spell. Where did he learn that spell? The only person who could have found that spell for him was Velatha, his own daughter, against him. He tried to make his way toward the stone but was stopped by some mages and warriors. Aldabus used his ironwood staff to knock the warriors away from him. He deflected the magic that the mages shot at him. He had to get to the alter before Ipion could finish his transfer. He knew that that is what he was doing. With the power transferred from here, there would be no getting back. He had to act quickly; he must stop Ipion. He was nearly there and was about to shoot a lightning bolt at Ipion's shield when Velatha came through the gateway and landed in front of him, "You will not harm him father." Aldabus waived his hand and said, "Get out of my way, traitorous daughter."

"Traitorous? You call me traitorous when it was you that trick Ipion into turning me into a dragon."

Angered by her accusation, he spouted, "It had to be done or..." Aldabus stopped from revealing his secret.

"Or what, father? You wouldn't be able to do this?" she said as she stood on her hind legs and brought her arms up in a gesturing motion around her.

"I needed to do this so that I could change the world," he retorted.

"The world will be change father, but not in the way you wanted it," Aldabus gave her a surprised look and said, "What do you mean? What are you and Ipion up to?"

"What needed to be done has been done and there is no stopping it now. Once Ipion is done, the gateway here will start to close for good. If you don't want to be trapped here, you best go through now."

Saphon was spinning his staff around, knocking Aldabus's men down. He kept looking at Velatha and Aldabus between fights. With Velatha, there he knew that Ipion was safe, so he wasn't worried about him. The thing that bothered him were the words being exchanged between Father and Daughter. After all, Aldabus did trick Ipion into turning Velatha into a dragon. He continued his fighting and kept Aldabus's men away from the alter stone. Suddenly, Uwrick came busting through the gateway in a frantic. Seeing that Ipion was just finishing his task at the altar, Uwrick ran up to Saphon and handed him a big satchel of potions, "Here, take these potions and hit the other dragons with them." Saphon looked up at the dragons flying around than back at the alchemist as if he were crazy, Uwrick realized his confusion and scoffed, "Semantics, get on Velatha and she will take you to the dragons. Now you have to hit them in the face, so that the potion seeps into their eyes and nostrils." Saphon looked at Velatha and saw that Aldabus was no longer talking to her. He looked around and saw him walking through the gateway and shortly after was followed by Ipion. "Quickly, boy, time is of the essence," Uwrick grabbed up his robe and ran toward the gateway. Saphon yelled at his men to quickly run for the gateway. As they all ran toward the gateway, Saphon jumped on Velatha and she flew him to each of the dragons.

Throwing the vials of potions at the dragon's face, Velatha yelled at them to fly through the gateway. There were many dragons that needed the potion but once the other dragon saw their fellow dragons fly through the gateway, they followed behind them. Saphon couldn't hit them all as some passed him before he could throw a vial at them. "Don't worry, Saphon, we can get them when we go through," Velatha circled the area until all the dragons flew through the gateway. With her eyes, she could see the portal growing smaller. She told Saphon to hold on as she flew with great speed toward the closing portal. She made it through with just enough time to only get nicked in the tale by the closing. On the other side, Ipion was staff to staff with Aldabus. Uwrick was yelling at them to hurry they needed to help Ipion, so he can open the gateway to New York.

Victor had not conquered New York like he thought he had. The armed forces pulled back enough just to reassess the situation. They recovered the president who was trying to think of ways to regain back control. One of the generals wanted to nuke the big cities where all the creatures had dispersed. Trump said, "Absolutely not, destroying our major cities would be the wrong thing to do. We will not use the weapons."

The general retorted and said, "Then why have this much bigger and more powerful nuclear button if you are not going to use it."

Trump crossed his arms and said, "Because it is only a scare tactic. To scare the other countries, they are not to be used in our own states."

The general was not a Trump supporter, so he grabbed some of his men and headed toward Nevada.

Access to the nuclear weapons base was easy for him to get in, he was a general after all. Once inside he shut himself in the control room with his men. He told them that they were safe in here even after the missiles have been released. When the nuclear clouds clear up, they can go back up top and see if they were successful. Some of the men did not agree with the general and a scuffled broke out. There was a tug of war with the keys and one of the keys was accidently toss across the room and slid under a secured desk. The general pulled his gun and held it on the other men, "Now I am going to release these missiles, so we can get rid of those diseased creatures."

"General, I just don't think we can do that, it could mean the end of this world."

The general was becoming crazed with fear over those creatures. He saw what they could do and what would happen to you if any of their blood or secretion got on you. He did not want to end up like some of those men. He had to convince at least one of them to be on the same page as him. The only way he could do it was to make them as afraid as he was. Anything would be better than to be like them.

"Now I have seen what those creatures can do to you. Their blood gets on you and seeps into your blood. Soon, your veins turn black, and this black ooze starts draining out of your eyes, nose, and ears. Then there is the screaming, the painful scream that they go through that would last for hours. Then the transformation takes place, you begin to lose your hair and your skin starts to sag. Then you start to grow talon like claws and your teeth turn this grayish tinge color and you grow fangs."

The sight he witnesses was so horrible he could barely finish what he was saying. He screamed at the men and asked, "Is that what you want. Do you want to turn into one of those things? How about your loved ones, do you want them to be turned into one of them?"

One of the men stepped forward and turned his gun on the men with the general. He had family, a little girl; he could not bear the thought of one of those things getting ahold of her. The general smiled a crazy smile and handed him some zip ties. He had him tie up the other men and help him to get the key out from underneath the desk. When they retrieved the key, he grabbed the book out of a drawer and began to read the instruction on how to use these missiles. He had to find the right coordinates, so that the missiles would hit the major cities. One of them men was trying to tell them to stop what they are doing, some of these missiles were too old and could leak inside. The general did not believe him; he just thought he was trying to scare them into stopping what they were doing. The man that was trying to talk them out of this craziness had been station to this room for five years and he knows what he was talking about, so he continued to tell them that he was not lying. The general heard enough and grabbed a napkin out of his pocket and stuffed it in the man's mouth.

When the coordinates were set, they each grabbed a key while the general counted. The man with the napkin in his mouth managed to spit it out, he started yelling, "Stop, this is madness, you have no idea what you will be doing."

He looked at the man who had a daughter and with his eyes, he pleaded with him, "Your children—" just then a bullet hole appeared in the man's forehead. The general continued his count down and they both turned the key. They felt the rumble of the missiles emerging from their silos. As soon as they heard them take off, they went to untie the men. As they were cutting the ties off with their knives, they all began to scream in pain. Their skin felt hot and began to melt off. The radiation from those missiles had accumulated for those many years and some seep out of the missiles into the so-called air locked room. The missiles were now on their way to the major cities and there was nobody around to stop them.

In New York, Victoria and Cullen had to fight their way through many grimlocks to get to Victor. They had to take the stairs because Victor had the elevators jammed, so that they couldn't use them the way he did. When they were getting close, Victoria caught a glimpse of something out the stair well window. "What, what is it?" Cullen asked when he saw her stop at the window.

"I don't know, I thought I saw something…" As Victoria got closer to the window, a blast of fire came toward her. Cullen grabbed Victoria and took a tumble down the stairs. As they hit the landing, Victoria could hear a loud crack and Cullen screamed in pain. She quickly got up to assess the damage that Cullen had incurred. Seeing the bone in his leg protruding out of his skin, Victoria felt a little faint, "I think I am going to be sick." She put her hand on her stomach and took in a deep breath. She knelt beside Cullen and put both hands around the bone protrusion. Closing her eyes, she tried to concentrate. Suddenly, she could feel warmth coming from her hands. She continued to hold onto his leg when she felt the bone slipping back into place. Then she could feel the skin healing up around the area. When she opened her eyes and let go of his leg, she wiped the blood away to see that the leg was healed. Cullen's pain had gone away, and he looked at his leg. "I would have to say you did a very good job, Victoria," he leaned over and gave her a quick kiss. "Thank you, it feels much better now," Victoria inhaled and said, "I would have to say that was my first time of healing somebody. That is with the knowledge that I can heal." Cullen got up and helped Victoria up, "Come on, we need to get up there."

"But I thought we should try and help Erross," Victoria said as they were walking pass the window. Cullen saw that he was about to shoot fire at them again and grabbed Victoria by the arm and ran up the steps, "I don't think he wants our help right now."

"But…" Cullen opened the door and pulled Victoria into the room before she could get another word out.

Down the hall and around the corner was a large opening where Victor had been waiting for them. As they entered the room, they found Victor sitting in an armchair with one leg hanging over the arm. When he saw them, he smiled and slowly clapped his hands and congratulated them for making it all the way up there to see him, "So, Erross let you through, did he?"

"Well, not quite, he shot a few fireballs at us on our way up," Victor began to laugh and said, "A few fireballs?" The smile left his face and he stopped laughing, "He was supposed to kill you. Why do I continue to be surrounded by incompetence?" He turned around and threw the chair across the room without touching it. This made Victoria jump as she watched the chair crash through the window. Victor was tired of everybody thinking that she was powerful than he was. He wanted to show her his strength as he pushed his hands forward toward the large window causing it to explode and shatter into a million pieces.

"Victor, stop this. It doesn't have to be this way."

Victor spun around to face her and said, "Yes it does."

"Why, what do you think you have to prove?"

"Everything, I have to prove to Grandmother and Grandfather that I am more powerful than you are."

"Is that all you wanted? To be more powerful? Well, you are, this is all new to me, I don't know what I am doing."

Victor squinted his eyes at her to try and figure her out. Was she just saying this to him to get him to lower his guard? Or could she be telling the truth?

"You lie."

"Why would I lie to you?"

"To try and trick me."

Victoria started to walk toward Victor, but Cullen reached out and stopped her, he didn't trust Victor.

"That's right, Guardian, you mustn't let her get too close, I just might have to throw her out the window."

Cullen put his hand on his sword and kept the other hand on Victoria; he was not going to let him throw her off the side like the last time. Victor smiled when he saw Cullen place his hand on his sword. Victor put his hands up as if to surrender and smiled. Then he pointed his finger at him and said, "Do you really thing you can stop me with that stick of yours. Or perhaps, maybe you can sing me a song."

He laughed and looked at Victoria with a smug look on his face.

The sound of an eagle screech through the broken window. It landed on the ledge and screech again then flapped its wings and flew away. Victoria was confused at first than she remembered Victor had turn Grandfather into an eagle. "An Eagle?" Victoria took that as a sign; she believed that deep down within Victor was that sweet boy she remembered. She was not going to give up so easily, she had to try, "Victor, why did you turn Grandfather into an eagle?"

Victor's smile faded, and a memory came to him when he was very young.

"I remembered him. He would take me fishing. When I caught my first fish, it wasn't very big, but he was proud of me. He said I had the soul of a warrior and I walked the good path. We saw an eagle snatch a fish right out of the lake. He told me one day, he hoped he could become an eagle so that his soul may fly freely through the sky."

A tear slowly glided down his cheek, he looked at Victoria and gave her a faint smile, "He was proud of me. I didn't want him to be in pain. I wanted his soul to fly free in the sky like an eagle."

Tears filled Victoria's eyes and she reached out to him. She believed she may get through to him.

As he tearfully looked out the window, he saw Velatha appear out of thin air, on top of her was Saphon, who was throwing potions at the other dragons. He could hear her shouting at the others to quickly fly through the gateway. Her voice sounded very urgent as she tried to usher the others on the ground through the gateway. Something was happening; both Victor and Victoria could feel it. Victor whistled for Erross, who quickly flew to his rescue. Victor jumped on Erross and left Victoria and Cullen stranded at the top of the building. He hesitated at first and was about to turn back but something changed his mind, and he flew Erross through the gateway. What caused him to turn so quickly and why was Velatha ushering everybody through the gateway. Something made Victoria turn around and, in the distance, she could see something flying toward them. Cullen said, "What is that?"

As Victoria focused harder an image came in her head, "Oh my God, it's a missile. We have to hurry and get down there."

"Is that a very dangerous weapon?"

"Yes, Cullen, it is a very dangerous weapon. It can destroy this entire area. We don't have very much time."

"Do we have time to get down all those stairs?"

Victoria grabbed Cullen and kissed him as if she was saying goodbye. Cullen was not going to give up that quickly.

"Start shooting fireballs or lightning to get their attention, they need to know we are up here."

Victoria did as she was told and got their attention. Within seconds Velatha flew up to them but was very tired, "Quickly get on." Seeing how tired she was, Victoria asked her, "Do you have the strength to carry us both."

"I can try."

"You can try? No. Take Victoria and get out of here."

"No, Cullen, I am not going without you."

"You have to," he grabbed her and held her tight, "I love you, Victoria, always remember that." He was about to force her up on Velatha when a deep voice said, "Anybody need a ride?"

"Barroth, am I glad to see you," Victoria put her arms around Barroth's neck and gave him a kiss on the cheek. Barroth smiled and rubbed the spot where she kissed him then in a thunderous voice he said, "Come on, we are running out of time. Cullen jump on Velatha, I will take Victoria."

Cullen did as Barroth said and jumped on Velatha. Barroth grabbed Victoria up in his arms and flew her out the window. The missile was just seconds away from them. Barroth had to dig deep within him to fly faster with the missile at his back. Everybody had made it through the gateway with Barroth and Victoria being the last ones through. When Ipion saw that they were safely through, he closed the gateway. The missile was so close, and they could feel the ground shake but there was no impact on their side of the gateway. Barroth landed next to Velatha and the others. They all sought each other out to be sure that nobody was missing. Victoria even got a hug from Wadester and his huge Teddy. Victoria wanted to know what happened, so she walked up to Ipion for some answers. Ipion sadly agreed to let her know what had transpired that day. He told Victoria when Velatha was rested enough she would take her.

Several hours went by and all Aldabus's men were gone. They all returned to Death Mountain. Even Victor had regretfully returned to his home at Death Mountain. The spell on Erross had worn off and he flew back to Dragon Island with the rest of the dragons. Velatha came up to Victoria and asked her if she was ready. She replied that she was and climbed on. As they soared through the sky, Velatha told Victoria to brace herself, this may come as a shock to her. She flew her across the great waters that separated them from the other lands. It took several hours for them to get to their destination, "Look before you, can you see that." In the distance, Victoria could see some land. As they got closer, there was a small island a short distance from a larger one, "Tell me, Victoria, what do you see?" She looked around and all she could see were some ruins overgrown with foliage. Velatha landed next to a large structure that had a strange shape to it, "Does this look familiar to you?" Victoria shrugged her shoulders and said, "No, not really. Well, it kind of looks like the statue of liberty."

Velatha looked at her and bowed her head, "No. No, that can't be. Where am I? I thought I was in the past or another dimension, or something."

Velatha sadly responded with, "It has been over 1000 years since that day went by. Those nuclear missiles destroyed nearly everything on the world. Years went by before things could grow again, and when it did, it covered the structures of the past."

Victoria thought about the things she dug up by Stonehenge, what was that all about. It was hard for Velatha to explain but she did her best. Victoria was home now, in her true home. She might have been born there and raised there, but she belonged here. It took a lot of deception from Velatha and Ipion to keep Victoria safe until she was old enough to come back. Hawke was truly her grandfather and while Velatha was explaining these things to her, an eagle flew low across the water to the island. When it flapped its wings, the tips just slightly touch the water as it crossed. Victoria smiled and said, "Grandfather?" The two of them spent a couple of days there as Velatha told Victoria everything. The horde was what was left of the people from the fallout. Some had made it to safe places underground. It was many years and she and Ipion still had not found out where the magic came from. Velatha had discovered books in her father's library that gave her some answers, but she had not found it all out. There were many books in that library that collected dust which might have the answers she sought. But getting to those books would be a challenge, maybe for another time. She was angry at first but then she understood. She was ready to go back. She wanted to be with her friends and Cullen who, by now, were all back at Mage Mountain.

Velatha flew Victoria home and landed on top of Mage Mountain. Ipion was waiting for them there. She walked up to Ipion and gave him a loving hug, "Thank you, grandfather. I love you." The words reached deep into his heart and he hugged her back, "Welcome home, granddaughter." He pulled her away to get a better look at her, a tear fell from his eye and he said as he was wiping his eyes, "Velatha, you always blow the dust around up here." Victoria looked at him and smiled, then she headed down to the dining room where Ipion said she could find her friends. The first person who saw her was Cullen. He ran to her and picked her up. Holding her tight and swinging her around, he stopped and kissed her long and passionately. The others saw her and came running to her and they all gave her a group hug. She did feel at home here, and these were her people and her friends. She never wanted to leave them. As the crowd slowly broke up, you could hear Fodgrel teasing Ryo and Clark. Then Clark said something to Barroth, and he got his usual response, "You couldn't handle this, goat boy." Both Cullen and Victoria laughed as he walked her up to the ballroom. The sun was the only thing that lit this room up. Walking her out to the balcony, Cullen asked her, "Marry me."

She looked at him and smiled saying, "I will."

Just when she thought her adventures were over, Ipion told her of another adventure she must go on. She sat there at a table in the small town that Cullen first took her. She was drawing a picture of a beautiful chest that had a woman on it with wings. She gave it to the elf that made the staff for Saphon. He was to carve this chest using the wood of an oak tree. He wanted to use better wood, but she told him it had to be oak. Then she went off to the blacksmith and showed him Cullen's ring and that he was to make some chain mail too. He was to make a ring, just like that one out of iron along with the chain mail. When she was done there, she walked over to the tailors to have them make a tunic similar to the guardians with cloth made of cotton. While she was waiting for these things to be finished, she sat back down at the table and began to write a letter. Cullen had been watching her and sat next to her, "You have been very busy here. Why are you having these things made?"

"Ipion told me that he can open the gateway to the past."

"Back to where you were from?" Cullen asked.

"No, much further than that."

He looked at her trying to understand, she stopped writing the letter to explain to him, "When I was back there, this guy and I found this chest, that chest."

She pointed toward the elf who made the carvings, "I need to make these things and go back 2600 years from my time so that I will find them again."

"Why?" Victoria placed her hand on his face and kissed him, "If I don't, I will never meet you and this place could have been destroyed by Aldabus."

Cullen smiled and said, "So you are writing yourself a note in order for these things that were to happen to come about." Victoria smiled when he caught on to what she was doing.

"Cullen, I don't know what life would have been like without you and I never want to find out. All I know is that I love you and I want to spend the rest of my life with you."

He smiled at her and said, "I love you too. Mind if I came along with you."

She was about to answer him when Barroth, Ryo, Clark, Claire, and Fodgrel asked if they could come with them. She smiled and said she would love to have them join her. Jumping out of a tree with his Teddy was Wadester saying, "Wadester go, too."

She smiled and said yes, they were to set off for another adventure.

CPSIA information can be obtained
at www.ICGtesting.com
Printed in the USA
BVHW040950210621
610126BV00002B/265